—Shotgun—
RIDGE

MINDY NEFF

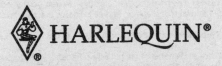

HARLEQUIN®

TORONTO • NEW YORK • LONDON
AMSTERDAM • PARIS • SYDNEY • HAMBURG
STOCKHOLM • ATHENS • TOKYO • MILAN • MADRID
PRAGUE • WARSAW • BUDAPEST • AUCKLAND

ISBN 0-373-83616-3

SHOTGUN RIDGE

Copyright © 2004 by Melinda Neff.

This edition published by arrangement with Harlequin Books S.A.

www.eHarlequin.com

Printed in U.S.A.

In memory of Della Mae Hillman, Donald Neff and Wayne Neff. I miss you more than I can say.

And for Vicky Rich—because you lived. I couldn't imagine a world without you in it.

With heartfelt gratitude to:
Marsha Zinberg, for your patience and kindness during an unusually trying time.
Annelise Robey, for being in my corner and never losing faith.
Charlotte Maclay and Sue Phillips, for your awesome talent, insights and hand-holding.

And to Gene
My soul mate and the love of my life.

CHAPTER ONE

SOMEONE LEFT a dead canary in Abbe Shea's mailbox.

She didn't need three guesses to figure out its meaning. The lifeless yellow bird—a *baby* bird—was the Mafia's way of warning her what happens to the children of people who "sing."

Forty-eight hours later, she was still trembling like an addict who needed a fix.

Damn it, she'd kept her silence for five months now. She hadn't told a soul that she'd witnessed her fiancé's murder—or that she could identify the shooter.

Shouldn't that prove something? Did these people actually think she'd risk her daughter's life?

In addition to front-page newspaper headlines, every television station in the country carried hourly reports on the Texas Rangers' apprehension and arrest of Lucca Ziggmorelli, a key member of a Las Vegas crime family. The charges were drug trafficking and money laundering.

Abbe knew he was guilty of much, much more.

And that made her a liability—to the Ziggmorellis and, worse, to her own daughter.

She took a final walk through her grandmother's house, where she'd been living for the past five months, her gaze touching items that brought both good memories and ones that made her cringe. She was leaving so much behind. But it couldn't be helped. Grandma Jane and Mama were gone now—Grandma taken home to Jesus, and Mama…well, that was a mystery. Abbe had no idea if her mother was alive or dead, and her regret was keen. There were so many things she wanted to say to her, to apologize for.

How had life become such a mess? Abbe had thought she could start over here in Hope Valley, Texas. It was the sort of place where acceptance was unconditional and people actually spoke to one another when they passed on the street.

She should have known better.

She should have known that one of the first places they would look for her was her mother's hometown.

"Jolie?" she called. "Sweetie babe, we need to hurry up now. It's time to go."

Jolene, her three-year-old, streaked through the living room, short blond pigtails bouncing, a fluffy white puppy hopping at her heels. The teacup Maltese, Harley, skidded on the hardwood floor and tumbled onto the rug.

"I gots to find Lambie-pie!" Jolene wailed. "Her's lost."

Abbe breathed deeply, trying to still the nerves clawing at her stomach. Jolene hardly made a move without her stuffed lamb, so how could it be lost?

"The last time I saw her, she was sitting on your potty chair."

Jolene's jaw dropped, and her eyes went round. "Oh! I forgetted. Her had to go tee-tee." With that announcement, Jolene dashed toward the bathroom. Neon-pink lights flashed from the soles of her tiny sneakers each time they connected with the cabbage-rose-patterned area rug. The puppy raced after her, clearly delighted with the blinking shoes.

Jolene had taken the news of their pending trip in stride. She was a happy, agreeable child, always ready for an adventure. Abbe couldn't bear the thought of anything happening to her little girl. The energetic cherub was her absolute heart.

Now, realizing that the Ziggmorelli family had found them so easily, especially the manner in which they'd let that be known, Abbe was totally spooked.

And that meant they needed to disappear. Go somewhere safe. To someone who could help *keep* them safe.

Her hands shook as she retrieved a manila file folder from the bottom drawer of her grandmother's Bombay chest and stuck it in her suitcase. The information in that file was something she didn't want falling into the wrong hands.

Compiled by a private investigator over a period of thirty years, it was a detailed dossier on Grant Callahan, his hometown of Shotgun Ridge, Montana, and the people who lived there. Reading through the mountain of papers five months ago, she'd gleaned that the small community of Shotgun Ridge was as far removed from the dirty hands of organized crime as possible.

And ever since she'd found the file on her father's computer and read it, she hadn't been able to get Grant Callahan out of her mind. According to the report, he was retired from the U.S. Army's Special Forces and dedicated himself to the horse-breeding farm he owned with his two brothers, but he still accepted assignments on occasion.

She'd made a call yesterday from a pay phone in town to the mayor of Shotgun Ridge, Ozzie Peyton. He'd come through for her just as the dossier had promised. As for Grant Callahan, if the man could infiltrate terrorist groups in foreign countries and rescue kidnapped executives, he could surely help her.

At least she hoped so. She'd been naive in the past, so trusting and gullible, accepting all the nice things money could buy, and never questioning where that money came from.

God, she'd made mistakes. She'd floated through life as though it were her own personal fairy tale, fallen in love, given birth to a beautiful little girl. Then, in a single day, all the security she'd ever known had been yanked out from under her in the most hideous, terrifying way—and she'd had to grow up in a hurry.

Looking back, she realized she'd been taken care of most of her life—first by her mom, then by her adoptive father, Stewart Shea, then by her fiancé, Tommy Donato.

Now she was on her own, and all the scary decisions rested solely on her shoulders.

Abbe hoped to God she was making the right ones.

Because her daughter's life was at stake.

With urgency pressing her chest, she loaded the rest of their suitcases into the car, put Harley into his pet carrier, then corralled Jolie and Lambie-pie, and strapped them into the car seat. They were traveling light—two cases each, plus a box of Jolie's toys, and some photo albums. The amount of baggage they could take was limited, due to the weight restrictions of the plane. She'd gone to the airfield earlier that day and calculated her fuel based on what she'd packed. She'd also gone over the aircraft inch by inch, sweeping it for signs of tampering or a tracking device, praying she'd know one if she saw it.

Jolene fell asleep before they even reached the main highway, and Abbe appreciated the silence. Her stomach was knotted with tension, her nerves were frayed, and somehow she had to pretend that nothing was amiss. Moms were supposed to be strong, to never let their children see their fears. Most moms, anyway. Her own had been just the opposite.

Abbe took the turnoff for Hope Field, the county airstrip where she kept her Beechcraft Baron B58. She was glad she hadn't let pride persuade her not to keep the plane—a gift from her father. After pulling her Jeep next to the Baron, she took her sleeping daughter out of the car seat and transferred her to the one in the back seat of the airplane. She left the cockpit door open while she went back for the puppy, then loaded their luggage into the cargo hold.

The cell phone in her purse rang, and a rush of adrenaline shot straight to her head. Annoyed with herself, she checked the caller ID.

Her father.

Her *adoptive* father.

She'd been waiting for him to return her phone call, but now she felt nervous about it. She hadn't spoken to him since she'd left Las Vegas in January—five months ago.

"Hello, Pop." Her voice was flat, with just the barest hint of a tremble.

"I got your message," Stewart Shea said in a deceptively gentle voice, one that revealed a slight trace of his Irish roots. "I suppose you've seen the news?"

"Who hasn't? The local stations here in Texas are liable to wear out the footage from playing it so often." She speared her fingers through her hair, surprised when her hand hit bare skin at her nape. She still wasn't used to the trendy short style Donetta Presley-Carmichael had given her two weeks ago.

"We need to talk about—"

"I received a special delivery from the Ziggmorellis," Abbe interrupted. "And it wasn't pretty." The image of that morbid calling card in her mailbox made her skin crawl. "Tell those bastards Jolie is innocent. She's only a baby—she didn't see anything. She can't hurt them. Baby birds don't sing!"

Stewart swore. "They left a dead canary on your doorstep? A baby one?"

She'd known he would understand exactly what she was talking about. "In my mailbox. Call them off, Pop."

"Abbe, Gil Ziggmorelli runs his organization different—"

"I don't care if he dances naked on the supper table. I just want him to rein in his henchmen and leave me and Jolene alone. Can you tell him that, Pop?" She felt weary and scared, caught up in something she hadn't chosen, didn't want any part of. "Gil and his family have nothing to fear from me. Does he honestly think I'd admit to even *knowing* any of those Mafioso goons?" Too late, she realized her words had insulted.

Pop was one of those goons.

Or had been. He'd recently retired—so he'd said. She wasn't sure if she believed him, was no longer even sure she knew who he was. A lump of pain and betrayal formed in her throat. He'd lied to her all her life, letting her believe his work was top-level security in some government agency when all along…

The sounds of traffic and honking horns filtered through the phone line. How many times had she seen Pop walk a short distance down the Vegas Strip and conduct business over his portable phone? She heard the snick of a lighter now, the deep inhalation of breath.

"I thought you quit smoking." Her voice was sharper than she'd intended.

"Tough habit to break."

"You went three years!" He'd supposedly thrown away his last pack of Camels the day Jolene was born.

"Listen to me, Abbe. If you hadn't called, I would have made the first move. You need to lay low for a while."

"I'm way ahead of you," she said. "Pop? Can I trust you?" Odd thing for a daughter to ask. Deep down she thought she could trust him—but a cynical voice inside, one created by the recent hard facts of her life, told her to be wary. And this inability to trust the one person she'd been closest to for so many years was like flying through fog with no instruments or landing gear.

"You ought to know that you *can,* punkin."

The anguish in his voice sounded so sincere. She nearly told him where she was going, what she planned to do, but at the last minute she changed her mind.

Maybe she *could* trust Pop. But she couldn't trust the people around him—people who kept the firearms, wiretap and tracking-device manufacturers in business.

"Just call someone, Pops, and relay my message, okay?"

"Oh, you better believe I will." The ice in his voice frightened her. She'd only heard him use that tone once before in her life—when she was barely into her teens and had pressed him to tell her about his secret spy work. He'd evaded her questions, but when she'd persisted, his temper had erupted. She'd never asked again.

"Regardless of what's happened between us, Abbe, you're my girl. Gil Ziggmorelli will know I raised you right. And if he doesn't, I've got enough clout and respect to make that known."

She wondered if that was still true. When she'd left Vegas, there'd been some muscle-flexing going on between the Ziggmorelli and Shea families.

Which was partly the reason Lucca Ziggmorelli had murdered Tommy.

"Tell me where you're going," Stewart said, gently now.

"I—I can't take the chance, Pop." Oh, God, she wanted to. Despite the breach in their relationship, she still loved him. He wasn't blood family, but he was the only family she had—or, at least, the only family whose whereabouts she knew. "If I could grant…grant you a wish, Pop, what would it be?"

He was silent for a moment, and she gripped the small cell phone, wondering if he'd picked up on her clue, or if he thought she'd lost her mind. She didn't know if a cellular telephone could be tapped, but she wasn't going to take the chance.

"I've got a shotgun load of wishes, punkin. The most important one is that you be safe and happy. I think I know my kid, though, which means I don't need wishes. You'll be okay."

He understood. Was he surprised? she wondered. That she'd chosen Grant Callahan and Shotgun Ridge to run to?

She checked her watch. Time was ticking away and she was standing out here in the open.

"Okay, Pop. I gotta go now. Take care."

"You, too, punkin."

Abbe pressed the end button on her cell phone, stared at it for a moment, then walked a few feet and tossed it into the trash barrel that rested in the patchy grass at the edge of the asphalt. Her body shuddered, despite the heat radiating from the pavement. She imagined this was probably what a fox experienced when he heard the distant bay of hunting dogs.

Shaking off the eerie sensation, she closed the Baron's cargo hold, glanced up to make sure Jolene was still asleep, then did another thorough walk-around inspection of the plane's exterior, looking for any skin cracks, corrosion on the trim tabs, loose bolts or anything out of the ordinary. She checked the engine oil, tested her fuel mixture, then turned and shaded her eyes as the AVGAS truck pulled alongside the plane. She'd told Dooley earlier that she'd be needing fuel, but hadn't wanted to get it then. She wanted to witness the fuel going into the tanks, wasn't taking any chances that someone could mess with it—as it went in or *after* it was in.

Her heart bumped when she saw Sheriff Storm Carmichael in the passenger seat of the fuel truck. He hopped down, strode over to the garbage bin, and retrieved her cell phone.

Abbe crossed her arms to disguise their trembling.

"Mornin', Sheriff. Are you moonlighting? Or did you lose the reelection vote?"

"Neither," Storm said with a grin. "I saw you pitch this."

He held up her cell phone. "Since my wife's been known to accidentally toss away her hair-cutting scissors when she gets in a hurry, I figured I'd run out here and see if you were afflicted with the same problem. Dooley said you needed fuel, so I saved myself a few steps and hitched a ride with him."

"Fill her up?" Dooley asked.

"Yes, please." She glanced back at the phone in Storm's hand and stepped farther away from the wing as Dooley began pumping fuel.

"This *is* your phone, isn't it?" Storm asked.

"Yes. I'm, uh, leaving town and won't be needing it."

"You could get one heck of a forwarding bill if someone fishes this out of the dump and decides to connect with long-lost relatives overseas."

"The service is scheduled for shutoff by five o'clock tonight. Um, maybe you could sort of keep it in custody until then?"

He nodded. "I could do that. Is anyone likely to come looking for it?"

Her head jerked up. That was a strange question. Storm Carmichael had once been a Texas Ranger. Injured in an undercover sting that had gone bad, he'd come back to his hometown, been elected Hope Valley Sheriff and married his sister's best friend, Donetta Presley.

Did he know about her connection to Lucca Ziggmorelli?

She hated all this distrust. It simply wasn't her nature. And Storm, after all, was one of the good guys.

Smiling, she said, "Well, if someone does come looking, won't they be surprised to find that my phone's been sent to jail?"

"Where you headed off to?" he asked as he slid the cell phone into his shirt pocket.

"Is it necessary for you to know?" She spoke as gently as she could, not wanting to sound rude.

He studied her, his cop's eyes shrewd and serious. "No," he said at last. "Just curious. I like to have an idea who's coming and going in town and for how long. And Donetta grills me something fierce over people's whereabouts. If you're planning an extended absence, she'll no doubt notice and I'll be the one she hounds for answers."

Abbe licked her lips. "I have a hair appointment booked for next month. I don't think I'll be back for it. Can you tell her for me?" She liked Donetta, liked most of the people here in Hope Valley, and would miss them.

"I can. But *you* could call and tell her."

When she didn't answer, he studied her some more. Abbe appreciated that he didn't pry for details, that he trusted her to know what she was doing. Before he could speak, Dooley interjected with "All topped off, Miss Abbe."

She handed Dooley her credit card. "You haven't seen anyone hanging around my plane since I was here this morning, have you?"

"I been here since before dawn, and you're the only one who's come around at all. And I kept a sharp eye out, just like you asked."

She smiled at the old man. "You're the best, Dooley." She watched as he went back to the fuel truck to write up the ticket and run the credit slip.

"Abbe, if you're in trouble," Storm said, "you know you can count on me to help."

She shook her head. "It's just best if I don't stay in Hope Valley." From her pocket, she retrieved the keys to her Jeep and handed them to Storm. "I wouldn't mind if my Jeep was incarcerated along with the cell phone." That was one thing she hadn't really thought about. What to do with her vehicle.

"Maybe you could keep an eye on my grandmother's

house, too? I can't really tell you more, because I just don't know when, or even *if* I'll be back to deal with things."

Dooley walked up with her credit card. She signed the slip. "Thanks, Dooley."

"Anytime, Miss Abbe." He looked back at Storm. "You ridin' back with me, Sheriff?"

"You go on ahead. I'll move Abbe's Jeep for her."

Dooley tipped his grease-stained cowboy hat and went back to the fuel truck.

Storm nodded toward the credit-card slip she held in her hand. "You know things like that are the equivalent of leaving a trail of bread crumbs. Assuming you're concerned about someone who might be interested in your whereabouts…"

"Yes, I realize that. I also filed a flight plan. To Jamestown, North Dakota. From there, it'll be anyone's guess which direction I might have headed." She gazed at Storm, waited a moment for her meaning to sink in. "This is a big country, and I'm an experienced pilot."

Storm nodded and reached out to shake her hand. "I hope we see you again, Abbe Shea. Meanwhile, take care of yourself and that little girl." He withdrew a card from his pocket and passed it to her. "If you ever need anything, don't hesitate to call. You have friends in Hope Valley."

Abbe had to get out of here before she embarrassed herself and bawled like a baby. She *did* know she had friends here. "Thanks. Give Donetta a hug for me."

Although she'd been there for the fueling of her plane, she drained a small amount from the tank into a glass vial and re-checked the color and clarity to make sure the gas was the proper grade and didn't contain any contaminants. Satisfied, she stepped onto the wing and climbed into the cockpit. Jolie was still fast asleep, and the puppy, curled up in his small crate next to the seat, was, too.

She'd filed a flight plan from Texas to North Dakota because she *wanted* to leave a trail—but only up to a point. Flying IFR—instrument flight rules—meant that air traffic control would monitor her journey, know her coordinates. Not only would she be easily traceable, but with Jolie on board, being followed by radar was the safest way to travel. From Jamestown, she would refuel, have a short rest and something to eat, then take off again, this time flying VFR— visual flight rules—for the shorter hop to Montana. She just prayed that the weather remained clear.

As always, when she started the Baron's twin engines, she felt a rush of excitement behind her breastbone. Flying was one of her passions. In the air she was free, with plenty of time and space to think and to dream.

With her feet firmly on the brakes, she did the prerequisite "run up" before takeoff, pushing the engines up to 1,700 rpm as she studied the gauges. Magneto, fuel flow, temperature and pressure all checked out, and with butterflies winging in her stomach, she taxied onto the short runway.

"Here we go," she whispered. Since there was no tower at the airport, she visually swept the cloudless blue sky for air traffic, then keyed the mike. "77Foxtrot is departing Hope Field on runway one-eight with a left turn to the east," she announced into the blind, letting any other aircraft in the area know she was taking off.

Pushing the throttles all the way forward, she watched the ground disappear rapidly beneath her. Sixty knots. Seventy. Eighty...eighty-five. She pulled back on the yoke, felt her stomach dip, watched the Baron's nose rise as the tires left solid ground, and the aircraft began its climb.

She was leaving behind the familiar and flying toward the unknown. At one time in her life, the adventure would have thrilled her. Now, however, she felt anxious. She needed to figure out exactly how she was going to present herself to the people of Shotgun Ridge, Montana—and more specifically, to Grant Callahan.

Being open and honest wasn't an option—at least not until she knew whom she could trust.

CHAPTER TWO

THE AIR IN THE STABLES was ripe with the smell of antiseptic solution, animal, and sexual anticipation. As many times as Grant Callahan had witnessed the sometimes violent act of equine mating, he still felt a tug of arousal himself at the fury and beauty of it all.

"Easy does it, War Party. Let's show the lady a good time." The muscles in his arms burned as he held firm to the powerful stallion's lead shank. Ethan and Clay, Grant's brothers and partners in Callahan and Sons Farms, quickly readied Irish Maiden in the breeding chute.

As a rule, War Party behaved like a gentleman when it came to "covering" the various mares in what he considered his personal harem. Irish Maiden was a little haughtier and more aloof than some of the other mares, but her behavior when the chestnut stallion curled his lip and screamed his mating call proved that the two magnificent champions were sweet on each other. Irish immediately urinated, enticing the stallion with both her scent and her readiness.

"Hussy," he murmured to Irish with a soft chuckle, and slackened his hold on War Party's lead. "Hold her head up and still," he said to Ethan while Clay pulled the mare's wrapped tail out of the way. "This girl's ready. Better let him at her while she's hot."

The stallion jumped a bit too eagerly and Grant swore,

shoving his shoulder against the horse's flank to help get him in position. The clumsy mounting might have spelled disaster with a less experienced stallion or handling team.

But Grant and his brothers had learned the business of breeding horses when they were mere boys, taught by their father, Fred Callahan, who'd shown up at a farm in Idaho one day to purchase quarter horses and ended up buying three little boys from their abusive foster parents, who believed children were good for slave work and little else. Not many bachelors would enlist the help of an entire town in adopting hard-luck kids who, at eight, six and five, had already developed attitudes, but Fred Callahan had been an exceptional man among men.

It was times like right now that Grant missed his dad the most. Fred Callahan had always delighted in being part of the process when excellent bloodlines were about to be mixed. But pancreatic cancer had claimed him several years ago, and Grant's heart still ached.

War Party's tail began to flag and Grant brought his concentration back where it belonged. Ten or fifteen seconds was all it took for the stallion to ejaculate. Irish Maiden didn't seem to mind the slam-bam-thank-you-ma'am style of the event.

Deeming the covering successful, Grant nodded to Ethan and Clay, and Irish Maiden was released and led away in the opposite direction from War Party.

"Hey, Grant!" He heard Manny Davis, his stable manager, call. "Phone for you."

Grant transferred War Party's lead into Clay's capable hands. The stallion would need to be washed and cooled down before being turned out to graze.

He removed his gloves and was heading for the phone in the barn when he heard a low-flying airplane buzz the area. It was the second time in the past few minutes. "Take a message, will ya, Manny?"

Grant stepped outside, shading his eyes against the mid-afternoon sun, and saw the twin-engine Baron circling their private landing strip. Shotgun Ridge was a small town and he knew every aircraft and pilot in the area who might be paying him a neighborly call. He didn't recognize this one.

He listened for sounds of engine distress, indicating a need for a forced landing, and didn't hear any, but it sure looked like that pilot was aiming for a place to set down. Knowing his brothers were handling the remainder of the breeding chores, he jumped into his truck and reached for the keys that always dangled from the ignition switch.

That was what he loved about this town—the lack of crime and ugliness. God knows he'd seen enough ugliness to last him a lifetime.

For a bare instant, a small boy's lifeless eyes flashed in his mind. Sweat dampened his spine, and his gut twisted. Slamming that mental door shut, he hit the gas and headed out across his large breeding farm, where million-dollar horses grazed in verdant pastures.

It took only a couple of minutes to reach the private airstrip. His hat brushed the windshield as he leaned forward, watching the twin-engine, B58 Baron's tires kiss the asphalt with barely a chirp. He took a moment to appreciate the pilot's skill, then stopped the truck and got out, surprised when the plane taxied right up to the hangar as though the pilot had mistaken his spread for a bed-and-breakfast with hangar parking included.

Not that he didn't have room for another aircraft. Containing only the Bell Ranger helicopter and his two Cessnas, his twelve-thousand-square-foot hangar echoed.

He watched as the Baron pivoted, the right wing pointing in his direction. The first thing he saw was an itty-bitty girl with her nose pressed to the back window, her little arm waving like crazy. Over her blond pigtails, she wore a tiny headset with a boom mike.

Grant chuckled. He couldn't see the pilot, but the pint-size passenger, with her wide smile, sure seemed happy enough. She looked to be close to his niece's age—Katie was nearly three and had her uncle Grant wrapped around her pinkie.

The right door opened and the pilot stepped out onto the wing.

A woman. Damn, he was a sucker for damsels in distress. Assuming this one was in distress.

She straightened and gave him a friendly wave before she flipped the seat's back forward to unstrap the child.

Appreciation jumped in his stomach in a way he hadn't felt in a long time as he walked toward her and stopped at the base of the wing. She had short blond hair and sun-kissed skin, which the cotton-candy-pink tank top over hip-hugging jeans set off to perfection.

"Need any help?" he called.

She ducked back out of the cockpit and looked over her shoulder, her smile as warm as the child's—but affecting him in a totally different way.

"Hey," she said in greeting. "I'm looking for Grant Callahan. Have I put down on the right strip?"

His surprise, and his hesitation, were only slight. She had a soft Southern drawl. Man, that got him every time. "You've found him."

"Well, I'm glad to hear that. I'm Abbe Shea, your new tenant and the schoolteacher come fall." She reached into the back seat and emerged with the toddler, who promptly waved at him again.

Grant's muscles tensed and his senses went on alert. His tenant? Since when? He had an unoccupied guest house, yes, but he hadn't advertised it for rent.

"You want to take this shameless little flirt," she asked, "or tackle the cargo hold?"

"I'll start with this one." He reached up and snagged the toddler. "Hey, squirt. You got a name?"

"Jo—lene," She drawled the name in that cute Southern accent, then giggled. "But Mommy calls me Jolie. I'm free years old. And dis is Lambie-pie." She shoved a stuffed lamb in his face, nearly knocking off his hat.

Despite his wariness, he couldn't help but grin. "You seem awfully happy for someone who's been cooped up in a plane. Somebody slip you a happy pill?"

Her pigtails smacked him in the face as she vigorously shook her head. He laughed.

The sexy-as-hell schoolteacher jumped off the wing holding a duffel bag and what appeared to be a pet carrier. He couldn't see what it contained.

"Jolene's *always* this happy," she declared. "Even at five in the morning, when she thinks I should get up and play." She set down her luggage, hooked her sunglasses into the scooped neck of her tank top and thrust out her hand. "Hey, again," she said when they shook hands.

Her eyes were clear green with tiny flecks of brown, her lips pouty and unadorned. There was a nervousness beneath her smile a less observant person would have missed, further putting him on guard. Grant was a detail man, trained—compliments of the United States Army—to read body language and sum up a person and their motives in a matter of seconds.

At one time, his life had depended on it.

He pegged her as coming from a moneyed background. It was in the way she carried herself, the obvious quality of her clothes, the Prada label on her sunglasses—not to mention that she flew her own airplane. Even if it was a rental, the fees and fuel would be steep.

So why would a woman of this apparent caliber apply for a teaching position in a town that was barely a dot on the map? If she needed money, she'd choose a cheaper mode of transportation—and work in a school district that paid higher wages than the community of Shotgun Ridge could afford.

"You don't fit my image of a schoolteacher." His gaze dipped to her modest cleavage and then swung to her plane.

"No? What did you expect?"

"Arrival by car, for starters. A little more meat on the bones and a few wrinkles. Pretty much like Mrs. Laboard, my third-grade teacher. The hairdo's close, but Mrs. Laboard wouldn't have looked good in that streaky shade of blond."

She thrust a hand through her short hair. Every strand fell right back into place. "I hope I'm not too big a disappointment."

"I can live with it. What's in the carrier?" He nodded at the thing as he set Jolie on the ground.

"Bad judgment," she said, releasing a little ball of fluff at his feet. "Meet Harley, our eight-month-old Maltese puppy."

"Darlin', that's no puppy. It's a coyote snack."

"Shh." Her gaze slid to Jolene, who was busy stepping on ants. "He's an indoor dog… I'm sorry. I forgot to ask Ozzie Peyton if you allowed pets. I just assumed…this being a ranch and all…" She tugged at the hem of her top. "Harley's house-broken and he doesn't bark."

Her expression was apologetic, her tone resolute. If he objected to the pitiful excuse for a canine—which he didn't, other than its miniature size—he'd obviously have to get over it in a hurry.

"You know our mayor?" Just the mention of Ozzie's name gave him a clearer picture of what was going on. That meddling old fool.

"Actually," Abbe said, "Ozzie is an acquaintance of…my father's. I called about a place to rent and he set me up here

and offered me the teaching job, to boot. I know it's short notice and all— Harley! Stop eating the rocks. Come here!" She
bent and fished a pebble from the dog's mouth.

Grant wondered about the slight hesitation at the mention
of her father, and at the way her green eyes flicked away.
Something wasn't quite right here—and Ozzie Peyton had
some explaining to do.

God help them all.

Ozzie, along with his cohorts Lloyd Brewer, Vernon Tillis
and Henry Jenkins were fondly known as "the geezers" and
fancied themselves the town matchmakers. They'd gotten it
into their heads that Shotgun Ridge had too many bachelors,
and several years back they'd set about correcting that situation by advertising for women and babies.

Hell, they'd roped in his brother Ethan that way—although
admittedly their meddling had turned out to be the best thing
that could have happened to his brother. Grant and Clay had
craftily ducked out of town when the geezers had staged a
bachelor auction. They'd come home to find Dora Watkins in
residence with Ethan's baby girl, Katie. A baby girl Ethan had
known nothing about.

Grant hoped this schoolteacher wasn't further evidence of
the geezers' shenanigans. He had a bad feeling about it.

"Mr. Peyton *did* tell you I was coming, didn't he?" she
asked, looking up at him. Her green eyes held a vulnerability
and, for an instant, desperation—as though her life depended
on his answer.

He'd been thinking about suggesting that she and her cute
little girl and pitiful excuse for a dog would be more comfortable in town at the boardinghouse of the widows Bagley, but
the momentary chink in her self-assured armor made him
pause. God almighty, he didn't know what to concentrate
on—the beautiful woman gazing up at him, the puppy doing

a fine imitation of a Hoover as he sniffed and sucked up another small stone, or the pint-size girl exuberantly skipping in circles with her stuffed lamb.

"I'm sure Ozzie just hasn't gotten around to making the call."

"Oh my gosh. You *weren't* expecting me." She pushed her hair out of her eyes and snagged a blue nylon leash, then clipped it to the puppy's collar and stood. "Do y'all even have a place for rent? I counted three houses when I flew over."

"I've got a guest house." Not necessarily for rent. "When did you talk to Ozzie?"

Again, her gaze skittered away. "Uh, a few days ago... Monday, I think."

He felt his hairline shift with his surprise. Today was Thursday. "And you just up and left...where did you say you were from?"

"Texas." She fished another pebble from the dog's mouth. "Look, if there's a problem, maybe we should call Mr. Peyton."

"Oh, I'll call him, all right" he said, his annoyance growing. Ozzie Peyton had a heart the size of Montana, but sometimes his antics were irritating enough to make a preacher cuss. Pastor Dan Lucas would surely attest to that.

"Mommy? Can we go swimming? 'Member you said there was a lake?"

"Not right now, sweetie babe. We have to unload the airplane." She looked at Grant, her smile a bit weary now. "Assuming we're welcome to stay..."

He nodded. "Obviously my manners need some polish. I imagine you're beat after a long flight."

He decided that if she intended to stay, it wouldn't hurt to have her in his guest house for a few days where he could keep an eye on her and figure out her story. She had to have one. Most people did.

"Why don't you take yourself and anything else that

moves and wait for me in the pickup." He gestured toward his truck that was parked beside the hangar. "I'll get the luggage. After you're settled in, I can come back and tie down the plane."

"Oh. I thought... Don't you have room in your hangar?"

"Well, yeah...."

"Great. I felt like I'd landed in clover when Mr. Peyton said the place came with hangar space. It'll just take a minute to put away the Baron. No sense in making another trip. Besides, the sun's murder on the paint job. Jolie, take Harley and stand right over here in the shade where Mommy can see you. We're just going to push the airplane into this building, okay?"

"'Kay." She tucked her stuffed lamb under one arm, and bypassing the dog's leash, she scooped up the puppy, burying her nose in the fluffy white fur as she walked toward the designated spot. "Let's go get in the shade, fweetie—no, no. No bite on da Lambie-pie," she admonished when the pup nipped at the stuffed animal.

"Cute kid," Grant observed. "Give me a minute to move the Cessna over to make room for the Baron."

"Thanks. I'll give you a hand." Abbe followed Grant into the hangar. She felt as though she'd been holding her breath for the past fifteen minutes. All the research and reading she'd done on Grant Callahan hadn't prepared her for the man in the flesh. He was so...so overwhelmingly *male*. And his shrewd blue eyes didn't appear to miss a trick.

She was normally an open-book type of person, and being so cagey was foreign to her. She wasn't used to guarding her words so carefully.

He clearly wasn't expecting her, and she wondered about that. Ozzie had made it sound as though the Callahans were actively seeking a tenant for their guest house. The airstrip and hangar had been a plus. She needed a place to hide the plane.

Still, whether he'd been expecting her or not, this was exactly where she wanted to be.

Months ago, she'd pried into Grant's life purely out of curiosity, never realizing she would actually one day seek him out. Now she hoped she hadn't made the wrong choice. He had a toughness and watchfulness about him, most likely gained during his army days. And of course, being abandoned by his parents when he was very young might have had something to do with the reserve.

Abbe simply couldn't fathom how a mother could give up her child.

Then again, here she was, prepared to contemplate that choice herself, if need be.

Albeit, the circumstances were very different. To harm Jolene, the Ziggmorellis would have to find her. To do that they'd have to locate Abbe. But if Abbe wasn't with her daughter, it would indicate that her daughter wasn't that important to her, and Jolene would no longer be part of the dangerous equation. She'd be safe.

And Abbe would go anywhere, do anything to keep her daughter safe. Even if it meant giving her up.

But she was getting ahead of herself here, pinning hopes on Grant Callahan as a potential guardian before she'd even gotten to know him. If he wasn't the right type of person, if she couldn't be sure Jolene would be safely hidden in this small town, she'd take her daughter and be out of here in a flash.

As they jockeyed the airplanes, pushing the heavy machines into position, she kept a watchful eye on Jolie. God, she was conflicted, her motherly instincts pulling at her from all directions. On the one hand, she wanted to clutch Jolie to her breast, not let her out of her sight for an instant, sure that she, as mother, was the best person to keep her child safe. Yet just as a parent wanted to protect their child, if danger approached, she'd be the first one to shove her daughter away, to scream for her to run! To survive. Regardless.

The push-pull born out of life-and-death terror was making her a wreck. She hoped that she'd retained some of the acting skills she'd learned in drama class her sophomore year of high school.

Although the interior of the hangar was cool, her top was damp by the time they got the Baron inside.

"Is this all you've got?" Grant asked, reaching into the cargo hold.

Abbe gave him a sassy grin. She saw him do a double take and nearly lose hold of the suitcase. Well, that was interesting. She was probably sending him mixed signals; but damn it, trying to act normal when her stomach and mind were churning like mad was about as easy as eating Jell-O with chopsticks. "It was a toss-up between the weight of full fuel tanks and my shoe collection. The fuel won out."

"Smart choice." He glanced down at her pink sandals. "I hope you brought something more substantial than those. Otherwise, the wildlife in the area will be real happy to see you. While the coyotes feast on your dog, the rattlers will be making a meal of your feet."

Abbe shivered and immediately looked down. They were standing on concrete but that didn't mean a rattler wouldn't come looking for a cool place to rest. "Do you have a lot of snakes around here?"

"We've got our share."

His muscles rippled as he hoisted the paisley suitcases from the Baron's cargo hold, and now it was Abbe's turn to stare, the image of snakes wiped clean out of her head.

The photos the private investigator had included in the file didn't even begin to do him justice. He was well over six feet and possessed a lean toughness that indicated he took care of his body. His white T-shirt hugged his torso and biceps, and was tucked into faded jeans sporting a brown leather belt with a large, silver buckle. His boots were scuffed, his hat well broken in. Despite his wealth, this was no gentleman rancher.

Grant Callahan was the real deal—a working cowboy.

"So, how long have you been a teacher?" he asked.

"Actually, I haven't taught since before Jolie was born. I carried a double major in college—English and aviation. Flying turned out to be a lot more fun than being cooped up inside a classroom. And when I had Jolie, she became my main focus."

"If you don't mind my asking, where's her father?"

"He died. Five months ago."

"Oh, man. I'm sorry." He lowered the luggage to the ground as though he wanted his hands free to offer comfort, yet he only tugged at the brim of his hat.

"Thanks." She tried not to think about Tommy, because the memories caused another conflict of emotions—the horror of witnessing his brutal death, and the stunning revelations that had come to light afterward. Revelations that had snatched away the very foundation of her world.

He met her gaze. "Are you looking to start a new life? Get away from memories?"

"I hope so."

"How long did you live in Texas?"

"Off and on since I was born." He was skirting close to questions she wasn't ready to answer. "Mr. Peyton didn't mention how much the rent is on your guest house. Will you be wanting a deposit plus the first and last month in advance?"

"Would that be a problem?"

"No. I can pay you cash."

He crossed his arms over his chest. "Just like that? I haven't even named an amount yet."

She nearly rolled her eyes, her patience thinning. "I was told you were fair."

"You agreed to rent a place without asking the price, so I'm assuming money isn't an issue." He paused, then added, "And this teaching position you got—did you even ask about the salary?"

"Well, no, but it's pretty standard, isn't it?"

"Not in this school district. Darlin', you're flying a honey of an airplane, your sunglasses cost more than some people make in a month, and call me cynical, but it just doesn't add up that you'd want to teach school in a small town, a town you just up and decided to move to in less than a week."

Abbe struggled to keep her voice calm. He was too smart. "Are you asking me a question, or just forming an opinion all on your own?"

"Most of the time my opinions are on target. Can't blame me for wanting to know a little about my potential tenant."

She put her hand on his arm. The word *potential* had her insides churning. "Grant, I've traveled a long way, driven mainly by hope. I want a normal life for my daughter, in a good solid town. When I read about Shotgun Ridge, I felt as though I'd had a private tour into a Norman Rockwell painting." She hesitated, wanting to stick as close to the truth as possible, unwilling to say *where* she'd read about the town.

"Jolie's father was killed in a drive-by shooting. I wanted to get my little girl as far away from that type of environment as possible. I'm hoping Shotgun Ridge is that place."

His eyes went from questioning doubt to compassion. "I don't usually greet folks with rudeness. Especially a fellow pilot. I'm just wary by nature."

"I understand. The new school year doesn't start for a couple of months yet. I need that time to see if this is a good fit for us. Will you rent me your guest house? I can't give you any credit references, but I promise I'll pay on time and you won't get a bounced check."

"Guess I won't have to go far to hunt you down if you do. Come on, let's get you and the squirt out of the heat."

CHAPTER THREE

GRANT HOISTED the two suitcases and box of toys. Abbe picked up the rest of her things, including the car seat, and followed him to the white pickup emblazoned with the dark green logo of Callahan and Sons Farms, gathering Jolie, Harley and Lambie-pie on the way.

She was breathing a little easier now that she knew she could settle in. The thought of having to make other living arrangements—or leave Shotgun Ridge altogether—was too much to contemplate.

She'd focused her hopes on Grant and hadn't given any consideration to a backup plan. God knows, if she'd had an alternative in mind when Grant had greeted her presence with suspicion, pride would have sent her right back into the plane. Instead, she'd had to swallow that pride and hope for the best.

Why had Ozzie given her the impression that the rental was a done deal, when it clearly hadn't been?

After the luggage was stowed in the truck bed, Grant fastened the car seat in the back of the cab, then reached for Jolene. "Up you go, squirt. You, too, pork chop."

Jolie giggled. "Her's not a pork chop, silly. Her's *Lambie*-pie."

"Don't be telling my horses she's a pie. They'll eat her up for supper."

Jolie gulped in a breath like a baby turtle snapping at air, and wrapped her arms around her stuffed lamb, squeezing it to her chest, her eyes dancing. The little flirt.

Abbe knew she ought to correct Jolie's grammar, but didn't bother. Her daughter was smart as a whip, and half the time said things just to be cute. At other times, she could sound so grown-up it was scary.

And one of the very reasons they were here was so that Jolie wouldn't be forced by terrible circumstances to grow up *too* quickly.

Or not at all.

Oh, God. The hideous thought nearly buckled her knees. She had to stop torturing herself this way, had to be strong—or at least pretend to be. Fake-it-till-you-make-it had become her new motto.

Before Abbe could coax Harley into his carrier, Grant plucked him up and perched him on the seat with Jolie and her lamb. "That's about the smallest eight-month-old dog I've ever seen. Is he going to get any more meat on his bones, or will he always be a dust mop?"

"Now how can you call something with a name like Harley a dust mop?" Abbe asked, determined to put aside their rocky beginning and start anew. "He's cute."

"Darlin', Harleys are cool, or sexy, or real fine pieces of machinery—not cute."

"Cute is in the eye of the beholder."

"I believe it's *beauty* that's in the eye of the beholder."

She brushed her hair out of her eyes and reached for the passenger door. "You're welcome to your own adage, I owned a Harley, and the Tweety Bird painted on my gas tank was *incredibly* cute."

She could tell she'd both surprised and impressed him. He rounded the hood of the truck and slid behind the wheel.

"You fly airplanes and ride motorcycles, too? You're a man's dream. Wanna get married?"

Her stomach jumped, even though she knew he was kidding, and that flustered her. She hadn't had this kind of reaction with Tommy. Maybe that was why she'd never pushed for anything more than an engagement ring—even after Jolie was born. Or maybe it was simply that she'd somehow sensed *she* wasn't Tommy's dream.

She plucked at her damp top. "I oughtta say yes just to watch you sweat."

His lips quirked as he put the truck in gear. "I'm already sweating."

Abbe pretended she didn't hear him. The air-conditioning blew on high, cooling the interior in a matter of minutes. In the back seat, Jolene entertained the dog and her lamb with a repetitious rendition of "Twinkle Twinkle, Little Star" pretty much nixing adult conversation. Which was fine with Abbe.

Her nerves were still frayed, but excitement twined through the anxiety as she took in the lush expanse of land. She'd been impressed when she'd seen the ranch from the air. On the ground, it was even more awesome.

Pristine white fences sectioned off acre upon acre of green grass where beautiful horses grazed. Between the stables and barns, all painted white and trimmed in green, several gleaming horses walked in a circle tethered to mechanical leads.

A long ribbon of paved private road stretched before them, lined by more white fencing and mature oak and sycamore trees. Up ahead, a cluster of trees surrounded an awesome Greek revival–style home adorned by green shutters and two-story Corinthian columns. A large garage sat to one side, and behind and off to the other side sat a smaller house, a bungalow. The guest house?

She turned to him. "This is so beautiful. How can you get anything done for looking at the view?"

"Mmm, it's my little slice of paradise."

A large pond dominated the front-yard landscape, and ducks paddled in the placid blue-green water that reflected the puffy white clouds overhead. The flagstone bridge they crossed caused an unexpected bubble of mirth to escape her throat.

Grant glanced at her. "What?"

"I just had a crazy image of a fairy-tale bridge complete with an evil troll."

Smile lines crinkled at the corners of his eyes. "No evil trolls allowed on Callahan land."

Which was exactly what she was counting on.

Instead of pulling up in front, he turned onto a side driveway that led to the bungalow. "This is it."

The exterior of the guest house was similar to that of the main house, all white wood and green trim. There was probably only a distance of about seventy-five feet between the two, but the separation still made her uneasy. She had a keen urge to ask him if she could rent one of the rooms in his house, instead.

But that would have been the old Abbe's way of operating. Even though she'd sought Grant out for a purpose, she was still on her own. From now on, *she* was the one who would make the decisions and act on them.

"I assume the minimansion over there is yours," she said, nodding toward the main house. "Do you live alone?"

"My younger brother, Clay, hangs his hat there, too. My older brother, Ethan, lives in the original house—you probably saw it from the air. I built *this* place after Ethan married Dora—figured they needed some privacy as a family."

"Do they have children?"

"Two. Ryan's a year old, and Katie's three. Jolie will have a playmate." He shoved the gearshift into Park and shut off the engine. "Dora's gonna go nuts over your dog. I hope he doesn't mind wearing costumes."

Huh? "You dress your dogs?"

"I'll leave that for my sister-in-law to explain." He got out of the truck and hauled the suitcases from the bed as though they were empty. Abbe tried not to gape.

"Mommy, did you bring my floaties?"

"Yes, sweetie babe, but they're packed."

"It's awful hot," Jolie said next, pouring on the charm. "Lambie-pie's hot, too."

"Well, Lambie-pie can make do with the air-conditioning for a while." She lifted Jolie out of the car seat, nearly dropping the dog in the process. "Now, promise Mommy that you won't go anywhere near the water unless I'm with you, okay?"

"'Kay. C'mon, Harley. Let's go see our new room."

Abbe wasn't overly concerned about the risk the pond presented because she intended to never let Jolie out of her sight. She had to practically sit on her lips now to keep from calling Jolie back and admonishing the child to wait for her. But they were only going into the house. And Grant was there— he'd already opened the front door and taken their bags in. It was too soon for anyone to have picked up her trail and followed. At least she hoped so.

The problem with a threat hanging over your head was that you never knew when the sword would drop. Typically, life went on as usual. Night turned into day, and day turned back into night. People went to and from work, watered the grass, pushed their kids on swings—let down their guards. You had no way of knowing if a private investigator kept tabs on you, perhaps watched your movements through the lens of a hidden, high-powered telescope, and reported all to an unknown interested party. You couldn't know when you might walk innocently out of the market with a bagful of groceries and collide with disaster.

Or in Abbe's case, merely step out onto the front porch.

Then again, maybe this mess would all blow over. Maybe Pop would convince the Ziggmorellis that she could be trusted with their nasty little secret.

But regardless of what might or might not happen, she could not—*would* not—pass on her fears to her daughter.

She mounted the front steps, promised herself she'd make time to come out here with a glass of lemonade or wine and sit on the porch swing.

The air inside the guest house was hotter than outside. Yet despite the temperature, she still found the place beautiful. The floors were glossy hardwood, softened by area rugs in muted shades of green and ivory. Vaulted ceilings created a feeling of spaciousness in the great room, which encompassed the kitchen, dining and family room. A short hallway led to two bedrooms, each with its own bath. Throughout, pale celery-colored walls were accented by crown molding and detailed trim with the color and appearance of frothy whipped cream.

The decor was inviting, neither too feminine nor too masculine. She glanced over at Grant standing in the hallway, leaning indolently against the wall. His posture and watchful expression made her uneasy. But God, he was sexy.

"It's perfect," she said. "Did you decorate it yourself?"

He pushed away from the wall and walked toward her. "Mostly. Although I had input from just about every female in town. They're a bossy lot. Most of them newlyweds, so they've got that nesting thing going. Can't be satisfied fixing up their own places, they feel obliged to get in the middle of their neighbors' business, too. You'll meet a good many of them tonight."

She did a mental rewind. "I will?"

"If you're up to it. Thursday night at Brewer's Saloon. It's like church on Sundays. If you don't show up, half the town'll be calling to find out why."

"Half the town doesn't even know I exist yet."

"That's what you think. Around here, news travels faster than God can get it. Besides, you want to see if we're a good fit. Show up at Brewer's and you can pretty much accomplish that goal in one night."

For a minute, she thought he was referring to the two of them as a good fit, then remembered those were the words she'd used in reference to herself and Jolie fitting into the town. "What about Jolene?"

"What about her?"

"I'm not in the habit of taking my daughter to saloons. Never mind the laws concerning minors."

"Brewer's is a family place. Best burgers and hot dogs you'll find in Montana."

"In that case, consider me up to it." She smiled. "By the way, I'll be needing a car. Where can I rent one?"

"Closest car rental place is over in Miles City." He hooked his thumbs in the waistband of his jeans, looked down at her. "I'll leave the truck for you until you get something permanent."

"You don't have to do that."

"No, I don't. But I'm offering."

"What are you going to drive?"

"Either the Suburban or the Vette—they're gathering dust over there in my garage." He nodded toward his house, only yards away. "Or another of the ranch pickups."

"Oh. Well, then…thank you. I appreciate it."

He tugged at his hat. "I'll take off so you can get settled in. The air's on, so it should cool down in here pretty quick.

The keys are in the pickup." He glanced at his watch. "It's four o'clock now. How about if I come back for you around six? You can ride into town with me and I'll introduce you to the neighbors."

She nodded. "I'll be ready. And, thank you, Grant."

"For what?"

"For being such a good sport. Now that I realize we truly landed on you by surprise, I feel a little embarrassed."

"No need. Just caught me off guard, is all. If you stay around, you'll find that I don't shake easily."

She watched him go, his stride easy, his shoulders erect.

She hoped what he said was true. Because in order to trust him, she would eventually have to tell him *why* he was the one she'd chosen for help.

And unless he was made of steel, that information was going to shake his entire world.

GRANT WALKED the short distance to his own house, strode into the kitchen and snatched up the phone, stabbing numbers by memory. He didn't bother with pleasantries when Ozzie answered.

"What the hell ever possessed you to rent out my guest house without discussing it with me first?"

"Now don't go gettin' up on your high horse. If you'd answer your telephone every once in a while when a person tries to call, you'd be in the loop, you bet."

"In the loop?" Grant repeated incredulously. "It's *my* house. I *am* the loop. Don't the Bagley widows have room at the boardinghouse?"

"Nope. Renovatin', is what they told me. Paintin' and sprucin' up the floors, you bet."

"And what's wrong with the new hotel Jake McCall spent so much time and effort to build?"

"It's a hotel, boy. You don't go tellin' a schoolteacher and her young'un to stay in no hotel."

"And that's another thing. Did you even check her credentials or references before you offered her a job?"

"I know all I need to know about her references, you bet. And what's got you all stirred up like a hornet's nest? I've never known you to be inhospitable."

Grant sighed and shoved his hand through his hair. He wasn't sure of that answer himself. And Ozzie's penchant for tacking on "you bet" to just about every sentence was grating on his nerves more than usual.

"Humor me, Ozzie. I'm a cynic, and I hate surprises. Just so that I'm fully in the *loop,* why don't you take it from the top and bring me up to speed? I'd appreciate the detailed version, if you don't mind."

"Well, now, I don't mind at all, you bet. Though there ain't as many details as you seem to think. I happen to be acquainted with Abbe Shea's father, so I recognized her when she called. Said she was lookin' for a good place to raise her little girl—poor thing's daddy was killed some months back. Heard tell he was shot down in broad daylight right in front of Abbe."

Grant swore softly. She hadn't told him she'd been a witness.

He knew what a bullet could do to a body. He'd seen the carnage firsthand—both as a bystander and as the one who'd pulled the trigger. Rigorous training had taught him to distance himself from the sight of death. But someone like Abbe Shea wouldn't have those skills. No wonder her eyes held so many shadows.

Still, he couldn't shake the feeling that there was more she wasn't saying.

"Anyway," Ozzie said, "I asked her what kind of work she did, and when she told me she had teachin' credentials, well, I couldn't let that pass. You know we need schoolteachers."

"So she didn't call you looking for a job?"

"No, but isn't it lucky for us that she fits the bill? Now, I'm countin' on you, boy, to make sure she feels right welcome, you hear? It's not every day that we get schoolteachers droppin' into town with an eye toward stayin'. And I expect you to watch over her real good, because she's been through a rough time."

"I'm no baby-sitter, Ozzie. And I hadn't planned on being a landlord, either."

"But you're a good man, you bet. I'd consider it a personal favor if you would take Abbe and the little one under your wing, and stick close." His tone lowered. "You just never know which way the wind'll blow when a delicate thing like Abbe goes through such trauma."

Grant went rigid. "Are you trying to tell me she's suicidal?"

"'Course not! I didn't say that at all."

Grant nearly laughed. The old man hadn't outright said it, but he was deliberately trying to plant the idea. Abbe might be vulnerable, but she was far from fragile. She flew airplanes, rode motorcycles and had given birth. Those three things took spine. Probably more than he had himself. Hell, he'd seen his sister-in-law give birth, and by God, nothing looked harder.

OZZIE PEYTON SET DOWN his favorite Bic pen with which he'd been writing in his journal before Grant had finally decided to call him back. Life was fickle at times, and it gave him peace to record his thoughts and the day's happenings in this leather-bound writing tablet.

His gaze rested on the painting of his late wife, Vanessa, which hung prominently over the fireplace mantel where most folks would show off their prized elk antlers. Vanessa had gone to the hereafter several years back, but he could feel her presence in the room just as strongly as the day he'd carried her over the threshold. She'd been his confidante and best friend, and he still discussed most everything with her. He kept that information tucked close to the vest, though. Some folks just wouldn't understand.

He felt a little guilty about not telling Grant the whole truth, but knowing the boy's past, that could get a mite ticklish. If there was any telling to be done, it ought to come from Abbe herself.

The fact that he'd had to let Mildred and Opal Bagley in on the details stuck in his craw some—those widows had all but shoved their way in on the action. The action being, of course, the matchmaking' business Ozzie and the boys— Lloyd, Henry and Vern—had started some years back when they'd realized the town was darn near all men.

Well, a person couldn't say the same thing now, and he was right proud of the fact that the sexes were close to being balanced now. Took credit for it, too. Though to be fair, there were a couple of gals that had pretty much dropped into their laps like ripe plums, Abbe Shea being one of them.

He gazed into his sweet Vanessa's eyes. The love of his life, she'd never been one to judge others harshly, and he supposed some of her gentle approach to life had naturally rubbed off on him. He couldn't say that he approved of how Stewart Shea made a livin', but that hadn't gotten in the way of the two of them becoming friends, albeit long-distance ones, over the years. Stewart had always been straight with him. Too bad the man hadn't carried over that honesty to his own kin.

Now, here they were, smack-dab on the horns of a dilemma the likes of which they'd run up against twenty-seven years ago.

And once again Ozzie had vowed to watch over something that was precious to Stewart Shea—the very man who was known in certain circles as the "quiet don."

"We might have bitten off more than we can chew this time, love," he said to Vanessa. "But the boys and me agreed that we had to pull some strings. Why, it's our God-given duty to offer safe haven to an angel—even if it means we might end up lurin' the devil into Shotgun Ridge."

CHAPTER FOUR

ABBE LOOKED FORWARD to meeting the people at Brewer's Saloon with nervous anticipation.

The smell of alfalfa and fresh-mown grass wafted through the open window of Grant's Suburban as they turned off the highway and headed toward the center of town, leaving behind the open ranges dotted with cattle. She loved the way summer days stayed light well into the evening. It put her in mind of backyard barbecues, family gatherings and carefree kids playing tag and dodging water balloons.

Not that she knew much about that kind of life. The only family she'd really had was Pop and his business associates, and most gatherings were held at Villa Shea's, Pop's restaurant in Las Vegas.

"I imagine you're hungry after traveling most of the day," Grant said.

"We had lunch in Jamestown when we stopped to refuel, but I admit I'm running on empty now."

"Me, too, Mommy," Jolie said from the back seat. "And Lambie-pie is starving half to death!"

Grant glanced in the rearview mirror, the corners of his eyes crinkling with amusement. "Hold your horses, squirt. We're almost there." He pressed on the brakes, observing the town's posted speed limit. "How come you stopped in North Dakota instead of flying straight through?"

"I didn't know if y'all were equipped to service the plane, and I didn't want to end up landing on fumes at a private strip with no fuel provisions." She was sticking as close to the truth as possible, yet she still felt guilty. The urge to just blurt out her entire story was fierce. But until she was fairly sure she could predict Grant's reaction, get his cooperation, she needed to hold her tongue.

"We've got our own pumps at the ranch."

"I noticed. But that information wasn't available to me starting out. You're not exactly listed on the map as a flight service station. Besides, I wasn't sure if I could hire a cab close by, or if I'd need to fly into Miles City to rent a car."

"Can't say as I've ever seen a taxi out this far. Around here all you need to do is ask, and any one of the neighbors will give you a ride anywhere you need to go."

"Or lend you their truck," she reminded him.

"That, too. Our ranches are from five to twenty miles apart, but we're a tight community. If you stub your toe, folks in town will know about it before you can make it to the clinic. Speaking of which, if you ever need to see the doc, Chance and Kelly Hammond are the only game in town. The medical clinic is up here on the right, just past Main Street. The vet is the next door down."

"I'm sure it'll take me a few days to get my bearings."

"Darlin', don't underestimate yourself. You can pretty much cover the whole town in a two-block loop. Not much chance of getting lost."

She smiled. "I wasn't worried. I am worried about the supermarket closing, though. The fridge in the guest house is bare."

"Hell, I forgot about that. The closest thing to a supermarket we have is the general store, but it's already closed. I happen to know the owners, though. I'll get Vera Tillis to open up before we head home."

Home. Abbe wondered if she'd ever again be able to call anyplace home.

With one hand on the steering wheel, Grant made a right turn. "This is it," he said. "Main Street in Shotgun Ridge."

On the left where the road ended at a T was a quaint white church with a gabled roof and a steeple atop. Next to it was a redbrick courthouse flying an American flag.

"You've got the church at this end," he said, "and the Bagley widows' boardinghouse and the sheriff's station at the other. If you spend much time with Mildred and Opal Bagley, you'll be heading back up here to repent."

Abbe laughed. "Now you've got me curious."

"That'll get you in trouble for sure."

For a moment, her chest filled with an odd sense of peace, as though she'd stepped back in time to a world that hadn't yet heard of the Internet superhighway, hadn't yet learned to rely on electronic calendar planners to govern their lives.

When, she wondered, had she stopped living in the moment, enjoying *now,* instead of worrying about tomorrow?

She'd thought Hope Valley was a small town, but it was practically a metropolis compared to tiny Shotgun Ridge. Here, diagonal parking spaces, crammed with SUVs and pickups, lined both sides of the street, and the overflow filled the dirt lot behind the bank.

Surprisingly, there was one open spot in front of Jenkins Feed and Seed, and Grant aimed the Suburban into it as easily as if he was turning into his own garage. She noticed the Callahan and Sons green logo on the truck next to them.

"Did you bribe someone to keep this spot open?"

A dimple flashed briefly in his cheek. "Didn't have to. Most people are creatures of habit. We're like dairy cows at the feeding trough—we tend to head for the same spot by rote. Ever seen cattle lined up to eat? Even if three of their neighbors are late or sent off to the butcher shop, it doesn't occur to them to move over and fill in the gap. I suppose that's the way it is with my parking space."

"Obviously, y'all have never been to Nordstrom's half-yearly sale. It's every man, woman and cow for herself. How do you feel about the back end of the truck you lent me?"

He tipped his hat slightly back on his forehead. "About the same as any other."

"Good answer, because I cut my teeth on parking-lot jockeying at the mall, so I'm bound to create major chaos the first time I come into town on my own. If I gamble wrong on which spaces belong to the latecomers or pot-roast victims, some old heifer set in her ways is liable to come barreling in and meet nose to tail with one heck of a surprise. That said, do you still want to lend me your pickup?"

His lips twitched and his eyes filled with amusement. "I'll take my chances."

She reached for the door handle. "Consider yourself warned."

Jolie had already unbelted herself from her car seat and was waiting impatiently to get out. Grant got to her first and swung her down from the SUV, keeping her hand in his.

Abbe wasn't used to having someone else see to her daughter's needs. Tommy had rarely offered, apparently unaware, or uncaring, that she might need help.

And frankly, it was scary how Jolene accepted Grant so easily. She was a friendly child, hardly ever considered anyone a stranger. That was a lovable, positive trait—within reason, of course. How was she supposed to introduce caution without transforming her daughter's sweet friendliness into fearful withdrawal?

"Get ready for the meet and greet," Grant said as they crossed the street. "How good is your memory?"

"Hit and miss."

"Okay. If you forget a name or face, tug on your ear and I'll rescue you."

The words, offered so simply, reminded her of the real reason she was here. To be safe. To place her and her daughter under Grant's protection. To let him come to their rescue. And the reason he might have to filled her with fear anew. She shivered.

"You okay?" he asked, his hand on the restaurant's door, his gaze steady and way too penetrating.

"I've made cross-country flights, landed at tons of unfamiliar airports, and never had a bit of trouble meeting or talking to new people." She put a hand to her chest. "Now, all of a sudden, my heart's racing."

Before she realized his intentions, he cupped her chin and tipped up her face.

Her breath stalled in her throat. The brim of his hat nearly brushed her head as he leaned in close. For one intense crazy moment, everything around them receded into a surreal haze and her anticipation was almost palpable. She could only *feel;* there wasn't a single, blessed thought in her brain.

"Breathe," he murmured, his own warm breath whispering over her lips. Then he abruptly stepped back. "Just breathe and you'll be fine. Pretend you've just landed at an airport if you like." He smiled. "Either way, I'll protect your back."

There it was again, she thought. The reminder of why she and Jolie were here. Yet Grant himself presented another threat. One that made her heart beat at Mach speed. She breathed deeply.

He glanced down at Jolie who was clutching her stuffed lamb and trying her best to peer through the café curtains that covered the lower half of the plate-glass window. "You ready for a hamburger, squirt?"

"Yup!"

"Then let's go put in our order before they run out."

The moment they stepped inside, Abbe could plainly see that Brewer's Saloon was the place to be on a Thursday night. The air was filled with laughter and noise, and the wonderful aroma of onions and burgers, beer, and the faintest hint of sweet cigar smoke.

There was a bar off to one side, vinyl booths and tables draped with red-checked cloths, and a jukebox in the far corner playing country-and-western music. A set of swinging double doors were propped open, leading to a back room. Grant led them in that direction.

The first thing she noticed was the sea of cowboy hats. Nearly every man in the place wore one—including Grant.

Two men were shooting pool while several people cheered them on. Others socialized in groups or at the tables while children streaked in and around the crowd playing follow-the-leader.

"About time you showed up, Callahan!"

Abbe wasn't sure who'd shouted, but every head in the place turned in their direction. Automatically, she placed her hand against Jolene's soft hair and drew her close.

"Hey, cut me some slack. I'm operating under a handicap tonight. Everybody listen up," he called out as conversations lulled. "This is Abbe Shea and her daughter, Jolie. Abbe's renting my guest house and checking out the town. If she likes us, she might hang around to teach school, so be nice to her."

Abbe smiled and spoke to Grant through gritted teeth. "Great. Now that I feel as conspicuous as fender skirts on a fire truck, you're excused."

He looked down at her, his eyes amused. "You asked me to introduce you around."

"Actually, you made the offer and I accepted. But somehow, I imagined a more…subtle approach."

"What can I say?" He grinned and winked. "I grew up in a house full of men."

Crossing the threshold into the saloon seemed to have flipped a switch in him. This was a very different man from the one she'd seen so far. This man was flirtatious, teasing, fun. Everything a woman could want in a male companion.

But damn it, she wasn't here for a male companion. She was here for protection, safety, and she'd do well to remember that. She had no business responding to his charisma.

Thankfully, a little girl of six or seven raced forward and skidded to a halt in front of Jolene.

"Hi! I'm Nikki Stratton. You want to come play with me and Ian?"

Jolene all but bounced in her excitement. "'Kay!"

"Hold on," Abbe said before Jolie could bolt. "I don't think I should let my daughter run off—"

"Hey, you talk just like my mom," Nikki said, clearly delighted. "Her name's Eden. She's from Texas, you know. We got to fly there after my sister was born—her name's Sarah. We went to visit my grandma—she's a judge and she gets to wear black jammies to work. Mom says it's really a robe and she wears it to look important. I still think it looks like jammies. Mom just had another baby—a brother this time—so maybe we'll get to go again. My grandpa's a chef. He cooks pretty good spaghetti." Nikki paused long enough to draw a breath and acknowledge the young boy who'd just joined their circle.

"This is Ian. He belongs to the Malones, and he has a little sister, too. Boy, you're gonna have a real hard time remembering all this. But that's okay, 'cuz you'll be sitting at our table and we'll help you. Isn't that right, Grant?" She didn't wait for an answer. "Grant always sits at our table."

Abbe looked at him. "You have reserved seating as well as parking?"

"Pretty much. I'm well liked."

"That's what we let him believe." The man speaking had a faint scar across his cheek, and a tiny girl perched on his arm. He held out his free hand. "I'm Stony Stratton. Nikki, the little social butterfly here, belongs to me."

Abbe shook his hand and decided she'd probably end up with a permanent crick in her neck. All these Montana cowboys were so tall! "It's nice to meet you. Hi, cutie," she said to the baby girl he held. Unable to resist, she brushed her fingers over the china-doll face. "I bet you're Sarah."

"Sure is," Stony said. "She's a little stingy with her words as yet. Tends to happen when big sisters do the talking for you." His expression barely changed, but pride rang loud and clear in his tone when he glanced from Sarah to Nikki. "Your daughter will be fine with Nikki. She's good with the younger kids. Watches them closer than a mother hen."

"Please, Mommy." Jolie hop-skipped in place.

"Might as well let her go," Grant said.

"All right. But don't go anywhere that I can't see you—or that you can't see me, okay?"

Nikki answered for Jolie. "We won't. C'mon, Jolie. We get to pick songs on the jukebox."

She watched the kids run off, anxiety twisting in her stomach. Warm breath brushed her ear and she jumped.

"Breathe," Grant whispered.

"I am." She noticed that Stony had moved away and was scooping up a toddler who'd almost managed to slip under one of the tables.

"Are you always so protective of your daughter?"

She shrugged, forcing herself to relax. "It's more of a recent thing. She's all I've got."

His eyes softened. "She'll be safe here, Abbe."

This was the first time he'd actually used her name. For a

moment, she almost thought he'd read her mind, knew her past and her future.

But he couldn't know. No one did—yet.

With a hand barely touching her back, he steered her past the pool table toward the long row of tables that had been pushed together family-style.

"That's Iris Brewer heading across the room," he said, the brim of his hat dipping in the woman's direction. "She and her husband, Lloyd, own the place. Looks like she's on a mission, and my money's on those four old codgers, one of them Lloyd, back there in the corner being her target. She pitches a fit over the cigar smoke when kids are here."

"Well, it's clearly marked as the smoking section." A gold velvet rope draped between two metal poles separated several tables from the rest of the restaurant. "Do the men listen to her?"

He chuckled. "Are you kidding? They sure do. Those old hell-raisers know good and well who runs the place—though Lloyd'll deny it. The one fanning the air to hide the evidence is Ozzie Peyton, our esteemed mayor."

"And unauthorized property renter," she added, studying the four old men.

"There you go."

"He kind of reminds me of Archie Bunker in *All In The Family*. Thinner, though."

"I suppose. I've never thought about it."

She glanced around the rest of the room. "Do you recognize all these people?"

"Yes. Why?"

She shrugged. "Just wondering. Forming impressions." She deliberately didn't look at him. Evasiveness was not one of her stronger suits. "Are your brothers here?"

"Yeah. That's Ethan over there chalking the cue stick. Clay's the one shooting. Do you play?"

"I've played a game or two." Her gaze skimmed over the group of children dancing by the jukebox. Jolie was smack in the center.

"Are you any good?"

She cocked her head, gave him a demure smile. "Maybe I'll let you find out for yourself. A girl's got to keep *some* secrets."

"Hmm. I have a feeling you have more than *some*."

"Don't we all?" she said lightly.

An arc of tension snapped between them as he remained silent, his gaze on her. Not for the first time in their short acquaintance, she felt as though he could see inside her. It was unnerving.

She wasn't ready for him to see her quiet desperation and the reasons behind it.

Iris Brewer broke the moment as she bustled back from scolding her husband and his pals. "Those old coots are stubborn as a pack of mules. Fancy themselves some sort of boys' club in a league with the Schwarzeneggers and Hefners—smoking them nasty cigars." She sighed and reached for both of Abbe's hands. "I apologize for not getting over sooner to welcome you, hon. I'm short a waitress—on a Thursday night of all things. We're so happy you've come to Shotgun Ridge, Abbe. You'll have no worries here." Her eyes on Abbe, she squeezed her hands for a long count of three before releasing.

Abbe's heart jumped. Why did she have the feeling that the story of her life had preceded her? Then she decided she was reading more into a look than was warranted.

"Thank you, Iris. Can I do anything to help? I waited tables one summer during college." She decided not to mention that it had been at her father's restaurant and that he'd felt the menial task was beneath her. "It's been a while, but I'm sure I can still manage to balance a tray."

"No—" Iris's protest was cut short by a small blond woman who didn't show an ounce of guilt over blatantly eavesdropping. She also didn't appear to realize that she was on the verge of losing the two trays she was balancing—or rather, not balancing—one in each hand.

Grant rescued one tray laden with burgers and fries, and Abbe caught the other.

"See there," the blonde said to Abbe. "You certainly *can* manage. You've handled that tray like a pro. I'm Dora Callahan, Ethan's better half and—" she nodded at Grant "—this guy's favorite sister-in-law."

"You're my *only* sister-in-law," Grant said.

She took the tray back from him. "Which still makes me your favorite. Now, shoo. Go annoy your brothers or something. If you keep hogging Abbe, it'll be a month before we get her introduced around."

"Dora," Grant said gently, "I hate to be the one to say this, but you're an accident looking for a place to happen. You better let me help you out with that tray."

"Hush. I've got it." Two baskets of fries nearly slid off the tray as Dora sidestepped his reaching hands. Luckily the jerking motion shifted the food back from the brink of disaster. "It's because you and your brothers constantly watch me, *expecting* the worst, that I end up being jinxed."

"Oh my gosh, Dora. Don't even say that word!" A pregnant woman, apparently also pitching in to pass out meals, stopped next to them. "I've gone a whole week without a mishap or speeding ticket." Balancing a tray of drinks on the shelf of her slightly rounded stomach, she turned to Abbe. "I'm Emily Bodine. And I'm really glad to hear you're going to teach school. I've got twins—they're just over a year old—plus I'm expecting again, as you can probably tell. So naturally education's becoming a very high priority in my life."

"Emily's married to the sheriff," Dora supplied helpfully. "Cheyenne Bodine."

"And you still get speeding tickets?" Abbe asked.

"One of the rookie deputies seems to have a grudge against me. I can't imagine why."

"Could be that you've threatened his life a time or two," Grant said. "That'll tend to get a man's back up."

Dora whipped around. "Are you still here, Grant? Go. We'll take care of Abbe. She can deliver meals and introduce herself at the same time."

"Now, Dora." Iris finally managed to get a word in. "I'll not be asking Abbe to work. This is her very first night in town. She's our guest."

"You didn't ask, Iris," Abbe said. "I offered."

Grant tipped his hat. "I believe I'll step out of the fray and let you ladies work this out among yourselves."

Abbe nodded, giving him silent permission to leave her side. It wasn't as though he was her date, after all. She didn't expect or want him to feel obligated to keep up with her for the rest of the evening. As he walked away, she turned back to Iris.

"Really, I'm happy to have something to do. And I'm not shy about meeting people." People who could well be very important in her daughter's life.

"All right. I know when I'm licked. Bless you, hon. An extra pair of hands is most welcome."

Iris hurried off to the kitchen. Abbe, Dora and Emily split the meal-delivering task between them, which was easy since everyone's order was the same. Burgers for the adults, hot dogs for the kids.

When she made it over to Ozzie Peyton's table, she raised an eyebrow, intending to find out if springing her on an unsuspecting landlord had been an oversight or by design. "Gentlemen—"

Ozzie jumped to his feet and snatched away the tray. "Here, now, missy. What are you doin' carting heavy dishes?" Before he could set the food on the table, one of the other men grabbed it from him and passed out the burgers.

This constant tug-of-war over the serving trays tickled her. "I'm Abbe Shea."

"Well, of course you are. And a beauty, too, you bet. Where's that little girl of yours?"

"Running amok with the rest of the kids, I'm afraid, Mr. Peyton."

"Ah. You probably recognize me from my voice."

"No, Grant point—"

"Good to meet ya, missy. This here's Lloyd Brewer—he owns this fine establishment. Henry Jenkins over there keeps our livestock fed, and Vernon Tillis sees to it that our pantries are stocked."

"Nice to meet you all."

"Now don't tell me Iris has done snatched you out from under my nose and hired you to wait on tables. I was countin' on you to sign on as our new schoolteacher come fall."

"I'm only helping out because she's so short-staffed."

"See there, boys? Didn't I tell you she'd fit right in? You bet." He turned back to Abbe. "Around here, you won't find the townsfolk treatin' new neighbors like outsiders. No, sir. We're all like family, you bet. And we watch out for each other, too. You can take that promise right to the bank. Good as gold, you bet."

Again, as she'd sensed with Iris, Abbe got the feeling that an entirely different conversation was taking place between the lines. Maybe it was. Lucca Ziggmorelli's arrest was national news. And Ozzie Peyton knew Pop. Putting those two significant puzzle pieces together would be a snap.

But did he know the *real* Stewart Shea? Or was he under the impression—as she had been until five months ago—that Pop was a top-secret government agent, as well as a restaurateur?

Tonight wasn't the time or place to probe that subject. However…

"Was it a family thing," she asked Ozzie, "that had you offering Grant Callahan's guest house for rent without his knowledge?"

"You bet." He gave a nod, totally unrepentant. "Those Callahan boys have a big old ranch and plenty of room for a young lady and her little girl to settle into. No sense in you stayin' in a motel room when there's a perfectly good house goin' begging."

She nearly smiled. "I don't believe Grant was aware it was begging."

Gray eyebrows beetled. "He better not have acted disrespectful toward you. That boy's a headstrong one, you bet, but I'm not too old to take him down a peg or two—"

"Oh, no. No. We've come to terms." Except for the amount of monthly rent. He'd yet to name a price. "We just had a couple of awkward moments, is all."

"Well, there you go. It's all settled then, just as it should be, you bet."

She smiled. "Why do I get the feeling you're used to getting your way?"

His vivid blue eyes twinkled. "That'd be because you're a right smart young lady."

Shaking her head, she went back to the kitchen to refill her tray, and by the time she'd served the last basket of burgers, she'd managed to meet almost everyone in the room. As was the tendency among friends, the men and women broke off into separate groups rather than pairing up in couples. Abbe sat with the women at the opposite end of the table from Grant, even though she could see that he'd left a place open beside him—a chair that Jolie occupied a few minutes later.

Never had she felt such an instant connection and sense of camaraderie as she did with these women. She lost track of time, and even relaxed her constant vigil of Jolie as Hannah Malone, Ian's mother, regaled the group with the latest antics of a billy goat that apparently fancied itself in love with her.

The kids sat at the men's end of the table, giving the mothers a welcome break. Abbe couldn't say with a hundred percent accuracy which kid belonged to which guy because they all pitched in equally. Babies fussed and were soothed by the closest set of masculine arms, hot dogs were rescued from crumbled buns, ketchup wiped from smiling cheeks and sticky hands.

As meals were finished and restless children excused to play, husbands and wives began pairing up on the dance floor. Abbe propped her chin on her hand and watched, surprised by a sharp nip of yearning she hadn't felt in a long while. That's what love looked like, she thought. Right there on the faces of Ethan and Dora, Stony and Eden, Hannah and Wyatt, Cheyenne and Emily.

That special something was what she'd been missing all her life, yet never been able to identify.

She jumped when someone ruffled her hair, and turned to find Grant standing behind her. He held out his hand, palm up.

"Wanna dance, Teach?"

CHAPTER FIVE

"YOU DON'T HAVE to dance with me," Abbe said. "I'm fine." Lord, she must be cracked in the head. "On second thought…" She snagged his hand and stood before he could withdraw the invitation. "I could use the diversion. I was sinking into a serious case of the poor-pitifuls."

"Can't have that." Keeping her hand in his, he led her to the dance floor. In one continuous move, he closed his arm around her waist, tucked her against his chest and swept her into a smooth two-step that had her feet gliding backward well before her brain caught up.

Her breath stalled in her lungs, and emotions collided all at once. She didn't know which to respond to first—her pleasure at his masculine self-assurance and the ease with which he held her, the hum of her nerve endings at the way their bodies fused from knees to chest, or the alarming fact that she'd never done this cowboy shuffle, and had no earthly idea what she was doing.

As soon as that last thought registered, the toes of her Doc Martens plowed head-on into the pointy tips of his Tony Lamas.

He stumbled to a stop. Only the strength of his arm around her waist kept them upright, and even that was touch and go. "Look up at me, Ace."

Ace? Feeling like an idiot, she tried to step back, but had about as much success as a mosquito against an armadillo. "I don't know how to do this dance."

"You were doing fine before you started to think."

Well, duh. Her legs felt as though they were made of cotton, and the way they were pressed against his thighs she might as well have been a rag doll standing on the tops of his boots. With little or no effort on her part, his forward motion had simply ushered her right along.

"Um...I'd probably do better if there was a little more space between us."

"The lack of space is exactly why you were doing so well in the first place."

"I don't see anybody else stuck together like taffy."

"That's because they know how to dance. Feel my body and move with me. Trust me to lead you."

"I don't think—" She sucked in a breath as his left thigh pushed against her right leg, propelling her backward.

"That's right," he murmured close to her ear. "Pretty much like walking, but with attitude. Slow. Slow. Quick, quick. Slow..."

It had been a long time since she'd danced with a man. Especially this close. She tried to imagine she was a puppet, letting him do all the work. Not the easiest of tasks when everything about him enticed her—the smell of his aftershave, the feel of his smooth cheek, the sheer size of his body, the utter confidence he exuded.

By the time they'd made a complete circle around the dance floor, she was beginning to catch the rhythm. The couple of times she faltered, he merely lifted her an inch or so off the floor, hummed the cadence for a few steps and then set her back down in the flow.

He was subtle, and she doubted anyone even noticed, but it was disconcerting nonetheless. At five foot seven, she didn't consider herself petite, and she wasn't accustomed to being so easily swept off her feet—literally.

"Do we get to trade off on who goes backward?"

He leaned his upper body back just enough to look down at her. "Nope. I always lead."

"No exceptions?" She saw something flare in his eyes and wondered what had possessed her to be so coy. The heat of friction from their bodies rubbing probably had something to do with it. She could *feel* every inch of him.

"I can be accommodating. With the right incentive. What did you have in mind?"

"Um…" She cleared her throat and glanced away. "Nothing. Sometimes I put my mouth in motion before my mind's in gear, and…" She paused, looked closely at him. "You're teasing me."

He loosened the arm around her waist and deftly put a little more space between them. She suffered a slight jump of panic, afraid she would shuffle "quick" when she was supposed to glide "slow" and would end up sprawled on her butt with her dignity smarting. But even without the pressure of his thighs, she could feel his energy through his hands and through his eyes. It was as though a magnetic field bound them, pulled them around the dance floor in a complementary mirror image of each other.

Grant tipped his head in acknowledgment. He knew he had no business flirting with Abbe Shea, but she just made it so damn easy—and irresistible. He made a concentrated effort not to stroke the soft strip of skin above the waistband of her jeans where her shirt had ridden up.

Dance lesson aside, putting distance between them seemed like a good idea. Certainly it made it easier to talk, and he hoped to hell it would allow his body to cool down. He didn't doubt that she'd felt his arousal. He was a healthy male, and such was the nature of the beast.

But this particular beast needed a distraction.

"You're two-stepping like a pro," he said.

"I don't know about pro status, but you're a very good teacher. Just don't let go, or we're liable to have a big wreck."

That was the problem. He didn't *want* to let go. The juke-box clicked over to a new song, and Grant nearly groaned over the slower tempo. He didn't ask if she wanted to keep dancing. He simply made the decision by drawing her closer—just not as close this time.

"How'd a girl from Texas get by without learning to dance?"

"I can dance. I just hadn't learned the two-step."

"How come?"

She frowned, then gave a soft chuckle. "You're awfully persistent."

"One of my most charming qualities."

"Modest, too, I see. I don't know why I didn't learn, other than the opportunity didn't present itself. I was a bit of a rebel, which meant I was grounded a lot, so I didn't go to many of the high-school dances. When I grew up, I favored nightclubs more than honky-tonks." She gave her head a shake as if shifting a long mane of hair back from her face. Interesting, since the silky, pale strands barely reached her earlobes.

"You're a puzzle, Abbe Shea. You're classy, apparently used to money, you drink beer from a glass, you've got the face and body of a cover model—I'd peg you as more of a city girl."

"I'm used to the city, yes. Why would that make me a puzzle?"

"Shotgun Ridge is the polar opposite of city life. There's not a whole lot to do around here."

"You don't think people change? Decide they want something different out of life?"

"Sure. I'm just trying to figure you out."

"And you think that'll happen in just one evening of socializing? I'd like to think I'm more interesting and complex than that."

"Darlin', if you were any more fascinating, my heart couldn't take it. I didn't mean any offense."

"None taken."

Her smile was gently chiding. They both knew she'd won that round—if they'd been keeping score. He wondered why he couldn't, just once, accept the company of a woman without searching for a hidden agenda.

"You said you ride motorcycles. How about horses?"

She shook her head. "I've never really been exposed to horses. But I'll take on anything with an engine."

"Maybe we'll do something about rounding out your experiences while you're here."

"Maybe. So tell me more about this town."

"Like what?" He noticed that she didn't comment on his insinuation that her stay wasn't permanent. That should have tripped a warning to steer clear, but when the jukebox changed to yet another ballad, he stayed right where he was, with her lithe body tucked against his, close enough to drive him mad. He hadn't realized he was this much of a masochist.

"Anything," she said. "Everything. In just a few hours, I've fallen in love with the town, yet all I really know about these people is that they've made me feel welcome."

"Oh, we've definitely got a welcome mat. Compliments of Ozzie Peyton and his pals."

She smiled. "The majority of you are longtime residents, then?"

"No. Until a few years ago, most of the men in this room were single and content to stay that way. But the geezers got it in their heads that the town was dying, and they advertised for brides and babies."

"You're kidding."

"Honest. They'd decided to try their hands at matchmaking. Started out small—with Hannah and Wyatt Malone. They ran Wyatt's picture in a magazine, listing his assets and his desire for a mail-order bride, then screened the applicants and picked Hannah. When she arrived, she was divorced, Ian was four and she was pregnant with Meredith. She thought Wyatt had been writing to her, but it was the four old guys."

"You mean Wyatt didn't know?"

"That's right. Plus, Hannah had never lived on a ranch and she was scared to death of the animals. But here she was with all her worldly possessions in a U-Haul trailer, and Wyatt didn't have the heart to send her away. We'd have skinned him alive if he had. Turned out fine, though. They're crazy about each other."

He saw her gaze rest wistfully on Hannah and Wyatt, then shift away in search of Jolene—who was happily playing beneath the pool table with the other kids. He would bet money that she'd had at least one eye trained on her daughter the entire night.

That was another thing he wanted to know about her. Why was she so protective of her little girl? She'd told him that the death of Jolie's father made her afraid of losing again, but his gut told him there was more. She had a habit of checking out her surroundings as though she expected terrorists to pop out of the woodwork.

"How many of these couples did they match up?" she asked.

He looked around the room, at his friends and at his brothers. "Six that I can recall."

"Six!"

"Yeah. And if you ask the old guys, they'll take credit for the kids, too."

"That's awfully enterprising of them."

"Mmm, hmm. After Wyatt, they staged a bachelor auction and conned Ethan into putting himself on the block—Clay and I managed to skip town that weekend."

"Cowards."

"Yep. Ozzie set it up so that Dora would win the bid. Turned out, she was buying a date to introduce Ethan to his daughter, Katie."

"I take it he hadn't seen Dora in a while?"

"He'd *never* seen her. Dora's not Katie's biological mom, but Ethan's her biological dad."

"What? How—"

"It's a long story. Basically, Ethan's playboy past came back to bite him in the ass. Turned out to be the best thing that could have happened to him." Grant, in fact, envied the love and family his brother had. It was an aching hole inside him, one that a man like him—with blood on his hands—didn't deserve to have filled. But it was there nonetheless.

"Who was next?" she prodded.

"Stony Stratton."

"Ah, the social butterfly's daddy."

"Actually, Nikki was his goddaughter. When her parents died in a fire, he adopted her. At the time, he was married to a real bitch. She left him over the whole episode—and good riddance to her. Then Eden showed up to be Stony's housekeeper while her aunt—his real housekeeper—took a vacation. The whole thing was planned with the geezers' help. Eden had some sort of medical condition and needed to get pregnant within a certain time frame, or the doctors were going to do one of those…operations. Make her infertile. She asked Stony to help her out, and the next thing we knew, they were married."

"She asked him to get her pregnant? And the men knew that?"

"Crazy, huh? I don't keep up with *all* the details, but that's the gist of it."

"Amazing," she said softly. "Have the old guys struck out yet? Picked the wrong woman?"

"Not that I've heard. And, believe me, it's gone to their heads. Which is pretty scary. Sometimes you can meddle in a person's life and really screw things up."

She sighed and laid her head on his shoulder. "But they haven't. Do you suppose there's something magical about this town?"

"No. Just blind luck." He didn't think she was even aware of how she'd melted into him. He, on the other hand, was very aware.

Her hair, with its clean scent of shampoo, brushed his chin. For a few brief moments, they merely swayed together to a ballad about a man in love with his woman. He didn't usually tune in to the lyrics of a song, but this time he did. Glancing around the room, he realized that many of the men here could have been singing this love song to their women. Oddly enough, the thought made him feel lonely.

Masculine laughter rang out in the room, the kind of laughter that invited participation, and Abbe jerked back, obviously just now realizing that she'd snuggled into his neck. Her hand tightened on his, her gaze immediately seeking out Jolene.

"A latecomer?" she asked.

He frowned. Her voice was slightly breathless, as though she'd experienced a sudden adrenaline surge. He'd like to think her response was due to him, to the closeness of their bodies, but the sudden grip of her hand, her widened eyes, suggested something else. Fear.

"That's Dan Lucas," he said. "The pastor."

"Oh."

He wasn't mistaken. As soon as he acknowledged recognition, she definitely relaxed. The back of his neck itched in the same way it had earlier when she'd asked him if he knew everyone in the room. Something or someone had made this woman wary, and despite himself, he felt his protective instincts rise.

"Since he came in by himself," she said, "I assume he's still single. Haven't the matchmakers tried to fix him up, or do they consider him off-limits?"

They were back to the subject at hand, he realized. He could have pinned her down about her reaction, probed for answers, but he decided to let it go for now.

"None of the above," he said. "Dan's married to Amy. The geezers show no mercy—although it was really an old war buddy of Ozzie's who kicked things off. That's a story you'll have to ask Amy and Dan about. All I know is there was some kind of marriage pact made between Dan's father and Amy's father before either of them was born."

"An arranged marriage in this day and age? With a *minister?*"

"I guess. But don't let the preacher title deceive you. Growing up, Dan was as rowdy as the rest of us. He's still a guy who knows how to have fun—and the most down-to-earth man I know."

"It's nice that you still hang out with the same friends you grew up with. So, what's Emily and Cheyenne's story?"

He chuckled. "Are you even going to remember all of this?"

"Absolutely."

"Okay," he said, his hold of her tightening briefly as he maneuvered them out of the way of another dancing couple. "They knew each other as kids. Emily moved away, and ended up working at an ad agency in Washington with Jimmy Bodine, Cheyenne's younger brother. She hooked him up with her sister and they got married. Turned out Debbie and Jimmy couldn't have kids, so Emily agreed to be a surrogate mother for them. When she was pregnant—with twins—her sister and Jimmy were killed in a car accident and she was left pregnant with two babies she hadn't planned on raising. She showed up here and told Cheyenne it was his family duty to help her cope because she was a career woman and didn't know the first thing about babies."

"How did the matchmakers come into play?"

"They rented her Cheyenne's house—and forgot to tell her he still lived there."

"Those guys are awfully free with the real estate around here."

"Seem to be," he murmured. She didn't appear to draw any parallels between that and the business with his *own* guest house, or if she did, she wasn't letting on. Grant wasn't, either. At least, not until he decided how he felt about the likelihood.

He'd told her he was a man rarely shaken, but he'd been staggered from the moment she'd stepped out of that plane. He didn't understand it, and didn't particularly like it. Beautiful women had come and gone in his life. He appreciated them, desired them, enjoyed the sexual intimacy. They were relationships where he controlled the depth of emotion—and he never allowed it much below the surface.

But his first glimpse of Abbe Shea had all but stopped his heart, and he hadn't been worth a damn the rest of the day. So much for control.

Dancing with her wasn't helping, either. She smelled like warm vanilla, both sexy and innocent. The combination made his knees weak.

"So, Emily and Cheyenne got married and are raising their siblings' kids," Abbe said. "And they're expecting another baby. That's so cool. Who was the sixth?"

She'd drawn her head back to meet his gaze, and her green eyes held a wistfulness he couldn't help but respond to. He couldn't remember a time in his life that he'd had this kind of conversation, dished up the neighbors' business as though he was the chairman of the tea-and-gossip club. But Abbe's obvious interest and enjoyment egged him on and he, a man most folks complained they couldn't get more than two words at a time out of, found himself having to watch that he didn't overembellish!

"We got a little out of order. Dan was number six. Before him, it was the doc, Chance Hammond, who took the fall. He married Kelly—she's also a doctor—and adopted her two little girls. One of the girls was traumatized after seeing her father get electrocuted in the garage by a faulty drill, and she didn't speak. She thought it was her fault."

"Oh, how awful." Abbe closed her eyes. The image of Jolene's little face peering out the front window of their house flashed in her mind. If it hadn't been for the hedgerow, Jolie might have witnessed *her* daddy's death.

"She came around," Grant continued, oblivious to her private nightmare. "I missed it, but half the town swears they saw an angel on Christmas Eve that looked a lot like Ozzie Peyton's late wife, Vanessa. That's the night little Kimberly started talking again."

Abbe got chills. *Miracles. Please, God. Let there be one here for me and Jolene.*

The song ended and Grant paused, looking down at her. "You want something to drink?"

"Sure." She'd lost track of time and knew they'd danced through several tunes. That might not have been such a great idea. People would talk, speculate. The last thing she wanted was to draw attention to herself. "Thanks for the two-stepping lesson."

"Was it a sufficient diversion to chase away the poor-pitifuls?"

She laughed as he led her off the dance floor. "Yes."

"What were you feeling sorry for yourself about?"

"Being a single in a room full of couples." She hadn't meant to say that aloud, and she felt her face heat.

"Why? Are you looking to get married again?"

"I wasn't married before."

"Oh. I just assumed."

"Most people do." She didn't elaborate, wondered if he would judge her. In Vegas, being a single mother was no big deal. Small towns were a different matter.

"What about you?" she asked. "How have you stayed under Ozzie and company's radar?"

"Luck, I suppose. Plus, I spent time in the army, so I wasn't ready to settle down."

She noticed that he used the past tense. She'd watched him with the kids tonight, heard the softness in his voice when he talked about his brother and friends who'd found love.

Perhaps he wasn't fully aware of it, she thought, but Grant Callahan was indeed ready to settle down. And here she was, dancing with him, taking up his time, living in his guest house—practically in his hip pocket—possibly blowing any opportunities that might come along for him to hook up with his potential soul mate.

She discounted the notion that *she* could be his soul mate. Chances were good that she'd have to, at some point, leave Shotgun Ridge and her daughter. Nothing was more important to her than Jolene's safety, and if leaving became her only option, she'd go. Grant deserved better.

Back at their table, he lifted a pitcher of iced tea and poured two glasses, handing one to her.

"Thanks," she said, and took a sip, surprised that her hand wasn't completely steady. She hoped he didn't notice. "I should probably go get Jolene."

"Why? She's having fun with the other kids."

"I've never let her go off by herself like this before."

"She's not by herself. And she's in plain view."

"I know." Abbe sighed. "I'm just not used to it."

He started to say something, but the preacher with the booming laugh came up to them.

"How in the world are you?" Dan asked, clapping Grant on the shoulder and shaking his hand.

"Better than you. I was a few minutes late, but at least I made it here by suppertime."

Dan laughed. "I have an 'excused' note straight from the doc. Are you going to spruce up your manners and introduce me to this pretty pilot?"

"I never claimed to have manners, and you obviously know who she is already." Grant grinned. "Abbe Shea, meet Dan Lucas, the man I told you about. He also happens to pray over our souls."

"Uh-oh. Whatever stories this guy's been telling, I have to deny." Dan gave another hearty laugh. "Nice to meet you, Abbe. I hear you're going to teach this fall."

"I'm still considering it." *Lord, girl, you're talking to a man of the cloth!* She half expected a lightning bolt to strike her, for the only thing she was truly considering was making it from one day to the next.

"We'll win you over. My wife, Amy, is dying to meet you, but she decided it was best one of stay home tonight. We've got a three-year-old with a summer cold and a fussy baby still cutting teeth."

"I know how that can be. My gosh, the grapevine around here is fast!"

"Yes. Well, I just wanted to stop by and welcome you to town—and Iris insisted I come get supper for Amy."

"Now the truth comes out," Grant teased.

"Iris is a much better cook than I am," Dan said on another laugh. "Will we see you at church this Sunday, Abbe?"

This man's joy was contagious and Abbe found herself smiling. "I'm told it's a not-to-be-missed deal. So I imagine you will."

"Great. Nikki already introduced me to your little girl. My daughter, Shayna, is the same age. She and Jolie will be good playmates."

"How old's the baby?"

"Benjamin's almost a year old. He's a handful, too—already trying to take his crib apart." Dan glanced toward the back where Ozzie and his cronies were sitting. "I suppose Iris is pouring water on the cigars again."

"Yes," Iris said from behind him. "I am." She thrust a white paper sack into his hands. "Besides, you don't have time to puff on a cigar. You get this food home to your wife. I'm sure she's had a difficult day with two sick babies on her hands."

"Only one is sick. And how come I don't get any sympathy? I had a hard day, too."

"Which is all the more reason you should take yourself home and have supper with your wife," Iris said.

"Yes, ma'am." Dan saluted and laughed. "Nice meeting you, Abbe. We're glad to have you in Shotgun Ridge."

Dan cast one last longing look at the smoking section, then turned and headed toward the door, stopping several times to speak to people on the way.

Iris slid her arm through Abbe's. "The girls are meeting in the kitchen over dessert. Come join us. Eden bakes like an absolute angel. We let the men think we're dishing up plates to serve, but we're really sampling the choicest selections before they get to it."

"I heard that," Grant said.

"Then I expect you to keep it to yourself."

He held up his hands in surrender. "No problem. I'm as scared of you as the next guy."

Iris whacked him on the arm. "Ready, Abbe?"

She looked toward Jolene.

"I'll watch her," Grant said, clearly reading her apprehension.

Iris evidently picked up on it, too. "She'll be just fine, hon. You try to relax now. Around here, we all take care of each other."

Although nerves tucked her stomach right up under her heart at the thought of Jolie being out of her sight even for a few minutes, Abbe allowed Iris to usher her in the direction of the kitchen. Sure enough, Eden, Hannah, Dora, Emily and Kelly were disappearing through the swinging doors.

"See there?" Iris said, pausing and nodding toward the pool table. Grant already had Jolie hoisted up on his shoulders, Lambie-pie resting on the crease of his hat. "That man is a natural with kids."

"My daughter's sure eating up the attention."

"And well she should."

The unconditional acceptance Abbe had received from these people tonight, along with the stories Grant had told her, made her feel as though she belonged. That was something she'd never truly felt before—not even in her hometown in Texas. She was starving for this kind of belonging. Wanted to feast like a greedy cat.

Odd how within the space of a day she could have found what she'd been seeking most of her life.

And at the same time, knew that it was still out of her reach.

CHAPTER SIX

THE TELEPHONE in the guest house rang at six-thirty Saturday morning, and Abbe's nerves jumped to attention. Thankfully, the handset was equipped with Caller ID. When she saw the Callahan name scrolled across the screen, her shoulders relaxed and she answered.

"Abbe? This is Dora. I hope I'm not calling too early."

"No. Jolie's awake at the crack of dawn, which means I am, too, whether I want to be or not."

Dora laughed. "I hear you. Listen, I'm fixing breakfast here at the house—mine and Ethan's place—and Katie's pestering me to see Jolie. We spent the day in Billings yesterday, and she still hasn't forgiven me for making her have an adult day when there was a perfectly good playmate just down the road. Why don't you and Jolie come join us?"

"Um, I said I was up, but I'm not fully at 'em yet. I forgot to buy coffee the other night when Vera opened the general store for us, so I'm moving a little slow."

"You should have said something. I've got plenty over here you could have borrowed. I'm sure Grant does, too, and he's steps from you."

"That's okay. I thought I'd make it back into town yesterday, but time got away from me." More like apprehension. Every time she started toward the door, she imagined unseen eyes watching her and a shiver crept up her spine.

"Well, I've got a pot of coffee on that'll get you going. You don't need to dress—though you might not want to come naked—just throw on a pair of jeans or shorts and call it good."

"I imagine I'll add a top, too," Abbe teased, deciding that she needed to be around people. Her life had been unsettled these past five months, and she'd had to be so cautious. She missed having friends to talk to.

"Well, it ain't the Playboy Mansion," Dora said, "so I suppose you'd better."

Abbe laughed. "How much time do I have?"

"How much do you need?"

She glanced in the mirror over the credenza. She was already dressed in jeans and a tank top, and her hair was so short it only required finger-combing. The only makeup she could claim, though, were the smudges of mascara under her eyes due to last night's laziness in not taking it off before bed. She'd have to fix that. "Fifteen or twenty minutes?"

"You got it," Dora said. "Oh—bring your puppy, too, if you want. I'm dying to see him. Grant said he's a cutie."

He did? Abbe hung up and called Jolie, who had her arm stuck in the cereal box and was digging around for the toy inside. "Come on, sweetie babe. You get to go have breakfast with Katie and Ryan."

Jolie shrieked and snatched her hand out of the box, scattering Cocoa Puffs over the table. She tucked Lambie-pie under her arm and climbed down from the chair. Harley, obviously thinking they were about to have a dog party, stood on his hind legs and danced.

Having children her age to play with was new to Jolie, and Abbe shared her daughter's excitement.

It took every bit of the fifteen minutes to settle the dog, clean up the cereal mess, wash her face, add more mascara and lip gloss, and find their shoes. Jolie had dressed herself the minute she'd gotten out of bed—anticipating, Abbe knew, that they would not spend the day indoors as they had yesterday. The pink polka-dot T-shirt under the orange-and-green-flowered sundress didn't exactly go together, but Jolie had become somewhat of a fashion maven lately—or so she thought—and constructive criticism on Abbe's part was met with deaf ears and a strong will. At least her socks were a match.

Remembering Grant's mention of snakes, Abbe traded her flip-flops for her Doc Martens—not that she planned to tromp through any bushes or tall grass. But no sense inviting trouble.

The truck was still parked in front of the guest house with the keys in the ignition. Her palms grew sweaty on the steering wheel, and it wasn't just from rushing.

Being out in the open made her feel vulnerable. She hated the feeling, hated looking over her shoulder, hated being afraid and having to pretend she wasn't. She consoled herself with the fact that the Callahan ranch was practically a small town in and of itself, and in the middle of nowhere. At least it seemed that way. Any strangers hanging around would be noticed.

Besides, who would even think to look for her here? Shotgun Ridge was merely a dot on the map in only one out of fifty-two states. And if by chance anyone had followed her trail to North Dakota, there were thousands of little dots just like this one in every direction between here and there.

It only took a few minutes to drive over the bridge and down the narrow private road to the main house. She could have easily walked, but she liked the comfort of having a vehicle at her disposal—just in case.

Men were already out working the horses. She didn't see Grant among them and wondered what exactly he did all day. She had no idea how business was handled on a ranch. She might have been born in Texas, but she'd been raised a city slicker.

She parked in front of the house, then collected the squirming dog, bouncing kid and lifeless lamb, and mounted the porch steps. She was about to knock on the door, when it opened.

"Morning," Grant said.

The air was sucked out of her lungs. She hadn't expected him, had thought it would just be her, Dora and the kids at breakfast. "Morning," Abbe said returned. "Dora called…"

"I know. I had strict instructions to watch for you. Come on in."

This was the first time she'd seen him without his hat. His light brown hair was short, almost military standard. Even without the hat, though, he still looked like a cowboy. A big tough one. He wasn't conventionally handsome, but any woman with a single active hormone would take a second look.

"Mommy said you had to work."

He looked down at Jolie and grinned. "I *was* working. But I'm the boss, so I can take time off whenever I want—especially when somebody's offering food."

"I don't know how you can be the boss when that's *my* title," Clay said, coming up behind them. Grant's younger brother reached down and chucked Jolie's chin. "Dora's ready to send out a search party, so will you people get on into the kitchen before she does any more damage? She's determined to cook, and Ethan won't let me talk her out of it." His tone was a good-natured whine.

"I thought you just claimed you were the boss," Grant said with a smirk. "And in case you forgot, that's not your kitchen anymore."

Clay sent him a mock scowl.

"Guess we better follow him," Grant said, nodding toward Clay's retreating back. "You want to let the little fluff mop down?"

"He's not a mop," Jolie said. "He's Harley, 'member?"

"Well, now, that might be a problem. Dora won't want a motorcycle in the house."

Jolie giggled. "You're silly."

"I'd better hold him until we get to the kitchen so I can show him his potty paper," Abbe said, walking beside Grant toward the hallway.

"Excuse me?" Grant said.

She held up the pad, which was similar to the ones hospitals used in the beds—a white cotton square with a blue plastic backing. "Potty paper. Or wee-wee pad, according to the package."

"You carry the dog's bathroom with you? Why doesn't he just go outside like a normal animal?"

"When we moved, I'd only had him for about three weeks, and he hadn't quite graduated to outdoors. Changing environments meant I had to start over with the potty training. He's so little he couldn't navigate the steps at my grandmother's house, so it was just easier to make him an inside dog."

"Moved from where?" he asked. "I got the impression you were a native Texan."

Heat rushed to her head, buzzed in her ears as she realized her mistake. Not that it was any big deal. It wasn't likely that he'd ever heard of Stewart Shea, much less his reputation, so he wouldn't have any reason to connect her last name to the Las Vegas Sheas.

"I *am* from Texas. But Jolie was born in Nevada. After Tommy…" She didn't want to mention his death in front of Jolie, and Grant's slight nod indicated he understood. "We went back to Texas for a while, then came here."

"So, you were only in Texas for what…five months?"

"Yes— Jolie, hon, don't touch." She steered her daughter away from the remote control lying atop an oak credenza, and nearly sighed with relief when the kitchen came into view.

This was only her third day here. She needed more time before she confided in him. All her life she'd trusted blindly, taken people at face value, assumed that like attracted like. Because of her own optimism and openness, she hadn't been *looking* for dishonesty or ulterior motives.

Now, sadly, she made it a point to look.

Perhaps she was sticking her head in the sand again, but fear and disappointment couldn't completely obliterate a naturally sunny disposition, and part of her still hoped that the bogeyman was merely a shadow in the dark that would fade away with the morning sun. That Pop would convince the Ziggmorellis she'd taken their warning seriously, and they'd be satisfied.

"There you are!" Dora exclaimed. "Come in and have a seat. Oh, look at this sweet baby dog! Aren't you a love," she said, pulling Harley out of Abbe's arms. "He's perfect."

For what? Abbe wondered. "Do you mind if I put this pad in the corner? He's trained to use it when he has to go."

"Oh, sure." A golden retriever wandered over and Dora held the puppy down so the dogs could sniff. "This is Harley, Max. Now, you be sweet to him. He's just a baby."

"Actually, he's eight months old," Abbe said. "But he barely weighs four pounds, so he looks like a puppy."

"Still looks like coyote bait to me."

Dora turned and glared at Grant. "Don't even start. I already told Abbe that you said Harley was cute."

Grant's scowl wasn't very convincing. He scooped up Jolie and settled her at the table next to Katie, then sat down.

The way he spontaneously attended to her daughter warmed Abbe, but still caught her by surprise.

Ethan came over and slapped him on the shoulder. "Told you to be careful what you tell my wife." He held out his hand to Abbe. "Welcome. Come have a seat where you'll be safe."

Abbe smiled. "I'm in danger?" Odd that she could say that so lightly when, in a different context, it was all too true.

"Could be," Grant answered for his brother. "As soon as Dora quits smooching with the little dog, she's going to notice that Clay has moved in on the bacon."

"Hey, you turkey," Dora said, thrusting Harley back into Abbe's arms and whirling around, her sights set on Clay. "Get away from my stove."

Clay quickly set down the tongs and backed away. "I'm just helping."

"I promised I'd cook a family breakfast, so sit down and relax, would you?"

Abbe noticed the gleam in Grant's eye. It seemed he'd deliberately stirred up trouble and was inordinately pleased with himself. She showed Harley his "paper," hoping he understood, then sat down at the table and watched the activity around her. She felt a little out of her element here at this *family* meal. Breakfast, furthermore.

The dynamics in this household were interesting. All the Callahan men clearly adored Dora, though her carefree approach in the kitchen seemed to clash with their orderly style, making them want to save her from herself. Clay hovered, visibly flinched when Dora splattered bacon drippings over the stove as she talked and wagged the spatula for emphasis, then cracked eggs in a bowl and tossed the shells willy-nilly toward the sink, missing more often than not. Ethan appeared to be the cleanup detail, wiping up the gooey trail across the granite countertop. Grant merely sat there taking it all in.

In an effort to get Katie and Jolie's attention, Ryan banged his spoon on the tray of his high chair, then lost interest and hung over the side, spoon dangling from his fingers, as Max darted under the table, clearly trying to get away from Harley's overzealous attention. The puppy skidded to a halt when he spied the spoon, and though the baby was all for letting him have a lick, Abbe jumped up and grabbed the fluffy white menace just in time.

She shooed the dog off, then righted Ryan in his high chair. "Better hang on to the spoon, doodle-bug. That's for big boys, not puppies."

"Is that dog afraid of *any*thing?" Grant asked. "He barely comes up to Max's knees, but look which one of them is hiding."

"He doesn't seem to know he's a dog, or that he's toy-size." She snapped her fingers. "Harley, go lie down."

Jolie's and Katie's heads ducked and disappeared under the table to watch as the puppy spun in a circle, then trotted to where Max had flopped down. Giggles erupted when Harley snuggled into the curve of Max's stomach. The beleaguered retriever raised his head in utter bewilderment, then with a long-suffering canine sigh, laid it back on the floor.

Several minutes later, Abbe couldn't understand why Clay had been fussing about Dora's kitchen skills.

"This is delicious," she declared of the light scrambled eggs, crisp bacon, golden hash-brown potatoes, buttery biscuits and milk gravy. And probably more calories and cholesterol in one meal than she'd eaten during the course of the entire year.

"Thank you," Dora said. "Contrary to what you might think with all these guys hovering, I do know my way around a kitchen. I'm just not as neat about it as they're used to."

"You do just fine, legs." Ethan kissed his wife, then deftly caught a jellied biscuit Ryan knocked off his high-chair tray.

"I didn't hover," Grant said.

"And I appreciate it," Dora replied. "So who's going to have a love match today?"

Abbe nearly dropped her fork.

Grant hardly paused eating. "Pride of Knight and Glory Days."

"Glory Days is the mare that came in from Sully Farms last week," Ethan said to Dora.

They were talking about horses, Abbe realized. Thank goodness. As she listened, she couldn't help but compare Ethan and Dora's relationship to hers and Tommy's. Although she and Tommy hadn't been married, they'd lived together, had a child together. But Tommy rarely sat down to breakfast with her and Jolie, and his eyes definitely didn't follow her the way Ethan's followed Dora.

There was something special between this couple—and the other couples she'd met last night.

Something special, she realized, that she and Tommy hadn't had.

"Abbe?"

She gave a start, then realized that Grant had asked her a question and she'd suddenly become the center of attention.

"What?"

"I said, do you want to come watch?"

"Um, I think my mind wandered. Watch what?"

"The breeding process."

"Oh." Did she? If it meant spending time with Grant, learning more about him, her answer would be yes. But witnessing the mating procedures of horses wasn't exactly appropriate show-and-tell material for a three-year-old. "I should probably pass. Jolie's a little young to learn about breeding, and Harley's a flat-out menace. We'd disrupt the whole process."

"Leave Jolie and Harley with me," Dora said. "Katie's thrilled to have a playmate, and I'm itching to try a couple of outfits on your puppy. I've about used up all the animals in Shotgun Ridge."

"Used up?" Abbe frowned in confusion, though Grant *had* mentioned that Dora would want to dress Harley.

Dora laughed. "I photograph animals for greeting cards. Sort of like Anne Geddes's work, except I use animals instead of babies."

"Oh. Well…"

"Pweeze, Mommy. Katie gots a Barbie house in her room."

Abbe glanced at Jolie. She hadn't thought the girls were listening to the conversation. Everyone at the table waited for her answer. Since all of her reasonable excuses had been allayed, it would seem foolish not to accept.

"Okay." She looked at Grant. "If you're sure I won't be in the way?"

"We'll keep you at a safe distance."

CONTROLLING MORE THAN a thousand pounds of pissed-off stallion was not a job for the fainthearted. One minute Callahan and Sons Farm was about to breed a champion, and the next, all hell broke loose.

Grant scrambled to avert disaster as the mare suddenly went berserk, squealing and pitching sideways in a frantic bid to be free of the restraints. The stallion reared up in defense, roaring his own outrage.

Grant swore and threw his whole body into subduing the high-strung stallion. "Whoa, boy! Back!"

Pride of Knight tucked in his chin, his neck and shoulder muscles bulging as he desperately tried to jerk free and get away from the thrashing mare. A horse's instinctive reaction when faced with danger.

"Hold her, damn it," Clay yelled to Ethan above the mare's panicked squeals.

Grant ignored what was going on with Glory Days and focused only on Pride, getting him away as quickly as possible. From the corner of his eye, he noted that Abbe was practically hugging the door of the barn.

When he'd promised to keep her at a safe distance, he hadn't thought the need would actually come up.

This was when expert training and trust between horse and handler paid off.

Pride responded to command—reluctantly, but who could blame him? At the "teasing rail," the bay mare had flirted like a tavern wench, displayed clear signs of peak sexual condition. Everything appeared ideal for the breeding, but the minute Ethan put her in restraints she'd erupted like a mistreated virgin.

"Sorry, boy," he murmured when he managed to get his breath back. "That was a little more teasing than we'd bargained for." He glanced under the horse's belly, saw that Pride's twenty-inch penis had retracted. "Don't blame you a bit. I'd have shriveled up, too."

He reached the door of the breeding shed and led the high-stepping horse outside, nodding at Abbe to fall in beside him.

"How do you feel about taking a tour of the stables instead?" he asked.

"Um…okay." She put plenty of distance between them, keeping her eye on the agitated animal. "What happened back there?"

"I'm not real sure— Settle down, Pride!" Damn animal was crowding him, acting more like a dog herding cattle rather than a valuable Thoroughbred stud. He loosened up on the lead rope and shoved his weight against the stallion's side, using sheer force to gain some elbowroom and reestablish who was in charge.

"The mare spooked when Ethan put her in restraints," he continued. "She was eager and willing up to that point, so none of us saw it coming."

"What will you do now?" she asked, sidestepping in the opposite direction.

"Call the owner, get some more background on Glory Days. Find out if this is her normal behavior or just a fluke. If it's typical, we should have been informed. Sully Farms is paying one hell of a stud fee to get a foal out of Pride, but no amount of money is worth injury to my stallion." He glanced down at her. "How you doing?"

"Recovering—I think. I don't know how y'all can get so close to a couple of excited animals like that. Or how you manage to hold on to them when they get in a fuss the way those two just did. Scared the tar out of me, and I was clear over by the door."

He chuckled. "I noticed."

"Hey, give me a break. I told you I haven't had much exposure to this lifestyle. These horses are beautiful, but I get the impression they either want to take a bite out of me or kick me into a funeral home."

He'd been utterly charmed by her Southern accent when she'd arrived, and today was no different. "Shame on you. All the males on this ranch are perfect gentlemen."

She raised an eyebrow, glanced from him to the powerful horse on his other side. The animal seemed to be finally settling down. "I think your dictionary has a different definition of 'gentleman' than mine does."

"There's where you'd be wrong. Pride, here, knows that when a lady says no, it means no. He displayed a fine sense of honor by backing off." He gave the horse a pat on the neck. "Can't blame a guy for being a little frustrated, though. She got him all hot and bothered, then told him to put his pants back on and denied him his ten seconds of pleasure."

Her head whipped around. "Ten seconds?"

"Give or take five."

"Good grief, what a waste." She shook her head, glanced

over at Pride. "All that impressive equipment, and turns out it's just big barker."

His lips twitched. "I'd say he's entitled to bragging rights. Pride's 'big barker' gets five hundred thousand for the pleasure of his command performance."

"Pleasure? Ha."

"So you're saying size doesn't matter?"

She opened her mouth, closed it, then simply gaped at him. "I'm not having this conversation with you."

She was flustered and Grant was charmed.

He smiled. Slowly. Deliberately. "If you want to change the subject, it's fine by me." His smile grew into a grin. "Your cheeks are red."

"Thank you for pointing that out."

"But you've got to admit, the sight of these guys when they're fully drawn is pretty damn impressive." He patted the stallion on the neck.

"Frightening, is more like it. No wonder that poor mare went to pitchin' and squealin'."

Grant threw back his head and laughed. He couldn't remember when he'd last been so enchanted by a woman.

CHAPTER SEVEN

As THEY NEARED the stables, Manny came forward to meet them. "That was fast," the stable manager said. "How'd it go?"

"It didn't. The mare balked at the last minute." Grant handed Pride's lead to Manny. The stallion had been born and raised at Callahan and Sons Farm, and wasn't one to pitch a fit over who handled him. "Manny, this is Abbe Shea. She and her little girl, Jolie, are staying in the guest house."

"Hey." Abbe greeted him with a warm smile.

Manny tipped his hat. A lifetime of experience showed in the lines of his weathered face and the ease with which he held the horse. "Pleased to meet you, ma'am."

"Go ahead and cool him down, Manny, then see if Stony Stratton's got time to come over and have a look at the mare. Ethan will probably want to phone Sully Farms, find out if she's had a bad experience with restraints or what. Either way, it won't hurt to get Stony's take on her."

"Sure thing, Grant." Manny led the gleaming black stallion toward the exercise arena.

Grant removed his gloves and looked at Abbe. "Well? You up for a tour of the place?" He saw her glance toward the main house, knew she was thinking about her daughter. He couldn't really blame her. He'd probably be wary of leaving his kid with someone he'd only known a couple of days.

"I hate to impose on Dora," she said.

"Believe me, you're not imposing." He stuffed the gloves in his back pocket. "Anytime she has a new animal to pose for her camera, she's in heaven."

"All right, then. Maybe just a quick tour."

"Got a pressing date or something?"

"You never know what might come up. At the moment, though, I'm all yours."

Hell. A part of his anatomy is what might come up. And if this woman truly was *all his,* they'd be touring a bedroom instead of a barn.

He kept those thoughts to himself. He couldn't quite tell if she was deliberately messing with him, or if his mind was merely stuck on a one-way track headed south. More than likely, the latter.

"All right, then," he said, gesturing her forward with a sweep of his hand. "This here's the harem stable. No boys allowed—at least, none with four legs. Just happy girls with nothing to worry about except being pampered."

"And being led off to the sultan's den."

"Darlin', that's the highlight of their day."

"I think Glory Days would beg to differ."

He grinned. "I suspect that had more to do with the ambience than the partner. The lady didn't like being tied up."

"Either that, or she got wind that her high-priced gigolo didn't have the staying power of a gnat."

Hmm, he thought. A few minutes ago she shied away from the topic. Now she was trading jokes about it. Interesting woman. "Shh," he said. "Darlin', have a care for the fragile male ego, would you? I'll end up with a bunch of stallions suffering from performance anxiety, and that'd be real bad for business."

She grinned and walked a few paces ahead of him. The interior of the pitched-roof structure was cool, thanks to superior insulation and a nice cross breeze. The air was sweet with the familiar smell of summer-dry hay and animals. Massive sliding doors remained open at both ends of the center aisle— a twenty-foot-wide corridor that would more than accommodate two horses passing or a tractor delivering straw or feed.

When he'd first seen this stable as a boy, he'd felt as though he was walking through an elaborate tunnel where horses draped their elegant heads over Dutch doors, their soft eyes watching to make sure he had a safe passage.

Oddly enough, it had been the first time in his life he'd ever felt completely secure and unafraid.

He didn't think it had the same effect on Abbe, judging by the way she jumped when an old barn cat darted past.

"We call her the watch cat," he said. "It's her job to make sure the rodents don't invite themselves to supper and send the girls screaming."

"What's her success rate?" She eyed the perimeter of the concrete aisle with a great deal of wariness.

"About ninety-eight percent."

Her shoulders squared, but her arms remained crossed beneath her breasts as she bravely moved ahead on her own.

His lips twitched. Tough woman, he thought now, amused.

Because she hadn't been in here before, he found himself trying to see it through her eyes, wondered if she would note the myriad details that still generated a catch of awe deep in his chest.

She certainly wouldn't find fault with the fastidious organization—a trait, thankfully, that he and his brothers shared. Their supplies and equipment were hi-tech and top of the line. The green-and-white Callahan and Sons logo was displayed on stable blankets, buckets, towels and every other tool of their trade. It was a stamp of ownership, advertisement, uniformity and pride.

At a glance, a person would know that this was a wealthy and well-run business—qualities that had earned them respect in the industry and were vital if that reputation was to be maintained.

He heard Clarabelle's friendly nicker of welcome, saw Abbe pause by the roan's stall. Leave it to Clara to draw in a visitor. That old girl was such a beggar, always looking for a treat. Out of all the horses here, Clara had the sweetest disposition…and patience to spare.

Excellent virtues to possess when faced with a skittish human.

He hung back for a few minutes, getting a kick out of Abbe's attempts to screw up her courage to pet the mare, then end up jerking her hand back as soon as Clarabelle opened her lips for a curious nibble.

At this rate, they'd be here all day and never make it past the first stall. He stepped in behind her, took her hand in his and guided it back to the mare's face.

"Clarabelle's a sweetheart. She won't hurt you." He could feel Abbe's resistance and he immediately eased up, let her make the choice on her own rather than forcing her. She clearly wasn't used to horses.

"It looked like she was fixing to bite." Her laughter was more breath than sound. "You must think I'm a wimp."

"Darlin', wimps don't pilot airplanes. You're doing fine. She just wanted to check out your hand to see if you were offering goodies. Clara's a favorite around here, and everyone spoils her with treats. Want to add your name to the list?" He fished a piece of carrot from his back pocket and placed it in her open palm, curling her fingers around it. "Best to hide it. No sense teasing her until you're ready to give it."

With his arm supporting hers from behind, the rest of his body had little choice but to mold her backside. Bent slightly at the waist, he was trying to hold his hips a respectful distance away so her butt wouldn't end up nestled against his crotch—or vice versa.

If she didn't make up her mind and relax her hand soon, he was going to be crippled.

"What do you think?" he prodded.

"Promise she won't go for the carrot and accidentally take a bite of my hand?"

"You got a biting phobia, or what?" He took a steadying breath when her muscles remained tense.

He was beginning to feel a kinship with Pride of Knight, and a much deeper level of sympathy and understanding over the stallion's earlier display of frustration.

"Horses use their lips to forage for food," he said. "I promise her teeth won't come anywhere near you, accidentally or deliberately."

She opened her fingers and he guided her hand beneath Clarabelle's mouth.

"Oh my gosh! It tickles." Her startled flinch was pure instinct, but Clara's dexterous lips managed to snag the prize.

Grant didn't fare as well. Abbe backed right into him, eliminating the space he'd so gallantly tried to maintain.

All he got for his trouble was a sharp elbow in the ribs. And an instant woody in his jeans.

He cleared his throat and sidestepped, handing her another carrot. "You're on your own this time."

"Sorry." Her gaze dipped below his belt, then away.

He decided not to comment. Frankly, that kind of reaction hadn't happened to him in a long time. She had a body that wouldn't quit, and a face that made a man want to spend a good long time just looking.

Intelligence radiated from her green eyes. She struck him as a woman used to being open and having fun, and he was seeing flashes of that person today.

But something, or someone, had taught her caution. Death of a loved one could do that. In his gut, though, he believed there was something more.

He wasn't a man to pry into other people's business. God knows, he had his own secrets. So it confounded him that he wanted so badly to know hers.

"That's better," he said when she fed the carrot to Clarabelle and managed to remain standing in the same spot.

"It probably seems alien to you that anyone could be uneasy around horses."

"No. It's all a matter of education. The more time you spend learning about something, the easier it becomes. You were probably apprehensive with the first puppy you ever had, too, until you figured out his needs and learned what to expect."

"Lord, isn't that the truth." She looked back at Clara with a little more understanding. "Harley's the first dog I've ever had, and I was nervous as all get out the first couple of days. I think I bought every puppy book ever printed, which actually was more confusing. One claimed they'd benefit from people food, and another said absolutely not. There were whole sections on supplemental vitamins, then dire warnings against supplementation because it could cause brain damage or something. The authors demonstrated how to teach commands, but didn't address dogs who would apparently rather break a bone than comply."

"So that's why you called the pup 'bad judgment.'" His tone was teasing because anyone with a set of eyes could see that she adored the little character.

She laughed. "Actually, that statement had more to do with him throwing up in my plane."

"Now, there's a hanging offense."

"Yes. But he just looked so pitiful and so darn cute. I had

to wash him *and* the plane when we stopped in Jamestown." She sighed and rubbed Clarabelle's cheek. Her touch was tentative, but it was progress.

"Jolie's father brought Harley home, unannounced, and just plopped him on the floor as if he were a stuffed animal we'd all know exactly what to do with. He didn't consider that a toddler and a two-pound puppy might be an iffy combination. Jolie needed to learn how to treat something so fragile, the puppy required a ton of time and attention, and Tommy wasn't around a lot to help. He was always showering us with gifts, and there were days I could have wrung his neck for this latest one."

"But you kept the dog."

"Of course. Who wouldn't fall head over heels in love with that little guy?"

She moved away from Clara's stall and continued through the stable, touching bridles or the occasional blanket that hung outside the stalls, yet staying out of reach of the horses who stretched their necks toward her in curiosity. Grant nonchalantly maneuvered around her, putting himself closest to the mares, noting that she was more relaxed with a buffer.

"Life hasn't been smooth flying this past year," she continued. "And moving was stressful enough with a three-year-old and her grungy Lambie-pie—I can hardly get the thing away from her long enough to wash it. Add a puppy to that mix, and it's a wonder I haven't ended up in a psychiatric ward."

"He's pretty well behaved."

"Despite all the books I've read, Jolie probably has more to do with that than me. They seem to communicate in their own language."

"I imagine you've contributed. Just looking at your daughter gives good insight into your puppy-parenting skills. Jolie's a great kid. You've done a fine job with her so far."

"She has her moments, believe me. But thank you for the compliment. I *do* seem to have this constant need for her to be well behaved, though. It's like I want everyone to love her the second they lay eyes on her, to ooh and aah over her and see the perfect angel that I know and love so much." She cut her eyes in his direction. "I love the devil side of her, too, but I just don't want her showing her horns in public."

He wondered what had happened in her lifetime to create her need for acceptance, wondered if she realized it was her own worthiness she sought, more so than her daughter's. If her daughter was deemed perfect, then so would she.

"Speaking of oohing and aahing, take a look over here." He steered her across the aisle to a stall that didn't have a mare looking over the top half of the door.

"Oh my gosh! A baby. Isn't she darling?" This time, instead of shying away, she pressed herself against the chest-high door, leaning in to get a better look.

"Actually, it's a *he*," Grant said. "Earl's Prince, sired by Duke of Earl." The top of the door was just the right height to push the swell of her breasts up and out from the scoop-neck tank top. Hell, his body had barely settled down as it was. He forced his gaze to the doorway at the back of the stall that opened to a fenced paddock for grazing—as did each of the other stalls.

"Shame, shame. What happened to 'no boys allowed'?"

"Stickler for details, aren't you? I should have said no boys past weaning age."

"You take the children away from their mothers?"

"Have to. It's not as though a mare can just button up her blouse and offer a bottle or glass."

She stood quietly for several moments, a look of anguish on her face. "The thought of being separated from my child is unbearable."

The utter poignancy in her hushed voice caught at something inside him. He draped his arm around her shoulders and squeezed, unsure if he was comforting her or himself.

"The equine world works a bit differently than ours. Let's go check out the gentlemen's quarters."

He urged her toward the open doors, then dropped his arm. From the main stable, they walked past the training and exercise areas where several horses were being worked, some attached to a longe line, others mounted by a rider.

One of his trainers, Jug Avery, was putting a two-year-old black filly through her paces, taking the horse from a gallop to an impressive, full-out run.

"That's one of the fillies out of Pride of Knight," he said, pausing to admire the fluid transition of gait and impressive speed. "She'll be a champion. No doubt about it."

"My gosh, I can almost feel the ground vibrating beneath me."

"Exciting, isn't it?"

"Yes." Eyeing the fenced arena as though there was no way it would stand firm if the horse decided to plow through, she skirted around to walk on his other side.

"Watch your step," he warned, steering her past a pile of horse droppings and into the stallion barn—which was a smaller version of the main stable.

They'd hardly made it to the second stall when for some reason Duke of Earl got a little pissy and began to take out his aggression on the walls of his stall.

"Whoa, that's it for me," Abbe said, and made an immediate beeline for the door.

Grant grinned and followed her back out into the bright sunshine, trusting the groom to settle Duke.

"I think I like the harem better," she said when he joined her. "And I'm buying you a new dictionary. Yours has obviously given you serious misinformation on the definition of a gentleman."

"Now, don't be too hard on them. This is merely a case like the kids you described. You brag about their manners, and they make liars out of you."

"Well, just so you won't think I dislike everything about your pride-and-joys, I'll concede that they are quite handsome and impressive."

"I'll tell them you said so. You had enough touring for one day?"

"There's more?"

"Just the surgical clinic and storage barns. But we don't have any injuries to patch up, and no one's scheduled for an enema, so there's no excitement to see."

"Somehow, I don't think I could get excited over an enema, so it's just as well. I had no idea y'all had such a big outfit here. Or that breeding horses was so lucrative."

"We're involved in a little more than just breeding—although the value of that end of the operation is nothing to sneeze at. We have an unrivaled reputation for consistently turning out champions that win big bucks in racing, so buyers pay top dollar for stud services *and* our foals. We've also got our own horses we run at various racetracks—that's mostly Clay's area of expertise. The rest of our financial dealings are in cattle—which we're phasing out—and the stock market."

"What in the world are you doing taking me for a tour? You're way too busy for this," she teased. "Seriously, how do you even have time for a life?"

"That's the beauty of a well-run business and the result of hiring qualified, loyal people. Leaves us plenty of time to play."

"Well. I'm impressed."

"Good. That's what I was hoping for."

"To impress me?"

"Yeah. I told you the other day. A woman who comes in

piloting her own aircraft and claims she recently sold her Harley-Davidson, tends to make a man feel envious, excited—and inadequate. Probably some caveman thing, but the need to show off robs us guys of rational thinking."

"You're so full of it." She grinned and ran her hand over the back of her neck in an upward movement, ruffling the hair at her nape. "It's going to be a scorcher by this afternoon. It's barely midmorning and it already feels like a furnace out here."

"Mmm, hmm." Unable to resist, he reached out and sifted his fingers through her short hair, intrigued by the way it shifted back into place. "Was your hair cut recently?"

She cocked her head slightly, a subtle move that discouraged further contact. "Don't tell me you're one of those men who thinks every woman should have long hair."

"No. I like that style on you. It's sexy. But a couple of times I've seen you start to fool with your hair, then seem surprised to find there's not more of it there."

"Wow. You're pretty observant for a guy. It is a new cut— pretty drastic for me since I wore it down to the middle of my back most of my life. I'm still getting used to it."

"So you're not one to test the waters before jumping in." In his experience, when it came to hair, most women made the change in stages, rather than all at once.

"There you go again, still trying to figure me out." Her eyebrows rose in a sexy arch that nearly disappeared beneath her wispy bangs.

"How am I doing?" He took a step closer, just to see what she'd do.

She retreated. Her back hit the outside wall of the barn. Nonchalantly, she leaned against the siding as though that had been her intention all along.

"I have no idea," she said, "since I don't know exactly what it is you want to figure out. As for your characterization of me testing the water, you're about half-right. I used to be a jumper, now I usually prefer to dip a toe in first."

"You went in a lot more than toe deep when you packed up and came here," he reminded her. "You decided to move and you acted on it within days. If that's not jumping, I don't know what is."

"Ah, but I didn't go in all the way, did I? I'm treading cautiously and—" She shot away from the wall as though she'd been spurred. "Why is my plane outside the hangar?"

He frowned, surprised by her sudden agitation, and looked toward the airstrip, which was clearly visible across the expanse of paddocks and green grass. Sure enough, the Baron was there. He shifted his gaze back to Abbe. "Clay probably moved it yesterday to get the Cessna out."

"Then why didn't he put it back?"

"Hell if I know. Maybe he was in a hurry when he left. I heard him come in late last night, so he was probably tired. You don't need to worry, though. He wouldn't leave the plane out without making sure it was secured. Clay's a stickler for details."

"Did you check it?"

"No. My brother's been around aircraft for as long as I have. He knows what he's doing."

"Someone could have called me. I'd have come over and taken care of it." Her tone dripped with censure.

"Abbe, I wasn't around when Clay left. For all I knew, you'd *told* him to leave the plane out."

"When there's a perfectly good shelter mere feet away?" She looked at him as though he'd suggested that cows were pink. "Why would I want my plane to sit outside where the sun can fade the paint, or a gusty wind might ding it with rocks and sand?"

"If you're so concerned about the thing, you should have gone over and checked on it yesterday."

"I had no idea that I needed to."

He studied her for a long moment. Her reaction was way out of proportion to the situation, and he'd bet his prize stallion this went a hell of a lot deeper than worry about a paint job. "What's the deal here, Abbe? What's going on?"

She sighed and shoved her bangs off her forehead. "I'd just…I'd just prefer the Baron stayed inside, that's all."

"Another one of your evasive nonanswers. Are we having a rerun of the other day when you insinuated you're rolling in dough, but can't provide any credit references?"

She shrugged. "I can't really say any more right now."

"Can't? Or won't?"

"Won't. I'm sorry." She met his gaze straight on, squared her shoulders. "Have I just rendered myself homeless?"

He hadn't been prepared for such candor. He didn't think he'd ever met a woman who appeared so genuine, yet so guarded. "Answer me this—are you in trouble with the law?"

"No." She crossed her arms. "Do I pack, or not?"

His stomach knotted. He was used to having his questions answered, knew more ways to guarantee cooperation than he cared to remember. Most involved violence. All were inappropriate for civilized society.

And that thought made him realize he didn't have any business demanding answers in the first place.

"Not," he replied, then turned on his heel and walked away before he changed his mind.

CHAPTER EIGHT

IT TOOK ABBE nearly week before she stopped jumping at shadows and began to relax. She still felt like an idiot for reacting so strongly eight days ago to the Baron sitting outside the hangar, but fear had a tendency to obliterate reason. For all she knew, the wrong person could drive by, or fly overhead and spot her plane.

She set her glass of lemonade on the flat wooden railing, then settled into the porch swing with her knitting needles and a ball of polyester yarn that resembled a fluffy angora cat. Her bare toes brushed the plank floor beneath her feet as she gently rocked, the chains suspended from the roof creaking with each back-and-forth movement.

Jolie had ridden home from church with Dora and Ethan, and Abbe had the quiet guest house and afternoon to herself. She could have sat inside under the air conditioner, but the lure of blue skies and birds singing had brought her out to the porch. It didn't matter that the weight of the yarn draped over her lap would soon make her sweat. The open air felt too good.

Metal clicked in a steady rhythm as she scooped, looped and transferred stitches from one needle to the other, the pattern so familiar she did it by rote. A slight breeze caressed skin exposed by shorts and a sleeveless top.

She loved the smells of wildflowers and fresh-mown grass, and the faint trace of animals. And she loved that small window of time between changing out of her church clothes and pulling on shorts, where her naked body felt ultrafree.

She heard a door close, looked up and saw Grant walking across the yard. Her knitting needles clicked faster.

She'd expected things to be strained between them after she'd thrown such a fit over the airplane, but when she'd seen him the next day at church and several times during the following week, he'd been cheerful and friendly. The subject of her plane hadn't even come up.

Butterflies took flight in her stomach as she watched him take the stone pathway that cut through the grass between his house and the guest house. Confidence radiated with every step of his booted feet. His hat shielded his face from the sun, and he'd either bought his green T-shirt a size too small or shrunk it in a too-hot dryer, because it molded every contour of his sexy torso.

In fact, he was one of the sexiest men she'd ever met, and she was having trouble reconciling her feelings of intense attraction with the fact that Tommy had been dead barely six months.

"You look awfully peaceful," Grant said, pausing at the foot of the porch steps. His gaze swept the area as though checking for anything out of place.

"I ate too much at the potluck after church this morning, and it made me lazy. Y'all just eat all the time out here, don't you?"

"Seems like it." He mounted the steps. "Where's your ferocious guard dog?"

"Cute," she drawled. "Dora came and got him. If my kid and my dog keep spending so much time over there, we'll have to change their name to Callahan so Ethan can claim them as a tax deduction." She spoke in jest, yet felt a jolt of pain. Because, ever lurking was the dreaded possibility that Jolene *could* end up as a legitimate dependent on someone else's IRS return.

He leaned his shoulder against the porch rail. "You know, I would have never pictured you as the type to knit."

"Are you kidding? It's all the rage. Just ask Julia Roberts."

"I'll take your word for it. What are you making?"

"A scarf." She paused and spread out the three-foot length she'd completed so far. "When it's finished it'll sort of look like a feather boa, but it's really a stretchy yarn knitted into a tube shape that you can wear in seven or eight different ways. I talked to Carly McCall in town the other day. She wants to sell them in her boutique."

"They should do pretty well there—at least come wintertime. Think you can keep up with supply and demand?"

"I haven't signed a contract for a specific order, so supply will be at my discretion regardless of demand. I'm pretty fast, though."

"Sounds like you've been busy this past week getting acclimated to the town. Have you just about met everyone?"

"Pretty much."

"So how're we doing? Is the town meeting your expectations?"

"More than meeting—" She looked up at the sound of gravel crunching under tires. A black sedan drove slowly toward the front of Grant's house, then backed up and came down the side driveway.

The blood in her veins turned to ice, freezing the breath in her lungs. She told herself to get a grip. The car had been heading for Grant's place, not hers. They'd probably seen him standing on her porch and were coming to seek him out.

She almost had herself convinced.

Until she saw their white shirts and ties.

"Looks like you've got some company," Grant said. He glanced back at Abbe, and what he saw caused his gut to knot. She was ashen with terror.

What the hell was going on? Several minutes ago, he'd been relaxing with a copy of *Horseman's Journal* magazine when Ozzie had called with the cryptic insistence that he rush right over to check up on Abbe. "You be on your toes, now, ya hear? And don't be lettin' on about nothin', either. Just stay a spell and see what's what."

Before Grant could ask questions, Ozzie had hung up.

Car doors slammed, drawing his attention away from Abbe. Two men approached, their button-down shirts, creased slacks and polished loafers branding them as outsiders.

Instinctive training kicked in and he straightened, blocking the porch entrance with his body. It didn't matter that there was three feet of space open on either side of him. He knew how to intimidate.

"Can I help you boys with something?"

"We're looking for Abbe Shea."

He sensed Abbe moving up behind him. "Mind telling me who you are?"

One of the men flipped open a leather case, showing his badge and identification, then looked at Abbe. "I'm Agent Snyder, FBI. This is Agent Bentley. Ma'am, we'd like to ask you some questions regarding Tommy Donato."

"I already gave my report to the Vegas police."

"Yes, but we'd like you to give it to us, as well," Bentley said.

"What's this all about?" Grant asked. Abbe looked like a cornered animal.

"We have reason to believe Ms. Shea has information that wasn't included in her initial interview following Donato's murder."

"And what reason would that be?"

"Are you a relative?" Snyder asked. He was the shorter of the two, with an acne-scared weasel face.

"No. But you're on my property. And unless you came with

some kind of warrant, it's up to me to decide whether or not you've worn out your welcome." He kept his gaze steady on the other man, refusing to back down. Snyder was the first to break eye contact. Pansy.

"We're working on a case that might be linked with Tommy Donato's murder. You're probably familiar with the name Lucca Ziggmorelli?" Snyder's expression shifted almost imperceptibly. "The fact that Ms. Shea's father is the head of a Las Vegas crime family, and that her fiancé, the deceased, was one of his underbosses, gives us valid reason to believe she might have information that didn't make it into the original homicide report."

Grant didn't let his stunned emotions show. That was one hell of a detail she'd left off her rental application.

"Why don't you gentlemen come inside," Abbe said as though inviting them to tea. She held open the screen door and the agents filed through.

Grant caught the metal edge of the door, pushing it a little wider, and looked down at her. "After you."

"You don't have to stay," she whispered. "I can—"

"Save your breath. I'm under strict orders to see what's what. I repeat. After you."

She didn't have a chance against him in a stare-down and she knew it. After a brief hesitation, she stepped through the door, and he followed.

"Nice place," Agent Bentley commented.

"Yes, it is." Abbe crossed her arms defensively, didn't ask them to sit. "How did you find me?"

"We have our ways. Listen, we don't want to take up any more of your time than necessary, but we've come across evidence that puts Lucca Ziggmorelli in the area of Barclay Street at approximately 10:00 a.m. on the sixteenth of January, driving a silver Mercedes SUV. Did you happen to notice a vehicle matching that description?"

"I was inside most of the morning."

"Are you acquainted with Lucca Ziggmorelli?" Bentley asked.

"No."

"But you know what he looks like?"

"Sure. His picture's been all over the news lately."

"And you didn't recognize him as the man who shot your fiancé?"

"Like I told the police, my focus was on Tommy, who happened to be bleeding to death on our front porch."

Grant noticed that she didn't quite answer the question. Frick and Frack didn't seem to realize it. A couple of bozos, he decided, who probably couldn't interrogate their way out of a paper bag.

"Did your fiancé know Lucca Ziggmorelli?" Bentley brushed his hand over the back of the sofa.

"I have no idea. Tommy never discussed his work or his friends."

"Do you really expect us to believe you're that uninformed?" Agent Snyder, this time. The weasel.

Grant decided to interrupt on the basic principle that this guy was an ass. "She said she didn't know, and the person who could answer that question is dead. Move on."

"Mr. Callahan, right?" Snyder said. "This isn't open court where you can object."

"Wrong. You're only on this property due to my good graces. Ms. Shea is a guest here, and I'm not going to stand by and let you badger her." Although he had some pressing questions of his own, at the moment he was on her team, and he was definitely going to watch her back.

"You're involved in the horse-racing industry, aren't you?" Snyder didn't wait for the answer he obviously knew. "Don't you think it might get a little bit sticky with the racing commission if they find out that you're housing a woman who has ties to organized crime? Seems to me there was quite a stir a while back at the Breeders' Cup."

"I have no ties to organized crime," Abbe said heatedly. "I wasn't even aware of my father or Tommy's business dealings until after Tommy was killed. When I found out, I severed my relationship with my father."

Bentley flipped through a pocket-size notebook. "According to phone records, you placed a call to Stewart Shea ten days ago—on a Thursday."

"Ten days ago, I was flying across country, and didn't have access to a telephone."

He rattled off a string of numbers. "Isn't that your cellphone number?"

"It *was*. I lost the phone."

"But you instructed the phone company to shut off the service at 5:00 p.m. that Thursday," he said, pouncing on the inconsistency.

"No. The phone company said it would be shut off *by* 5:00 p.m. I merely acknowledged what they said."

"Did you know that the Ziggmorellis had put out a contract on Tommy?"

"I told you, I didn't know anything about those people. I thought Tommy worked for the government—along with my father."

"For the Treasury Department, perhaps?" Snyder offered sarcastically. "Recirculating money to increase economic spending? Is that what you thought when you flew Donato to the Yucatán Peninsula to pick up counterfeit bills?"

"That was a vacation!"

"Apparently, it was a *working* vacation for your fiancé. Lucca Ziggmorelli was part of a counterfeiting ring in Yucatán. We believe Donato was proving his loyalty by picking up and delivering a shipment of money to Ziggmorelli."

"No way. We'd have never cleared customs with counterfeit money on board."

"Haven't you made quite a few trips across the border? Know several of the agents by name? You're a beautiful woman. Our customs agents aren't infallible, and if they're used to seeing you…"

"I've never asked for preferential treatment from customs. I went through the same process as everyone else did." Abbe clenched her fists, dimly aware of her nails digging into her palms. Her insides were a kinetic mass of nerves. She could hardly think straight.

She remembered that Tommy had been especially attentive to one of the customs agents that day, had made a big to-do over showing Jolene's latest pictures, bragging about his angelic baby daughter and how much she looked like her beautiful mama.

Abbe had thought he was simply in a great mood because they'd had a few days away all to themselves—except for the few hours Tommy had left her sunning herself by the hotel pool while he went out to take care of some business.

She also recalled that Pop had been livid when he'd found out where they'd gone, had nearly come to blows with Tommy over the trip. She'd thought he was just angry over the possibility of his and Tommy's integrity being called in question over a perceived breach of their security clearance and confidentiality rules.

In her wildest dreams, she wouldn't have guessed counterfeiting or organized crime was at the root of the argument.

God, she felt like such an idiot. How the hell had she floated through life with her head so stuck in the sand? If she were in Snyder and Bentley's shoes, she'd find her claim of ignorance a little tough to believe, too.

"Tommy worked for my father," she said. "So why would he involve himself with Lucca? And if he was doing something with Lucca, why would they put out a contract on him?"

"Maybe he was playing both sides," Snyder said. "Or he got greedy and skimmed from the counterfeit bills. If you're not a man of respect in the Mafia, your lifespan is often short. Word is, there's also a contract on your head." His tone was just this side of gleeful as he confirmed what she'd been fearing.

Bile rose in her throat and her skin grew clammy. She felt a firm grip on her elbow, realized Grant had reached out to steady her.

"Do you know that for a fact?" Grant's deep voice was icy, a direct contrast to the warmth of his hand on her arm. She wasn't sure if his unfriendliness was rooted in what he was hearing about her or toward the men doing the telling.

"The information came through an informant. Whether or not it's factual…" Bentley shrugged.

"What is it you want?" Grant asked.

"To pin a murder charge on Lucca Ziggmorelli that his high-priced lawyers can't get him out of. We want to guarantee he doesn't walk on some technicality. We're fully prepared to put Ms. Shea in protective custody in exchange for her testimony as an eyewitness to Tommy Donato's murder."

"I won't be testifying."

"We have a witness who said you saw the hit."

"Then get them to testify!" She didn't know if Snyder was bluffing. One of the neighbors could have seen her, she supposed. But she didn't think so. Maybe someone who worked for Pop had spilled the beans. Surely Pop would know if one of his people had become a police informant. She had to believe that if that were the case, Pop would have found a way to let her know.

"Who are you protecting?" Snyder's voice raised, and he

visibly battled for calm. "Are you afraid of implicating yourself in your fiancé's illegal activities?"

A scream built inside her, clawing for release. Abbe refused
to answer the asinine accusation, refused to be baited. She
wanted these men out of here. What if the Ziggmorellis had
someone watching her?

The feds had found her, so the Mafia probably wouldn't
be far behind. For all she knew, these agents had led the enemy
right to her door. If the wrong people saw her talking to the
FBI, they would naturally assume she was ratting on Lucca.

Dear God.

As much as she hated this whole nasty business of organized crime, would love to see Lucca locked up for good, she
couldn't give the government what they wanted.

Not at the expense of her daughter's life.

The sound of more vehicles arriving outside distracted the
agents. Grant stepped over to the window and glanced out.
The next thing she knew, people were streaming in through
the front door, filling the living room of the small guest house.

Mildred and Opal Bagley, the widows who ran the boardinghouse in town, were the first in the door.

"Land sakes," Mildred said, fanning herself. "It's hot
enough to fry an egg on the pavement."

"What's wrong with you, Sister," Opal demanded. "I declare, you have the manners of a goat. Can't you see Abbe has
company?"

Mildred glared at Opal, then fluffed her ash-blond, page-
boy cut. Her false fingernails were painted firecracker red and
adorned with ladybug decals. "I'm not blind. Just because you
always want to be the first one in the door is no call to criti-
cize my social conduct. And what's wrong with commenting
on the weather? I'm sure these nice gentlemen share my opinion—why, just look at the way their shirts are wilted." She

turned to Snyder. "I don't believe we've had the pleasure of meeting."

"Agents Snyder and Bentley," Snyder said. "FBI. We're in the middle of conducting—"

"FBI? Why, I've watched nearly every episode of *America's Most Wanted*. Never ran into any of those rascals whose pictures are hanging in the post office, but you can be sure I keep my eyes peeled. It's a crying shame, some of the meanness that goes on in this world."

"Yes, ma'am. Now—"

"Do you know that nice young man, John Walsh? Why, I could hardly imagine getting to work next to a big TV star like that. So sad about his little boy."

"John Walsh isn't an FBI agent, ma'am. He only hosts the television show. Now please excuse—"

"Well, that's a bit of false advertising, if you ask me!" Mildred complained.

Opal snorted. "You're always thinking someone's trying to pull a fast one on you. If you'd read something besides those gossipy *National Enquirers*, you might be able to have a decent conversation in polite company without looking like an old fool."

"Sticks and stones..." Mildred turned to Snyder. "Don't pay her any mind. She's just jealous that I got to you first. You ever give any of those ride-alongs while you're out doing whatever it is that you do? I hitched me a ride with Sheriff Bodine a while back. 'Course, the only excitement all day was when Winona Tate reported Cooter Granville for riding his tractor in his birthday suit. Claimed he stood up and wagged his dog at her. 'Course me and the sheriff had to go see about it. Believe me, what Cooter has to wag is no big deal, so I don't know why Winona made such a fuss. Now, me, I've always fancied the dangerous, powerful type of man. You're a little short for my tastes, but this other fellow over here—"

"Sister!" Opal pressed her hand to her bosom. "What kind of talk is that? The whole town knows you're stepping out with Lester Russo. You should have the decency to show some loyalty."

"Oh, don't be such a prude. Nothing wrong with window-shopping if I don't paw the merchandise."

Despite the gravity of the situation, Abbe had a great deal of trouble stifling a laugh. Agents Snyder and Bentley seemed to have been rendered speechless. She'd learned that the sisters had a penchant for bickering. It was a long-standing routine, purely for show. A means of distraction, or an attempt to lighten a mood. Or simply to entertain.

Today's performance appeared to be a combination of the three. And they'd all found out a little more about Cooter Granville's anatomy than was strictly necessary.

Just as the agents attempted to step away from the Bagley widows, Ozzie moved in, introducing himself as the mayor. Abbe noticed that Ethan and Clay stood just inside the front door, expressions stoic, looking like bouncers at a nightclub who were ready, willing and able to keep peace and order.

"Don't get too many feds out this way," Ozzie said. "Saw you boys come through town. Thought we'd come on over and see what's what, you bet."

Vernon and Vera Tillis, along with Iris and Lloyd Brewer, and Henry Jenkins pushed in behind Ozzie, creating a human shield between her and the agents.

It was deliberate, Abbe realized. They were protecting her. She was incredibly touched.

"Anything we can help you boys with?" Ozzie asked.

"Our business is with Ms. Shea."

"Well, that don't mean nothin'. Ain't no secrets around here. Figure you're lookin' into that Ziggy-whatever fellow that got hisself arrested, you bet. Just because our Abbe, here, happens to be kin with some folks who might'a associated with the man don't mean any of the rest of us can't be of help, you bet. If you ask me, it's a pure shame to come singlin' out this girl when she's still recoverin' from a tragedy. Seems to me you oughtta be offerin' compassion and protection."

Until just now, Abbe hadn't realized how much of her background Ozzie was actually aware of. She noticed that besides herself, Grant and his brothers were the only ones who appeared the least bit surprised over Ozzie mentioning a link between her family and the Ziggmorellis. Which meant that the rest of the people in this living room had already known.

Everyone began talking at once, nonsense small talk, hounding questions, subtle censure and suggestions that perhaps the men might want to move on before the wind kicked up over the plains. Clearly overwhelmed by the chaos and realizing their interrogation couldn't continue, the agents began inching toward the door.

"You haven't seen the last of us, Ms. Shea," Snyder said. "The federal prosecutor will likely subpoena your testimony in court. Meanwhile, withholding information is called obstruction of justice. If you're holding out on us, the next time we come we'll have a sworn warrant for your arrest—if you manage to live that long."

Iris Brewer reached out and slid her arm around Abbe's waist. For the space of several heartbeats, the silence in the room was almost deafening. Then, in some part of Abbe's mind, she was aware of the agents leaving, the screen door shutting, the townsfolk recovering their voices and expressing outrage, Ozzie and the rest of the men converging on Grant with advice and demands, the women rallying around her in compassion and support, Ethan and Clay still standing like riot police at a political protest.

But she felt as though she was in a glass bubble, able to see, but unable hear or feel. Insulated, isolated and numb.

My God. It wasn't Snyder's parting remark over her life being in danger that had her frozen in place. She'd already known that. It was the threat of being arrested. Throughout this whole horrible mess, that possibility hadn't even crossed her mind. Why would it? The only thing she was guilty of was stupidity.

But innocent people went to jail all the time.

At least with a death threat she could run and hide, defend herself. That gave her some semblance of control. If she was locked up, she'd be helpless. Unable to protect Jolie.

A person could fight their enemy in self-defense—society accepted that, even lauded it. But the law was an entirely different matter. If the FBI came back for her, there wasn't a thing in the world anyone could do to stop them from handcuffing her and taking her away.

"Now you try not to worry," Iris said, penetrating her stupor. "We're all on your side. Anyone who comes looking will have to go through the whole lot of us to get to you and your precious little girl."

Through the open doorway, she saw the sheriff's Bronco pull in behind the black sedan. Cheyenne Bodine got out and intercepted the agents. He was a tall man, with dark hair that brushed the collar of his uniform shirt and the distinct bone structure of his Cheyenne ancestors. The men filed out the door to join him.

Abbe's insides trembled to the point where she feared she might be sick. She looked at Iris. "I don't understand. How did you know?"

"Your father was worried about you. He called and spoke to Ozzie before you got here."

No doubt now that Pop had understood her "granting a wish" hint.

"Ozzie felt he should share the problem with the rest of us," Iris continued. "Mind you, he doesn't condone that side of your father's business, but he judges a man differently than most, looks to a person's heart, and once he gives his friendship, you won't find anyone more loyal."

"We've all been on alert in case any strangers showed up in town," Vera Tillis added. "Those two stopped in at the store when we opened up after church—bought Pepsi's and candy bars—and Vern got to talking to them. Next thing I knew, Vern was giving them directions that took them out around the old Homestead Road and clear over to Butte Hill Creek. I caught on to what he was doing and went directly to the back store room and called Ozzie."

"Butte Hill Creek lets out several miles past the Malones place," Opal explained. "Which meant they'd have to take gravel roads that would slow them down considerably, then double back toward town for quite a way to get here—smart thinking on Vern's part because it gave us all a little extra time to rally our troops."

"And let me tell you, the phone lines were burning up and we were scurrying," Mildred said, taking up the story. "Why, I wouldn't be surprised if Sister forgot her drawers. She was on the pot when we got the call—"

Opal gasped. "I did *not* forget my drawers! Clearly, what I *did* forget was a sock to stuff in your mouth."

"I didn't say you *had* forgotten them. And I was trying to pay you a compliment on your spry reactions." Mildred laughed. "You should have seen yourself—streaked right past me, hooked your purse on the fly and cleared the porch steps in a single bound. Pretty doggone impressive for an old woman."

"I declare." Opal sniffed and fiddled with her short hair, looking secretly pleased. "I think Lester Russo is influencing you poorly."

"He's a judge, Opal. The worry should be over how I'm influencing him." Mildred turned to Abbe. "Now, you listen, honey. If you ever get afraid out here by yourself, you just pack up Jolie and come stay with Sister and me. Ozzie told us to claim we were renovating and didn't have any rooms to rent, but that was only his matchmaking attempts. He wanted to fix you up with Grant and see what kind of sparks would fly. But that was before we knew a bunch of hooligans might try to do you harm. We keep a shotgun right by the front door, and the sheriff's station is smack-dab across the street."

It was a ridiculous offer in view of the type of "hooligans" she was dealing with, but Abbe was moved nearly to tears. "Thank you," she said softly. "You have no idea how much your support means to me." Her gaze rested on each of the women.

"Oh, now, don't be getting misty-eyed," Iris said on a watery laugh. "You'll have the whole lot of us bawling."

Car engines started, drawing their attention. Cheyenne backed up his Bronco, giving the black sedan room to turn around, then followed the agents out of the driveway. Lloyd Brewer beckoned to the ladies, and after hugs all around, they filed out the door.

Abbe stayed inside. Sinking down on the sofa, she put her head in her hands, thankful that Jolie was still at Dora's. Being alone gave her a few, much-needed minutes where she could let down her guard, where she didn't have to pretend she was the strong, invincible mom who would always keep the monsters under the bed at bay.

Right now, she just wanted *her* mom.

The thought came out of nowhere, caused her heart to lodge in her throat. Dear God, she had no idea where her mom was—or if Cynthia Shea was even alive. That was wrong. A daughter should know if her mother was alive or dead, and vice versa.

Her thoughts were interrupted when Grant came back inside. Alone.

He shut the door behind him and just stood there, his blue eyes icy.

"Now, why don't you tell me the *real* reason you're here."

CHAPTER NINE

THE UTTER SOFTNESS of his voice split the silence more effectively than a full-out roar.

"I had nowhere else to go." She stood up, holding her courage in both hands. "I need your help, Grant. I know you were in the Special Forces—"

"Not anymore."

His curt tone made her flinch. She hadn't considered that he might not want to help her. All she'd thought about was whether or not he was the right person to ask.

That just went to show the state of her fear and how it skewed her thinking. Once she'd made a decision to come here, her mind had simply recorded the rest as a done deal.

"I—It doesn't matter. You still have the skills."

"And how would you know that?"

This was the tough part. "You're not going to like it."

"I don't like the FBI barging into my home, either." His voice was still eerily quiet, his demeanor calm, contained, yet anger clearly simmered below the surface. "Start talking, lady, or you're out of here."

Despite his outward composure, she didn't dare make the mistake of underestimating him. This man meant business and wouldn't give second chances.

"My…Jolene's father was murdered…"

"In a drive-by shooting, I believe you said."

He was clearly baiting her to find out how big a liar she was. Thankfully, she'd stayed relatively close to the truth—at least with Grant. The only thing he could fault her on was omission.

She lifted her chin. "Yes. He was gunned down right outside our front door. I was just a few steps behind him. I heard several strange *pops* and the next thing I knew, Tommy was on the ground with blood pooling around him. I saw the shooter, and I *can* actually identify that piece of crud, but that's not what I told the police or anyone else."

"Why?"

"Weren't you listening to those two agents? Lucca Ziggmorelli is the son of a Mafia don, for crying out loud! This guy makes Hells Angels look like choirboys. The son of a bitch emptied a clip of bullets into a man's chest in broad daylight, then had the gall to calmly get out of the car and point his thumb and finger at my front window as though he was still holding the gun."

With her own hand, she replicated the threatening gesture, the one that she saw every night in her dreams.

"When I looked through the hedge, I saw Jolie playing peekaboo with the front-room drapes. It didn't take a Harvard degree to figure out the meaning of Lucca's brazen little charade, and that's all it took for me to come down with a convincing case of blindness. If I talk, I sign my daughter's death certificate."

Grant swore, then prowled across the room—away from her. "That baby saw her daddy get shot?"

"No, thank God. There was a hedge that ran along the front walkway leading to the porch, and the window was on the other side of it, so her view was blocked. But Lucca could see her from the street." She'd since wondered why Lucca had used the hand gesture instead of actually pointing the weapon at Jolie. Optimism had her hoping that perhaps he was a killer with a conscience—that he might actually draw the line at hurting a child.

Of course, that wouldn't stop his people from using a child to get to *her*.

Grant was watching her. Silently. She couldn't tell if he was responding to her dilemma, or if he was getting ready to tell her she wasn't his problem.

Desperation clawed at her. She'd just taken the biggest leap of faith possible, trusted him with information she'd told no other.

And she'd done so right on the heels of lying to the FBI.

Oh, she'd been careful not to actually verbalize a lie—she knew how that could trip you up—but she'd deliberately given them the wrong impression.

"I don't have anyone else to turn to, Grant. These aren't the kind of people who jump out of the bushes and say, 'just kidding.' They mean business. I left Las Vegas and moved back to Texas, figuring if I just stayed out of the Ziggmorellis' way we'd have a sort of gentlemen's agreement and they'd leave us alone. Then Lucca got arrested, and the next day I found a dead canary, a dead *baby* canary, in my mailbox. It means—"

"I know what it means." He stopped pacing, his unwavering gaze so piercing and intense, she felt like a butterfly pinned to the wall by its fragile wings. Wings that were slowly tearing, dissolving into dust.

"Then you know that I'm the one they want, but if they have to, they'll use Jolie to get to me." She was pleading and didn't care. "I can't let that happen. I couldn't bear to see my daughter used as a pawn, threatened right before my eyes. Harmed."

He leaned against the granite-topped island that separated

the kitchen from the rest of the great room, his arms crossed over his chest.

His silence was driving her crazy.

"Would you please say something?"

"You still haven't told me how you know so much about me." His voice remained calm, but the vein pulsing at his temple was anything but.

"My pop had you investigated."

He frowned. "Why?"

"He's…Stewart Shea, the man who adopted me when he married my mom, is…" Lord, this was a mess. All of a sudden it didn't seem like such a great idea to drop the next bombshell. She needed time to plan the words, not just dump it on him.

But she was at the point of no return.

"Stewart Shea is your biological father," she said in a rush.

He shot away from the counter. "The hell you say!"

"I have the file to prove it."

"Show me." His words were like ice.

She went to the bedroom and retrieved the manila folder. When she returned, he hadn't moved an inch, nor was his expression any lighter.

He took the folder from her, and she waited while he flipped through the pages. She wanted to tell him to slow down, to savor the chronicled account of his life, to take pride in the accomplishments and growth recorded over the years. To see the exceptional man he'd become within the beauty, love and support of this town, his family and friends.

It was all there in those pages, a gift few people were lucky enough to behold. She wondered if he would share the pages with his brothers. Although Ethan and Clay weren't Stewart's own—the men each had different fathers—their lives were depicted in this file, as well. But it had been Grant who had captivated her, and she wanted him to see the man the words in that file had revealed to her.

But he merely skimmed the highlights. Detached. Without a word, he finally closed the folder, but didn't give it back.

"Who else knows about this?"

By *this* she assumed he meant the information listing him as Stewart's son. "No one—that I'm aware of."

"What about Ozzie? He apparently knows your father." A muscle clenched in his jaw when he said that last word. "How'd you manage to wind up here—at my ranch—which you say was your destination to begin with? Was that Ozzie's doing?"

"Not totally. I knew you had the only landing strip in the area." She glanced away out of guilt. "I'm sorry, Grant. I didn't hire the investigator. You can hardly blame me for reading the report, though. Curiosity is human nature. You'd have done the same thing."

He didn't comment. Putting herself in his place, she could understand his anger, why he would feel violated. A person deserved to choose which parts of their lives they wanted to share with the world. The dossier Stewart Shea's investigator had compiled on Grant over a period of thirty years—no matter how stirring she'd perceived it—had taken away his choice.

"I specifically asked Ozzie for a place to rent that would be close to an airstrip, and crossed my fingers that you didn't already have your guest house rented out."

"Which you knew about from this report." He set the folder on the counter, stared at it for a minute. "I think we need to back up. I'm a little confused over some of the details. Stewart Shea is affiliated with organized crime, but he's not part of Ziggmorelli's outfit?"

"Right. They're sort of like friendly rivals, I think."

"Not so friendly if they're offing each other's members. And you're, what…twenty-five?"

"Thirty."

His eyebrows rose. "How old were you when Shea adopted you?"

"Eight."

"You've known the man for twenty-two years and didn't know how he made his money?"

"I only lived with him off and on for about twelve of those years. He and Mama divorced when I was fourteen, and we returned to Texas. But I went back to Vegas right after my high-school graduation. I was in and out during college, then I lived on my own. Anyway, he told me his work was top secret. I didn't have any reason not to believe him. As a kid who'd never had a father, the mystery was kind of glamorous. Plus, I assumed that most of his money came from his restaurant."

"So what tipped you off?"

She went to the kitchen cupboard and pulled out a bottle of Scotch. It was only the middle of the afternoon, but this conversation called for something much stronger than the lemonade she'd left outside with her knitting supplies.

She reached for a glass and held up the bottle. "Want some?"

"No thanks."

"Would you rather have a beer?"

He shook his head. "I'd just as soon keep my wits about me."

She shrugged, dropped ice cubes in the glass and poured two fingers of Scotch over them. "Suit yourself. Mine could use some numbing." She took a sip, felt a bracing path of fire burn all the way to her belly and tried not to shudder. The second sip went down more smoothly.

"Not much of a drinker, are you?" he noted.

"I usually lean toward the sweet stuff that comes in pretty colors and has an umbrella and pineapple sticking out of it."

She skirted the counter and sat on one of the upholstered bar stools. "This'll do for now. Why don't you sit down? I'll see if I can fill in some of the blanks, but I don't want to end up with a kink in my neck from trying to look up at you."

He tossed his hat on the countertop, sat and swiveled the bar stool toward her, their knees nearly bumping. "You've got the floor."

"Yes, and I wish I didn't." She took another sip of Scotch. "I met Tommy about five years ago in Baja. He said he worked with Pop and had recognized me from pictures he'd seen. He was having transportation problems, so I told him he could hitch a ride back with me in the Baron. He was charming, very smooth, and I fell for him. We moved in together, I got pregnant."

"But you didn't marry him." It was a statement rather than a question.

"No. He bought me a ring when I told him about the baby, but he didn't seem to be in any rush to set a date. That didn't matter to me. I thought I was living the perfect fairy tale, had all the comforts money could buy, and when Jolene was born, I was so content with motherhood that marriage rarely crossed my mind. Sometimes I think it was Pop's attitude that kept me from pressing Tommy to make things legal. Pop didn't openly disapprove of the relationship and he didn't interfere when we moved in together, but sometimes I sensed a hint of censure."

She shrugged. "Hard to explain. Anyway, when Tommy was gunned down right in front of me, I was in total shock. I didn't even think to dial 911. I called Pop, instead. One of the neighbors eventually phoned the police, and Pop arrived just minutes before they did. He told me not to say a word until our attorney got there. I couldn't believe it. First, I'd been given a gag order by the murderer—when he'd made that gun gesture toward Jolie—and then by my father."

"Where was Jolie during all this?"

"My neighbor came over and got her. Pop went with me to the police station, but they put us in separate rooms. Turned out the attorney couldn't meet us right away, but I didn't see that as a problem—until the cops started interrogating me as if I was a suspect. I finally lost it. I said I was sure Tommy's death had something to do with whatever high-security gig he'd been working on, and if the detective would just call somebody who kept the database of secret agents, he'd probably find all the information he needed. Of course, I couldn't tell him which branch of the government either Tommy or Pop worked for. That was the first time I felt really foolish about not knowing exactly what they did for a living."

She took another drink of Scotch, tucked her hair behind her ear. "The detective was more than happy to remove my rose-colored glasses, telling me that Tommy was a member of organized crime, and that he'd been recruited by my own father. I didn't want to believe him. Pop is one of the nicest men you could ever meet—at least I thought so. He's gentle and compassionate, a dedicated family man and father."

The moment the words left her mouth, she wanted to call them back. "I'm sorry. That was—"

He raised his hand, stopping her apology. "Go on."

She glanced at the clock, worrying because Jolie had been at Dora's for so long. It took her a minute to collect her thoughts.

"They were still questioning Pop when I left the police station, so instead of going home, I went to his house to wait. I kept thinking the whole day was just a bizarre nightmare, that I'd wake up and realize none of it had actually happened. I decided to pry into his computer, to see if there was any incriminating organized-crime information. That's when I found the file on you."

He didn't comment, merely stared into her eyes as though he was carefully reading the printout of a polygraph test, watching for inconsistencies. The intensity of his quiet scrutiny made her squirm.

"I'm not sure why I did it, but I printed a copy of the report and stuffed it in my purse. When Pop got home, it was obvious that I'd been snooping in his computer. He finally admitted everything—who he was. People call him the 'quiet don' because he stays so low profile. He showed me some photos of the Ziggmorellis, and that's when I recognized Lucca."

"What made him suspect the other family?"

"I don't know. I was so distraught, I didn't even think to ask. Oddly enough, I was more upset by the implications of that file than I was by anything else." She nodded to the folder lying on the counter. "As a mother, I wanted to know what kind of man turns his back on a child."

"A Mafioso 'wiseguy' evidently," Grant said coolly.

"Ironically, that's the reason he gave for not being in your life. He's the last blood member of an Irish/Sicilian crime family. He felt he didn't have any choice about following in the family tradition—and once a person's in, they're stuck. He said when he found out your mom gave birth to a boy, he backed away because he didn't want you exposed to his lifestyle. Sons are expected to go into the business, and by not acknowledging you, he thought he was protecting you."

"Oh, yeah. I felt real protected in a rat-infested apartment in Chicago."

She reached out and laid her hand on his knee, gave an apologetic squeeze. He glanced down as if the gesture was offensive, and she pulled back her hand, hurt but unable to blame him for his attitude. She hadn't considered how Grant would translate such a sacrifice by a father.

But for her, Pop's words had come as a severe blow. His real flesh-and-blood kid had to be kept safe. Abbe had only come as part of a marriage package. *"I'm just the throw-away kid. Right, Pop? My safety's not nearly as important as your real kid."*

Pop had tried to explain that he hadn't meant the words the way they'd sounded, that Abbe and Jolene were the center of his life. But she hadn't believed him. Especially after he'd lied to her all these years.

"I'm not making excuses for him. I'm just telling you what he told me. After that awful day, I felt like I didn't know him anymore. Just as I hadn't known Tommy. I left, told him I was cutting all ties with him, and moved back to Texas where I thought we'd be safe from all that ugliness. Five months later, I found out how wrong I was. That's when I came here. I thought I was just running from the Ziggmorellis. It never even crossed my mind that the FBI would come looking for me—as far as I knew, the police had closed Tommy's case. The impression the detective gave me was that one less member of organized crime was no big loss."

She glanced toward the front windows. "I wish I knew how those agents found me. If it was so easy, then Lucca's people probably aren't far behind."

"Not necessarily. The FBI have a whole system of computers and other connections that the Mob doesn't have."

"I've heard of organized crime infiltrating law enforcement," she said.

"Did you file a flight plan?"

"Yes—"

His expression seemed to indicate her IQ was less than half her shoe size. "Big mistake."

"No. I did it deliberately." By damn, she deserved some credit here. "I'm instrument rated and I wanted flight following as far as Jamestown, North Dakota. I wasn't comfortable flying VFR clear across the country with Jolie onboard. Even though flight service reported clear weather, you never know what you might run into. My flight plan ended in Jamestown, so I figured it would be anyone's guess where I went from there. I even headed east, just in case, then doubled back. The chances of pinpointing my final destination should have been about the same as trying to find a lily in the desert. I closed out my bank account, and I haven't used my credit cards or any computers."

"What about this file? You didn't think this information would give someone a leg up? Point them in this direction on a hunch?"

"No one knows about…you." Lord, that sounded awful. "Other than the investigator."

"What makes you so sure?"

"Pop told me."

"And you believe him? Seems like you've made a habit of swallowing anything he feeds you."

"I understand your hurt, Grant—"

"Hurt? Baby, you're way off course. I'm pissed that you've known this information and didn't bother to tell me until now. I'm damn upset that there's a target on your back—from the Mob, for God's sake. And I'm mad as hell that you came here endangering my town, my family and my friends. It's not just physical danger, either. Snyder might be an ass, but he got one thing right. If anyone in the horse-racing industry finds out I've got the adopted daughter of a Mob boss living on my ranch, my brothers and I might as well kiss our reputation goodbye."

"Why? I keep telling you, I don't have anything to do with that stuff. I didn't even know my father was a mobster."

"That doesn't mean shit. Once a rumor starts, it spreads like the plague. My stallions are worth millions. I already told you the kind of stud fee they bring in. Our yearlings are in high demand because we consistently breed winning stock. People might start to wonder if that phenomenon is honestly based on excellent bloodlines, or if we're involved in race-fixing—which organized crime, very recently, has had a hand in. Ever since the 2002 Breeders' Cup scandal, breeders, jockeys and owners are all being closely scrutinized, and the slightest hint of foul play prompts investigation."

Abbe felt like an outcast, accused of spreading a disease of danger and ruin. She might as well be wearing a bright scarlet M on her chest—*Mafia*. Her relationship to Stewart Shea was public record for anyone who cared to look.

And folks wouldn't have to search too hard if the Ziggmorellis found her first.

A Mob hit would have the media converging on Callahan and Sons Farm in nothing flat. Because of her, Grant's livelihood could well be at stake.

Not to mention the *lives* at stake.

Because innocent bystanders often got caught in the cross fire of evil.

Shame stung her like a thousand angry wasps. His words made it abundantly clear that if he had known about her in advance, she would not have been welcome. But she refused to let her hurt show. She had to put aside her own feelings and think about Jolene.

Once again, she felt the horrible push-pull battle of a mother's need to protect her child at all costs.

And getting the next words past her throat was the hardest thing she'd ever done in her life.

"You won't have to worry about rumors because I won't be here. You asked why I came to you. Maybe it's because I convinced myself that you were the closest thing to family that

Jolie and I had left. I know it sounds wild. We're not related, but there's a link—however small."

She took a gulp of Scotch, set the glass back on the counter, smearing the ring of water left by condensation. She would not cry.

"I want you to take Jolene." Her heart pounded so hard she thought she'd be sick.

For a moment, there was dead silence. Then he reached out and snagged her glass. "I think you've had enough to drink."

"I'm not drunk. My adrenaline is pumping so fast it's probably burning up the alcohol before it even hits my stomach. I'm dead serious. Now that you know the whole story, surely you can see that she's not safe with me. No one is. I have no choice but to leave. If Jolie's with you, she can't be used as a pawn to get to me."

She leaned forward and gripped his arm. "I need to know she's safe, Grant. You're her best hope. I read every word in that file and formed a picture of you in my mind. I know about the time you spent in the Special Forces, and the kind of life you've lived here on this ranch. That you have good values, and that Shotgun Ridge is far removed from the world of organized crime. But I was afraid I'd created a perfect fantasy and embellished it over the months. That's why I didn't say anything right away. I had to be sure you were the man I'd hoped you were, and that this town was as special as it seemed. I had to be positive I was making the right decision."

"Abbe, you're building me up to be somebody I'm not."

She shook her head, realized her fingernails were digging into his arm and let go. "I don't think so. I've seen the way you are with Jolie, and the way she responds to you. In a little over a week, you've probably spent more time with her than Tommy did in two and a half years."

"I'm sure that's an exaggeration."

"Not much." She rubbed the center of her forehead where a headache was trying to take hold, noticed that her hands were trembling, and dropped them in her lap.

"You're my little girl's best hope for a normal secure life." Her throat was so tight she could hardly speak.

Please, God. Let me get through this without breaking down.

"I have to give her up, Grant. As long as I'm around, she'll always be in danger."

Grant stood up, nearly knocking over the bar stool, and raked his hands through his hair. He was stunned by Abbe's sacrifice, could see what a toll it was taking on her just to say the words. She loved that little girl more than life itself. He'd watched them together.

But, damn it, he was still reeling from Abbe's revelation about Stewart Shea being his biological father.

And he sure as hell didn't want to be anyone's hero.

His last mission had cured him of seeking that rush.

Despite the nightmares that still haunted him, these were different circumstances, a different environment. He was on his own turf, not in a Third World country ruled by a dictator.

Abbe was right. He had the skills to protect his property—and his family.

But he could no more guarantee a successful outcome than she could. That was a simple fact of life.

He snatched up his hat and the file folder, strode to the door and opened it, then remembered that Abbe was still standing in the middle of the room, waiting for an answer.

He didn't have one. Damn it, this was insane. "You're not giving up your kid."

CHAPTER TEN

GRANT STORMED OUT of the guest house, the chaos in his mind propelling him across the lawn and around to his truck on the main driveway. He opened the door, tossed the file on the front seat and climbed in. He switched on the engine, stomped on the accelerator and headed toward Ethan's place, figuring he'd find Clay there, too.

The air conditioner blew full blast, but it didn't cool the burning in his gut.

He and his brothers shared the same mother, but they all had different fathers—and none of them knew the identity of those men.

Until now.

His hand fisted around the steering wheel. Growing up, he'd wondered about the nameless, faceless man who hadn't had the balls to step up to his responsibilities of making a baby. Granted, his mother wasn't any prize. Most of the time she'd either been drunk or high, leaving her boys to fend for themselves while she partied, blew what little money she had, then spread her legs for any man who showed an ounce of interest or offered her a cheap high.

Despite her behavior and lack of morality, though, it took two to get knocked up. And in his very early years, Grant's resentment for the missing half of that duo had grown into hate.

Once Fred Callahan had found him, taught him about love and loyalty and trust, Grant had rarely thought about his roots.

He wished like hell it could have stayed that way.

Parking in back of Ethan and Dora's house, he tucked the folder under his arm and went inside without knocking.

The first thing he saw when he walked in the door was Jolie carting her dog across the room. She was following Katie out of the kitchen, and Max was traipsing right behind them. No telling what kind of mischief they had in their little minds. Jolie had her arms wrapped around the puppy, and her ever-present stuffed lamb was sandwiched between her chest and Harley's white fur.

Emotions flooded him. In the first five minutes after he'd laid eyes on the little girl waving and grinning at him from the airplane's window, the kid had streaked past his cynicism and wormed her way right into his heart.

He'd always wondered how Fred Callahan could truly love three boys who were not of his blood.

Now he understood.

Ethan and Clay sat at the kitchen table, watching him as though they expected him to…hell, he didn't know what they expected him to do. He didn't even know himself. It was a toss-up between putting his fist through a solid object, and crying.

Neither one of those options held any appeal.

"You okay?" Ethan asked.

He snorted. "Hell, no."

"Language!" Ethan and Clay said at once. They'd adopted a no-swearing-in-the-house-or-around-the-kids rule when Dora and Katie had moved in.

Dora flipped a dishrag over her shoulder and rolled her eyes. "The kids aren't even in the room."

"Want to sit?" Clay asked.

"Why don't we take a walk, instead? I imagine Abbe'll be here any minute now to pick up Jolie and Harley. I'd just as soon not run into her until I've sorted things out in my mind and made some decisions." He glanced over at Dora. "I don't mean to exclude you."

She stood on tiptoe and kissed his cheek. "I'm not worried. Ethan will tell me everything anyway."

"Legs," Ethan warned, his eyes brimming with amusement, "you're not supposed to admit that."

"As if they don't know." She kissed Ethan—on the lips— then urged them all toward the door. "You guys go discuss your battle plan. I'll hold down the fort."

Obviously Ethan and Clay had already told Dora what had taken place at the guest house—and she naturally believed they were going to circle the wagons and lay siege in anticipation of unsavory characters gunning for Abbe.

He wondered how she would react if he told her what Abbe was planning.

"What's in the file?" Ethan asked as they walked toward the corral.

"Skeletons from my closet." Grant stopped at the fence, propped his booted foot on the bottom rung and leaned his arms on the top.

For a moment, he merely stared across the flowing green grass to the airstrip and hangar. Rainbirds chugged in a soothing, monotonous rhythm, creating an occasional rainbow as beads of moisture glistened in the sun, hovering over the verdant blades before the thirsty earth could drink them in.

He didn't feel soothed, though. He was off balance, fighting a boiling anger he couldn't wholly define. It wasn't Abbe's fault that his father had abandoned him, or that Stewart had *chosen* to raise her, fully knowing he had a son somewhere in the world that he'd elected not to meet.

She was the innocent in all of this—at least she *had* been...right up until she'd made the decision to come here under false pretenses.

If she'd told him her circumstances right away, and how their backgrounds intertwined, he would have had a choice whether to distance himself or to let himself get tangled up in her life. Now he didn't have the option. He was emotionally invested—in her and in her kid.

But his brothers *did* have a choice.

"Seems to me, any bones in your closet are likely rattling in ours, too," Ethan said.

"No. Just mine. Turns out the guy who married Abbe's mother and adopted Abbe happens to be my dear old deadbeat daddy. Stewart—the quiet don—Shea."

"Get out!" Clay said.

"There's some sort of lab-test results in the file. I didn't read it all." His jaw ached from clenching his teeth. "How the hell could someone get proof without me knowing about it?"

"Mind if I look at what's in that folder?" Clay asked.

Grant shrugged and passed him the file. "This presents a problem for all of us. Other than what's in that report, there's no record of anything tying me to Stewart Shea. But Abbe's another matter. With the FBI and the Mafia on her tail there's a good chance the media will pick up the scent and we won't be able to keep a lid on her identity."

"Snyder indicated there are people who might want her dead," Ethan said. "Was he right, or just blowing smoke?"

"He was right." As they all settled with their arms propped on the fence, Grant filled his brothers in on everything Abbe had told him.

"By association—with her living here on the ranch," he added, "we'll be the target of speculation. This could ruin us. I was pissed—I still am—and it crossed my mind to toss her off our property. Then, damn it to hell, she asked me to take her little girl."

Clay's head whipped around and he frowned, the folder closed and dangling from his hand. "What do you mean, *take* her?"

"Abbe came here to find a good home for her daughter. She thinks the only way to keep Jolie safe is to give her up…to me. Her intentions are to disappear, lead any possible danger away from her kid—and from us. I've dealt with this type of situation enough times to know that her fears are founded. The scum of the earth prey on the weak and innocent, using them as pawns. It's easier to snatch a baby than it is to struggle with a grown man or woman. A parent will voluntarily step in front of the firing squad if it means saving her child."

"Well, she can't leave," Ethan said. "That's just plain stupid."

"I know." Grant looked at both his brothers. He couldn't explain it, but he felt like an outsider. Before today, they'd all been Fred Callahan's sons. All of them had the same life circumstances.

Now that had changed. Grant knew his biological father's name.

"But this isn't your fight," he said. "If Abbe stays, the two of you will be linked to any rumors that might circulate, and you'll be dragged into the fallout. We'll take a hit with the stud fees, and at the track—I'm willing to bet Shea's illegal dealings included bookmaking."

"Best not be *betting* on it, then." Ethan flashed a smile, tipped his hat back on his head.

"Smart-ass," Grant muttered. "Every time one of our horses wins a big purse, whether we own him or just bred him, race-fixing will enter people's minds. I need to know your thoughts on Abbe staying, or if you'd rather I relocate her. God help us if it leaks out that I'm related to the guy, too. If that happens, I'll take myself out of the business."

"Now you're talking like an idiot," Clay said. "I can handle the racing bureau, or any other bozo who wants to question our integrity."

Ethan put his hand on Grant's shoulder. "Don't let the identity of your sperm donor take up space in your head. You know damn well anybody can plant a seed—it doesn't mean crap. Fred Callahan was our father in every sense of the word. We bear his name and we're the product of everything he was."

"And Dad would have never turned his back on someone who got caught up in circumstances that weren't of their own making," Clay added. "I know without even asking that I'm speaking for Ethan, too, when I say we're willing to ride out any possible repercussions to the ranch stemming from rumor. Because that's all it would be—rumor."

Ethan nodded. "A person in the right doesn't run from trouble. They stand and fight—together. Dad taught us that."

Grant felt his throat thicken with emotion. How could he have thought, even for a moment, that their brotherly bond had been weakened? "You have a family to think about," he said, determined to remind both his brothers of the danger they could be facing. "If these Ziggmorelli characters decide Abbe's too big a liability, she won't be the only one in harm's way."

"I can take care of my own family, and if you're suggesting otherwise, I might have to slug you," Ethan said.

"I'll hold him for you," Clay offered helpfully.

Grant breathed deeply. He couldn't imagine being an only child—like Abbe. Not having these two guys in his life.

"Thanks," he said. "I had to ask. What I'd really like to know is how the feds found Abbe so quickly. She seems to have done all the right things—using cash, instead of checks or credit cards, no cell phone. She filed a flight plan as far as

Jamestown, North Dakota, then took off flying VFR, thinking anyone following her would concentrate their search there and come up with a dead end. Seems it should have taken more time to comb all of North Dakota and the surrounding states."

"Could have been someone just got lucky," Ethan said. "Maybe they spotted her plane or something."

"It's possible. They'd have the Baron's description from the times she's landed in Mexico and gone through U.S. Customs."

"Shit." Clay took off his hat, raked a hand through his hair, then replaced the hat. "I left the Baron out last week. I'm sorry, Grant."

"No need to apologize. None of us knew. Abbe flipped out when she noticed the plane was outside the hangar, but she didn't tell me why it bothered her. She had the perfect opportunity and didn't take it—which means, if any of us feels guilt, it's misplaced. Besides, we don't even know if it *was* the plane that tipped off the feds."

He glanced around when he heard the sound of a truck. Just as he'd thought, Abbe had come for Jolene. At least she hadn't left.

He'd pretty much known she wouldn't—not until she had clear and solid plans for her daughter. And right now, she didn't have a firm commitment from him or anyone else.

"Could be a locator on the plane," Ethan said.

Grant dragged his attention back to his brothers. "Could be. I'll check it out. I imagine Abbe would have thought of that, though."

"She said she didn't know about Shea's criminal life," Clay said. "I doubt she'd even know what to look for. Hell, I probably wouldn't even know."

"Luckily, I do." Grant brushed a piece of grass off his shirtsleeve.

Ethan turned sideways. "I think we ought to move Abbe and Jolie out of the guest house so we can keep a closer eye on them. There's plenty of room here at the main house."

"They'll be staying at my place."

"Grant, I know how pigheaded you can be at times. You want to take everything on your shoulders, instead of sharing the load. I think it would be best if you and Clay came back to stay at the house with us for a while, too. If danger's gonna come knocking at the door, I'd feel better if we were all in the same place."

"Forget it. I'm not putting Dora and the kids in harm's way any more than they already are. Besides, my place is rigged with an alarm. Between Clay, me and the security measures, we can make sure Abbe's safe."

Ethan shook his head. "I thought you were nuts when you built a house in Shotgun Ridge and rigged it with an alarm when everybody else leaves their doors wide open. Guess your cynicism paid off."

"If you'd seen and done half the things I have, you'd want good solid protection around your family, too."

Grant took the folder back from Clay and pushed away from the fence. "I don't imagine we'll see any more excitement tonight. Aside from dealing with Abbe, I'll try to keep up my end of the work around here, as well."

"You deserve time off if you need it," Ethan said. "Clay and I can pick up the slack on the ranch."

"In case you've forgotten," Clay said in mock indignation. "I'm standing right here while you volunteer me for hard labor and physical danger."

Ethan slapped his brother on the back. "Curse of being the youngest, Clay. Us older dudes get to pull rank."

"Good thing I have such a willing and charming nature."

Grant felt his lips tug at his brother's teasing conceit. They were making light of the situation—obviously for his bene-fit. His brothers both knew what it would cost him emotion-ally to assume the responsibility of life-and-death stakes.

Something he'd sworn he'd never do again.

FOR THE SECOND TIME that day, Abbe saw Grant cover the short distance from the main house and the guest house. She'd picked up Jolene from Ethan's place, had noticed Grant talking to his brothers. She'd driven home, wondering…

Now she unlocked the door and opened it, saw that his de-meanor didn't look any friendlier than it had earlier. Her heart pounded and her palms grew sweaty.

She'd asked him to take her daughter. Now that the time was at hand, she wanted to retract the plea.

But it was for the best. If she kept telling herself that, maybe she'd start believing it.

"Where's Jolie?" he asked. He stood on the porch, not making a move to come in.

"Sulking in her bedroom because I cut short her playtime with Katie. Do you want to come inside?" She felt exposed with the door open.

"Pack your stuff. You're moving in with me." He stepped across the threshold and she automatically moved aside.

"You mean Jolie is."

"I mean *both* of you. I told you, you're not giving up your kid."

"Do you think I want to? My God, Grant, she's my world! What I *want* to do is sit down in the middle of the floor and bawl. But that's not going to do any of us any good."

"You came here for my help, and I've decided to give it. But we'll do this on my terms, my way."

"Grant—"

"You can't just hand over your child to a stranger. And set-ting up legal guardianship isn't something that can be accomplished overnight. What if she needs medical attention? Have you thought about that?"

"I haven't thought about *anything* except keeping her safe." Her voice was a whispered hiss. She glanced around to make sure Jolie hadn't come out of her room.

"Well, you seem to think I'm capable enough in that area, so pack your things. It's just as easy to protect two of you as just one."

"What about your brothers? Won't they be upset if I stay?" Her heart was beating so hard she wondered if it was visible through her shirt. She'd been preparing herself for the unthinkable. Now Grant was offering her her heart's desire. To stay with her child.

"They're the ones who insisted."

She could tell nothing from his stoic expression. But his words told their own story.

Ethan and Clay wanted her here. Grant didn't.

She would only be a job to him, much like the Special Forces assignments he no longer accepted.

But she would take anything she was offered if it meant keeping her daughter close and safe—even if only for a few more days.

"All right. For now, we'll do it your way." She shoved her hair off her forehead, her hand shaking. "Thank you. It shouldn't take me long to get our things together. I'll call you when we're ready so you don't have to stand around and wait."

"I'll wait." With his arms crossed, it was clear he didn't intend to budge.

She shrugged and headed toward Jolie's room. It broke her heart to see her normally happy little girl lying on the bed with her lip poked out. The puppy was snuggled beside her, his head on his paws, brown eyes accusing. Great, *two* upset babies.

Usually she didn't tolerate sulky behavior. But with all she was facing, and even though she knew she could end up with a very spoiled three-year-old, she simply couldn't bear the thought of discipline.

"Come on, sweetie babe. We're going to pack our things."

Fat tears rolled down Jolie's face. "No! I don't want to go nowhere. I want to play wif Katie! And Max!"

Abbe sat on the bed and gathered her daughter in her arms. "It's okay, baby. We're not going far. Just to Grant's house."

"Hey, squirt," Grant said from behind her.

"Gwant!" Jolie pulled out of Abbe's arms and crawled across the bed, throwing her arms around Grant's waist.

Abbe glanced up. She hadn't realized he'd followed her. A razor-sharp pang of hurt and jealousy sliced from her stomach to her heart.

Never before had her daughter sought comfort from anyone but her. But how could she be so petty? Less than an hour ago she'd been trying to arrange a new home for Jolie, intending to ease herself out of her little girl's life.

A sure guarantee that all future comfort *would* come from someone else.

But she wasn't gone yet. And, damn it, it hurt to sit back and watch while Jolie latched onto Grant.

Harley danced exuberantly on his hind legs, then put on a show by chasing his tail. Although her throat ached with tears she refused to shed, Abbe forced a smile when Jolie giggled at the puppy's antics.

As though sensing Abbe's sadness, Harley leaped across the bed, nosed his way into her lap and licked her chin. She speared her fingers through the puppy's soft hair, cuddling the little body next to her heart.

"How would you like to come stay in a big room over at my house?" Grant asked.

Jolie's eyes lit up, then she glanced at Abbe. "Can Mommy have a big room, too?"

"Yep. Right down the hall from yours."

"'Kay, Mom?"

Abbe nodded, glad that she hadn't been totally replaced in her daughter's affections. Children bounced back so quickly. She only wished she could do the same. "I think that sounds like fun."

Jolie looked back at Grant. "Can Harley sleep wif me if he promises to potty on the papers?"

"Yep."

"And Lambie-pie, too?"

"The lamb's gonna go on the papers?"

"No, silly." Jolie giggled. "Her doesn't potty. Her's just a pretend lamb."

"Does she know that?"

"Huh?" Jolie didn't quite understand. One thing was clear, though. Just the sight of Grant had banished her sulks in an instant.

"Never mind. Hop down and show me your suitcase, and we'll get you packed." He lifted her off the bed, looked at Abbe. "I've got this one covered. You go get your stuff together."

Abbe wanted to object to his bossiness purely on principle. She didn't like the way his tone had changed when he spoke to her. He'd been sweet and fun with Jolie, yet monotone and stoic with her.

Oh, his behavior was subtle, but she'd picked up on the nuances. Struggling and fearing for her future was forcing her to live more deeply, more fully, to tune in to the moment and really see the world and people around her, rather than skimming the surface.

Watching Grant, she would describe him as consistent and calm.

Good traits to possess in a crisis.

After today's visit by the FBI, Abbe wasn't all that keen on being alone. Grant was offering his home and his protection.

Under other circumstances, moving in with a man like this would have been exciting—a man who made her heart speed up, made her long for romance and the delicious anticipation of figuring out if they were compatible, if perhaps he was "the one."

But she couldn't allow herself to consider any such possibility. A person couldn't set their sights on building a relationship knowing there would always be the threat of having to leave at a moment's notice.

She would take his offer of protection. For Jolie's sake.

But she wouldn't allow herself to dream of more.

STEWART SHEA'S DOORBELL rang at the ungodly hour of 6:30 a.m. Tying the sash of his paisley silk bathrobe, Stewart walked across the terra-cotta tile atrium and checked the security camera that zoomed in on the early-morning visitor.

Gil Ziggmorelli.

His cordial adversary.

Waiting beyond the wrought-iron gates of the courtyard, Gil was impeccably dressed in a dark business suit. His thinning hair was pulled back in a short ponytail that, in Stewart's opinion, no man in his sixties should be caught dead wearing.

Hair fashion aside, Gil might appear pleasant, but it would be a big mistake to underestimate the natty dresser. The man was as lethal as a bullet to the heart, and Stewart knew better than to let down his guard.

He pressed a button and the gates opened, as did the front door.

"Good morning, Stewart," Gil said as he flipped a coin into the burbling courtyard fountain. Ziggmorelli never passed a fountain without tossing in a quarter and making a wish. Claimed it was bad luck not to. "I hope you'll forgive me for calling so early in the day. I don't tolerate the heat as well as I once did."

Stewart shook hands with the other man, aware of the double entendre. Although the Nevada temperature would rise to triple digits by noon, lately, Gil's family was feeling even more heat from the feds.

"We've been around a long time, you and I," Stewart said. "Bound to be some intolerances. I'm weary of the desert heat, too. I'm about ready to cash in my chips and find a friendlier climate. Meanwhile, would you like to come in?"

"No need to inconvenience you. I won't be staying long, and your courtyard is quite lovely."

And, Stewart thought, it was out in the semi-open. If Ziggmorelli came inside, the two men lurking by the gate wouldn't be able to protect his back.

"What can I do for you, then?"

The soothing sound of water trickling over the stone fountain vied with the jingling coins Gil fiddled with in his pants pocket.

"We had an agreement, I know," Gil began in a slightly apologetic tone, "that we would let the matter of an incriminating computer disk drop unless—or until—you decided to retire. A show of good faith after the unfortunate incident with Donato."

"We still do have that agreement," Stewart said as both an acknowledgment and a reminder.

"In light of my son's dilemma and upcoming trial, I find myself somewhat twitchy over the possible existence of delicate data. I've come to ask, man to man, that you surrender the disk earlier than we agreed upon."

"I don't have a problem with that." He had the dates, names and places committed to memory, anyway. Normally, in their line of work, absolutely nothing was documented—in any form.

But Tommy Donato hadn't honored the Omerta—the code of silence a Mafioso takes when he's initiated into a crime family—as he should have. He'd been a cocky kid wanting to run before he learned to crawl. So he'd recorded information on Stewart's computer, hoping to make it look as though Stewart was planning to turn informer. Armed with the lie, Tommy had gone to the Ziggmorellis and asked them to make a hit on Stewart.

He'd wanted Stewart out of the way so he could take over the position as head of the Shea family.

That miscalculation had gotten him whacked.

Not by the Sheas, but by the Ziggmorellis. Gil had taken a dislike to Tommy, felt he was a loose cannon and a disgrace because he'd proved he couldn't be trusted, was loyal only to himself.

A man doesn't play on both sides of the fence and live to tell about it.

"I would also ask," Gil continued, "that you turn over your computer to me, as well. I mean no disrespect. If you were in my position, I am sure you would want to personally see to it that any information lurking in the bowels of such a machine was destroyed."

"I'll deliver the computer by this evening," he said to Gil. The sooner this information was out of his hands, the safer Abbe and Jolene would be.

"Good enough. I will trust your word."

When Gil left, Stewart went into the study and booted up the computer, wondering how the other man had managed to run his operation so smoothly all these years when he was clearly ignorant of the computer age. If Stewart wanted to double-cross the Ziggmorellis, all he had to do was make another backup diskette.

But he was tired of the game, tired of the business he hadn't chosen. A family business he'd been sucked into against his will. Sadly, once he'd been caught in the greedy jaws of the money trap, opting out had been nearly impossible—not to mention potentially bad for the state of his continued health.

He drummed his fingers on the desk as the machine took its sweet time loading. He'd only looked up this particular file once—right after Tommy's death—just to make sure it actually existed, since the disk Tommy had claimed he possessed had never materialized.

Finally the computer indicated it was ready to access the program. Damn technology. This was supposed to be the fastest model on the market.

He typed in his password and the file name, then leaned back and tapped out a cigarette from the pack of filtered Camels that rested on his desk. He thumbed the wheel on his sterling-silver Zippo. The flint sparked but it never caught flame.

Staring at him from the computer screen was a message straight from the grave.

Once is all it takes. KABOOM! Gotcha. Information destroyed...destroyed...destroyed...

The entire computer screen went black.

His mouth went desert dry. The cigarette clung to his lower lip even as his jaw went slack.

Abandoning the cigarette and lighter, he rebooted the computer, his gut burning as he waited, and waited, and waited for the damned machine to load whatever the hell it needed to before it would accept a command. He changed his mind about the cigarette, lit it and dragged smoke deep into his lungs.

Finally the cursor blinked at him. He dropped the cigarette in a leaded-crystal ashtray and quickly retyped the file's name.

Nothing. Good God. Smoke curled up from the ashtray, stinging his eyes as he typed command after command, searching the hard drive and every other area of the computer he could think to try.

At last he came up with a file named Second Try. It was another one of Tommy's taunts. The kid had been a computer whiz, and a fan of *Mission Impossible.*

"Shit! You snotty little bastard!" Stewart leaped up and his chair shot out from behind him. Tommy had programmed the file to destroy itself if it was opened more than once.

With both anger and fear roiling inside him, he heaved the monitor across the room, ignoring the destructive sounds of shattering glass and wood as the equipment skidded across the credenza.

He'd thought he could keep Abbe out of this mess. But if he told Gil the file was gone, admitted that he'd never found the disk Tommy had supposedly made, Ziggmorelli would automatically go after Abbe, believing that she had the one and only original copy.

They knew she'd seen Lucca kill Tommy. It would make perfect sense if she'd also found the disk among Tommy's belongings, held on to it as a means of leverage and protection.

By tonight, when he didn't show up with the promised computer and disk, events would be set in motion that couldn't be stopped.

And unless he could come up with a very convincing story, Stewart knew that he'd just hammered the final nail in Abbe's coffin.

CHAPTER ELEVEN

THE NEXT MORNING Grant was in her room before daylight.

"Get up."

"What?" Abbe grabbed for the covers he'd snatched away, disoriented for a moment. Where was she?

Then she remembered. Grant's house. In the guest bedroom that was decorated in soothing shades of yellow and cream.

"Boot camp starts today," he said. "Your ass is mine. I can't trust you to be honest, so I may as well make sure you have the best chance of not getting yourself, or someone else, killed."

He yanked open the closet, took out her tennis shoes, then snagged a pair of sweatpants and a tank top, and tossed them on the bed.

"Get dressed and be downstairs in fifteen minutes."

"Or?" she prompted, fully awake now.

"Or I'll come back and take you down myself."

Well, no more Mr. Nice Guy, she thought, annoyed. Although he hadn't been overly charming last night when he'd moved her into his house, either.

"I can't just leave Jolene—"

"She's taken care of." He started to walk away.

"Oh, no you don't." Now she was angry. Who did he think he was? Invading her privacy and issuing orders as though she was nothing more than something he'd bought and paid for.

She flung back the covers, stormed across the room and clamped her hand around his arm.

"Let's get something straight right now. When it comes to my daughter, *I* make the decisions. And neither of us will budge until I'm satisfied with whatever arrangements you apparently have in mind."

"So you're a tough girl now? That wasn't the tune you were singing yesterday. I distinctly recall that you were pretty damn eager to hand over your daughter to a near stranger and hightail it out of here."

"Well, I *didn't* hightail it anywhere." She could have strangled him for throwing her emotional plea back in her face.

He'd known damn well what that had cost her.

Her stomach twisted, her anger boiling.

"I'm still here. I might not be some hard-ass mercenary, but don't you dare underestimate me, buddy. You'll learn right quick that a *mother* is more dangerous than you and your whole stinking army put together!"

His expression hardly changed. They were chest to chest, both breathing hard. He looked down at the fingernails digging into his arm.

"Prove it. Be downstairs in fifteen minutes," he repeated.

"Go to hell."

"I made that trip long before you arrived, darlin'." His hand fisted around the doorjamb, his eyes glittering and hard. "Dora will be over in a half an hour to take care of Jolie. Clay's sticking around until I'm free. Satisfied?"

"Not even close."

"Tough. From now on, your days of privacy are history. You and Jolie don't go anywhere unless me or one of my brothers is stuck to you like glue. As for who makes the decisions, there can only be one squad commander. And I'm it." With that, he turned and left the room.

Abbe was horrified at the way she'd lost her temper. She didn't let go often, but when she did, she had a tendency to say and do rash things.

Fine. If he wanted to play drill sergeant, she'd give him a run for his money. She snatched up her sweatpants and shoved her legs in.

Boot camp? Ha!

She yanked the tank top over her head and raced into the bathroom to brush her teeth.

She'd show him she could take anything he could dish out.

SEVERAL HOURS LATER, Abbe was seriously rethinking her cocksure attitude. They'd already jogged three miles, lifted weights in his fully equipped gym and exercised every muscle her body possessed.

Now she was standing on a mat, her limbs feeling like limp spaghetti, and he was insisting on seeing her repertoire of self-defense moves.

"I've never been in a fight," she said, "so I don't know what you want me to show you."

His face was a stone mask. "A man is most vulnerable in five places—eyes, nose, throat, groin and knee. Go for one of them."

"Yours?"

"Do you see any other man standing around?"

She desperately wanted to mimic his words in a defiant singsong just to provoke a reaction, but she doubted it would work. He was like a statue; not an ounce of warmth in him. She'd understood his initial anger yesterday, but had expected him to get over it. Clearly he hadn't, and his nasty mood was contagious. It didn't take any thought at all to decide on a target point.

She aimed a kick at his crotch, knew in an instant she'd made a big mistake.

His hand shot out. The room upended when he grabbed her ankle and jerked her out feet from under her. Air whooshed out of her lungs as her back hit the mat. Hard.

Panting, she lay looking up at him, wishing she had the skill to wipe that gloating expression off his face.

"First lesson," he said, standing over her. "Every guy in the world has been kicked in the groin at least once, and he knows that if a female's ticked-off or afraid, that's the first place she's going to try to hit."

"Then why did you offer it as an option?"

"Because it's an effective target—for the second or third shot. Just not the first one, because he'll be expecting it."

She sat up and managed to get her feet under her—unaided. Obviously a gentlemanly helping hand was out of the question in boot camp.

She'd barely straightened her legs when he grabbed her arm and twisted it behind her. The unexpected attack scared the living daylights out of her. Her muscles were already shaking with fatigue. Now her adrenal glands were burning jet fuel.

"Your objective is to escape," he said, his breath stirring the hair next to her ear. "Using any means. Head, hands, feet, teeth. I have the advantage of size, so you have to think smart and fight dirty. Make sure your moves are aimed to inflict maximum pain."

She dropped her head back against his chest, allowed her body to sag into his. "Sugar, right now I don't have the strength to squish an ant, much less hurt something." Even more pitiful, she didn't have enough energy to appreciate the virile body propping her up.

His muscles went rigid for a minute, then he released her wrist and stepped back—well before she'd had a chance to rest and recharge her batteries. Only quick instincts and pride kept her from falling. His actions made it abundantly clear that he had no patience for slackers—and her in particular—which was just the reminder she needed in order to get a grip.

She realized that she was in danger of letting him best her, and that would never do. Not after she'd been so determined to prove her fortitude.

Although she really wanted to find a corner and go lick her wounds in private, she gave him a cheeky grin and held out her arm. "Okay. Brief insanity. For a second I forgot we were in boot camp, and transported myself to a spa in Vegas. Let's try that again, and I promise to show no mercy."

Her attempt to lighten his mood fell flat. What *was* his problem?

"You don't have the luxury of forgetting." His arms were crossed over his chest. He didn't make a move to pick up where they'd left off. "There are no second chances when you're faced with life and death."

"I'm all too aware of that, Grant. Which is why I was trying to inject a little levity here. I refuse to roll into a sniveling ball and give in to all the 'what if' fears that dog me night and day. You might think you're helping by whipping my butt into shape, but the whole exercise'll be useless if I end up so sore I can't move. I've never owned a membership to a gym, and these muscles are virgins when it comes to exercise."

She snagged a towel off the weight bench and wiped the back of her neck. "You do what you want. I'm done."

She attempted to make a dignified exit, but he grabbed her arm.

"You wouldn't last a day in the army."

"Good thing I never enlisted, then, isn't it?" She held his gaze, refused to look away even though every instinct she possessed screamed for her to do so. He made her feel things she didn't want to feel—attraction, anger, lust, fear. Her emotions were a tangled mess.

At last he let go of her arm and stepped away. "Have you ever handled a firearm?"

"No."

"Does Jolie still take a nap?"

"What in the world does that have to do with guns?" she asked.

"I'd like your undivided attention when we practice weaponry later. If she's with Dora *and* she's sleeping, you're less likely to be distracted."

He had a point. She suspected he was attempting to make concessions, and that would have been a nice gesture if he would at least relax his shoulders and not stare at her as if she was a skunk that'd wandered into the middle of his mama's garden party.

She wasn't used to being treated so coldly, and frankly, it hurt. If she'd been a rotten person, his behavior would make sense. But she wasn't. And she hadn't chosen any of this.

"When I can, I try to get Jolie to lie down around one in the afternoon."

"Fine." Arms still folded, he kept his distance. "Meet me by the kitchen door at one-thirty. It's nine-thirty now. That gives you four hours to rest and recuperate."

She rolled her eyes. "Spoken like a man who's never parented a three-year-old or owned a puppy who constantly wants to play. I can guarantee you, I won't have time for rest."

Grant's gaze raked her from head to toe. "I'll say one thing. Your body looks damn good for being so out of shape."

Not sure if that was a compliment or an insult, she automatically stood straighter, sucking in her stomach. So what if her muscles weren't as toned as they used to be? She was thirty, and she'd had a baby, for crying out loud.

"Rome wasn't built in a day," she said, even though it was a partial admission that she wasn't as fit as she'd been in her earlier twenties.

"Baby, that might be all the time you've got to get yourself in condition."

"I'm not as soft as you think. It's perfectly natural to be shaky and out of breath after running three miles and contorting my body every which way on those torture contraptions." She indicated the exercise equipment with a tilt of her head. "I'm human. Not a machine with replaceable parts."

"I'm human, but I'm steady and have plenty of breath," he pointed out, showing no mercy.

She raised her eyebrow. With his rigid body and expressionless features, he looked very much like a lethal machine ready for action. "If the robotic parts fit…go ahead and brag."

Turning, she walked away. He didn't follow her as she left the indoor gym. He probably thought she wasn't taking the lessons seriously. She was. But concentrating was difficult when she was worried about Jolie's whereabouts, nearly fainting from hunger and trying to stay vertical on fatigued muscles that threatened to collapse in on themselves—not to mention achieving that upright footing from a horizontal position after the breath had been knocked out of her.

Being attracted to her surly instructor wasn't helping her equilibrium, either. She needed to put those nonsense thoughts out of her mind. She had more important things to worry about.

Besides, the interest was clearly one-sided. Oh, sure, he'd said her body looked good, but that didn't mean anything special. He was male, after all, and he wasn't blind.

Grandma Jane had always said actions spoke louder than words. And Grant's behavior indicated that as far as he was concerned, she would always be tainted by the affluent, corrupt environment in which she'd been raised.

Guilty by association.

Ironically, she'd been tarnished by the very father who'd abandoned him.

THE NEXT MORNING was the same drill. Running, weight lifting, getting tossed around in self-defense lessons, then target practice in the afternoon—which they were engaged in right now.

Despite feeling vulnerable out here in the open where anyone with a pair of binoculars could spy on them—or worse, through a high-powered scope on a rifle—Abbe had another reason for wanting the day to end. She was sore in places she didn't know could get sore. Even the roots of her hair hurt. Wearing a baseball cap, protective goggles and electronic ear protectors only magnified the discomfort.

Sweat trickled between her breasts as she lifted the 9 mm pistol off the folding table Grant had set up for them to work from. They were on the back section of the ranch, about a quarter of a mile behind Grant's house where a small creek, bordered by a cluster of cottonwoods, elms, aspens and Douglas fir, shielded them from view of the house.

In front of her, dirt and clumps of grass flowed into a gentle knoll scattered with sagebrush baking in the sun. Serving as a backdrop for the watermelon, paper silhouette target, water jug and tin cans Grant had propped on various rocks was a hill rising out of the prairielike landscape. She certainly had enough objects to aim at.

Very aware that Grant was watching her, she tried to remember the proper sequence of steps to check and load the gun. He'd practically taken the darn thing apart.

"I find it hard to believe that you were never exposed to firearms," he said from behind her. "Even if you thought Shea and Donato worked for the government, seems you'd notice them carrying concealed weapons."

"Of course I did. That doesn't mean I'd have any desire to handle one. Pop deliberately kept that part of his life low-key. And when Jolie was born, I made it clear to him and Tommy that I didn't want guns in the house around the baby."

"And no one thought you should learn to defend yourself against disgruntled spies?"

"No." Hoping her tone conveyed her disinterest in continuing this subject, she picked up the loaded magazine from the table. She didn't need any reminders of her past stupidity and gullibility, thank you very much. Nor did she need Grant's sarcasm.

"Why is the action open?" he asked.

For a minute she stared at the gun as though it was an alien's thing, which in a way it was, her mind going blank. He *would* have to give her a pop quiz. Yesterday's practice session had been mainly learning about gun safety and how the weapon worked. Which was a whole lot of information for a novice shooter to retain. "Um, because that's the way you left it?"

"Wrong answer."

Finally memory kicked in. "Oh. It's open so you can see it's unloaded."

"Did you check the chamber to make sure?"

"No."

"Why not?"

"Because *you* already did."

"Strike two. Whenever you pick up a firearm that's been out of your control, don't rely on someone else's word about the weapon's condition. Check it yourself. A *click* when you're expecting a *bang!* can be as deadly as a *bang!* when you expect a *click*."

She sucked in a deep breath and counted to five. No wonder they were using blank ammo. He'd probably had occasion to teach firearms in the army and was well aware of how irritating he could be.

Then again, she understood the importance of safety, as well as the confidence that comes with intimately knowing how something worked. As a licensed flight instructor, she demanded no less from any of the students she'd trained. The more familiar they were with the aircraft, the better chance they stood of reacting calmly and averting disaster in an unforeseen crisis in the air.

Taking her time, she carefully rechecked the gun, then closed the action. Her hands trembled as she inserted the magazine clip. Nerves, she realized. She couldn't seem to do anything about them.

Being a mechanically inclined individual, she hated appearing inept at anything. Especially when someone else was watching.

She pulled back on the action slide to chamber the first round, turned toward the targets and tried like the devil to get the little red dot on the rear sight to align itself with the one on the front of the gun, *and* on the chest portion of the paper silhouette in the background. Invariably, about the time that happened, the gun wiggled, growing increasingly heavy in her fatigued, two-handed hold.

"Spread your legs," Grant said from right behind her.

She jolted and the gun wobbled. Cursing beneath her breath, she planted her feet a shoulder width apart as he'd taught her to do. The fancy ear protectors they both wore blocked out excessive noise, but amplified lower-level tones—like the shiver-inducing baritone of his voice, making it sound softly seductive.

"My hands are sweating," she said. "If you want to know the truth, I'd rather face a screaming stall light in a spiraling plane over the ocean than fool with this gun." The aversion probably had more to do with why she was learning to shoot in the first place—in anticipation of having to defend her life or her daughter's.

He reached both arms around her and steadied the gun. "Wipe them on your jeans."

Confident that he had a solid grasp, she let go of the Glock and scrubbed her palms against her thighs, thinking it wasn't going to do a whole lot of good—at least not while he was practically pressed against her back with his mouth inches from her cheek.

For Pete's sake, she could smell the fresh-air scent of his shirt.

Sliding her hands back beneath his, she gripped the stock of the gun once more.

"Keep your finger out of the trigger guard until you're prepared to shoot," he cautioned. "And make sure your thumbs are below the action's slide range, otherwise it'll hammer back and take a chunk of skin with it." He used his own hands to correct her position.

"Gee, thanks," she drawled. "Another thing to worry about. One end might shoot me and the other end's waiting to whack off my thumb. Swell."

"Weapons aren't capable of acting on their own, Ace." Even through the slight distortion of the electronic ear protectors, she could hear a trace of amusement in his voice. "This is only a tool. What it does depends solely on what *you* do with it. Now close your left eye and sight straight down the barrel with your right."

"I don't see why I'm aiming at stuff clear across the way. I'm certainly not going to draw a bead on somebody and deliberately assassinate him. Besides, if I'm ever forced to point a gun at a live target, it would only be at very close range." Although she appreciated the support of his hands beneath her shaky arms, she really wished he'd step back a pace or two. His closeness wasn't helping matters any.

"First off, when you're dealing with the scum of the earth, you don't get to choose the ideal circumstances. The enemy can threaten from any range. The second rule of handling a firearm is, never point your weapon at anything you aren't fully prepared to destroy. If that turns out to be a living target, you better be sure that person's destruction is a consequence you're willing to face."

Her arms went slack against his. He didn't try to prevent her from lowering the gun. "Are you trying to scare me half to death so I'll give up? This wasn't *my* idea. You're the one who insisted I learn to shoot a gun."

"Don't try to tell me you never considered buying a handgun for protection."

"Of course I thought about it. But since I don't know how to use one, or if I could even bring myself to pull the trigger if confronted, I dismissed the notion."

"Mafia soldiers carry high-powered, automatic weapons, Abbe. They don't hesitate to use them."

She turned her head to look at him, wondering if he was deliberately being stupid. "I'm more aware of their murderous tools than most people are."

"Yet you hesitate over whether or not you can pull a trigger? What were your plans? To defend yourself with a kitchen knife or deflect a bullet with a can of Mace?"

"I hadn't thought about hands-on defense. That's what I came to *you* for. My only instincts were to take Jolie and run." Saying the words aloud appalled her. Her life was turned upside down because she'd trusted so blindly, counted on the men in her life to take care of her. She'd come to Shotgun Ridge for much the same thing. Was she merely repeating the cycle? The realization, examined in a literal context, had her spine stiffening.

She was no longer the happy-go-lucky woman who took wealth, comfort and safety for granted, looked to others to make her decisions. She'd left Las Vegas with the determination to be proactive, not to repeat past behavior.

She reminded herself to be careful. She needed Grant, yes. She wasn't living in fairy-tale land. But she wouldn't let him take over, wouldn't simply hand him the controls and say, "Fly anywhere you want, and I'll merely come along for the ride."

"Let's see if we can clarify your thinking," Grant said, his voice devoid of emotion except for that recently adopted hint of anger simmering just beneath the surface.

"Get a real clear picture in your mind. There's a depraved thug coming toward you. He doesn't have a shred of conscience, doesn't care about either the sex or the age of his prey. All he's interested in is the kill. He's holding a bullwhip, snapping it, taunting you, but his slimy eyes are on your baby girl. One vicious slap of that whip can easily slice off her arm, maim her for life, cause her endless, relentless suffering…or death. If she's lucky, that is. It's come down to the final hour and you have to make a split-second decision. It's either you and Jolie, or him. There's no way that three people can walk out alive. Even though you don't see a gun in his hand, the bullwhip is a weapon. A deadly one. What are you going to do? Your daughter's crying, begging, clutching at your pant leg. *Now* can you pull the trigger?"

"Yes." The single word was a guttural hiss, uttered without hesitation between clenched teeth, her finger already squeezing the outside of the curved metal that guarded the trigger. If her finger had been inside the semicircle, she would have reflexively pulled.

He guided her arms back into firing position. Every vivid word of his descriptive image branded itself inside her, sickened her. The possibility of such a vile occurrence was very real, causing fear to ball in her stomach like hell's fire, her throat nearly closing against the burning ache above her windpipe.

"Good." He let go of her hands and stepped back. "Keep your wrists straight," he coached quietly. "Use your arms to push out and maintain a positive tension against your weapon, but don't lock them. That'll transfer all of the weapon's energy into your shoulders and won't allow you to work with the recoil. Don't strangle the gun, but hold it firmly so you stay in control. Now press the safety release. Sight your target. Take your time. When you're ready, squeeze the trigger with the pad of your index finger, not the whole joint."

His monotone instructions helped her to focus, nearly banished the horrible images he'd conjured up a few moments earlier. For a split second, everything lined up, and she quickly squeezed, simultaneously closing her eyes. The recoil of the gun pushed her hands upward and shoved her right into Grant's chest.

She hadn't realized he'd moved back in so close. Clearly, she'd locked her arms instead of her wrists, because an ache penetrated clear to the bone in her shoulders.

"It might help if you opened your eyes," Grant said.

She complied. "Did I hit anything?"

"That depends. What were you aiming at?"

"The silhouette."

"Well, you hit a bunny rabbit on the hill, ten feet above the watermelon."

"Oh, no! Oh my God, are you kidding?" Horrified, she squinted her eyes, searching for the carnage.

"Yes."

She whipped around to look at his unsmiling face. Would it hurt him to act a little friendlier? "Kidding?" she asked.

"Proving a point. When you pull that trigger, you want to know exactly where your bullet's going to go. Once it leaves the bore, there's no way to call it back."

"I told you I'd never fired a gun before."

"That's pretty obvious. Let's try it again. Get a good grip on your weapon, steady your wrists and try not to anticipate the recoil. You're flinching upward right when you pull the trigger."

"Easy for you to say—not to anticipate the recoil," she clarified. "It feels like the gun's going to flip right out of my hands. And I'm not *even* going to tell you how my shoulders feel."

She lifted the gun, determined to hit something other than nonexistent rabbits halfway up the hill.

She could land an airplane on a pigtail road between the edge of the ocean and a dense forest, and never once have the wheels stray outside the ruts. By dog, surely she could manage to hit the side of a big fat watermelon—even without aligning that stupid little dot to within a hair on a gnat's ass.

She lined up the barrel and squeezed the trigger. Even wearing ear protectors and fully expecting the sound, the gun blast scared her silly, causing her to jump.

"You're not concentrating," Grant said when the recoil of the Glock nearly *did* send the gun sailing out of her hands. Again.

Well, duh. Holding the weight of a gun after the second day of being put through a full workout that had included thirty push-ups was just a tad difficult. Plus, she couldn't get those ugly bullwhip images out of her mind.

She hadn't been sleeping well lately. Now she'd be lucky if she could sleep at all.

She squinted toward the target area. The watermelon wasn't smashed to smithereens or oozing any pink fluids, so it was a safe bet that she'd missed completely.

"I'm worried about Jolie," she said in excuse of her poor marksmanship. "I know she's with Dora, but I still don't like her being out of my sight."

"You were willing to give her up," he reminded Abbe. "You wouldn't be seeing her at all, then."

She clicked on the safety, slammed the gun down on the table and spun around to face him.

"I'm sick and tired of you tossing that back in my face. I know damn well what I was prepared to sacrifice. That doesn't mean I'd be any less distraught over my daughter's safety— whether there was no more than a yard between us or if we were separated by a thousand miles." Without thought, she hooked her leg behind his knee and swept his legs out from under him.

She was so startled to see him lying flat on his back in the dirt that she simply stared for several seconds. Slowly, pride swelled inside her, pushing away the fog of surprise. Earlier today, *she'd* been the one sprawled on the floor most of the time.

She brushed her hands together in a dusting-off "so-there" gesture. "How's that for concentration?"

He got to his feet. "Don't get too cocky, Ace. I let you have that one."

"You did not."

"Did you see me put up a fight?"

"You didn't have time to resist. I caught you off guard. But even if you did fall down on purpose, you could at least be a gentleman and keep the ruse to yourself, let me believe I'm making progress."

"I'm afraid you've mistaken me for someone else. I'm no gentleman." His voice was deep and dangerously quiet, his blue eyes trained on hers like the laser sight on a rifle. "If you want praise from me, you'll have to earn it. I won't blow smoke up your ass just so you can puff up with false confidence. That'll only get you killed."

"Gee. Aren't you a merry ray of sunshine."

"Listen up, sweetheart. Taking you on essentially makes us partners. If someone comes gunning for you, they're going to run into me, too. Since that's the case, I intend to be damn sure that the person watching my back is at least halfway prepared for the job." He deliberately picked up the gun and ejected the magazine, paused to give her a long, pointed look, then opened the action to empty the firing chamber, and placed both the gun and the ammo back on the table.

The silent reproach was blatant. She could have kicked herself for forgetting the proper rules of safe handling, for allowing him to goad her into reacting rashly. At least she'd remembered to push the damn safety button.

"Now, if you're through gloating," he said, "do you think we can get back to work?"

CHAPTER TWELVE

"IF YOU CAN'T HIT any harder than that, then you're in deep trouble and I'm wasting my time."

After four days of the same grueling routine, coupled with Grant's surliness, Abbe had finally had enough.

She flopped onto the mat in his state-of-the-art gym and refused to move. He could stand there holding that stupid punching bag for the rest of the week for all she cared.

By God, she was proud of the slight definition that was developing in her arms. And the tightening of her abs made her look damn hot when she wore her low-rise jeans. She could splatter a watermelon at fifty paces with a handgun, or turn a plastic water jug into a fountain, and every once in a while, she could flip Grant onto the floor by design instead of by luck.

Yet the more she progressed, the more he demanded of her.

His criticism wasn't helping her morale at all. Every morning she woke up wondering if this would be the day that evil found her. She constantly tortured herself by imagining how few hours she might have left to hold her daughter in her arms, to smell the sweet scent of baby shampoo clinging to silky-fine hair. To listen to the happy sound of childish giggles and belly laughs. To marvel over the teeny-tiny white teeth. To look into the mischievous green eyes so like her own.

Dear God, she loved Jolene more than she'd ever thought possible to love another human being.

Anguish over the uncertainty surrounding their lives was ripping her insides to shreds. She'd come to Shotgun Ridge with a nebulous hope of finding an ally, of not being alone, of having someone who would understand the depth and validity of her fears.

Yet the man she'd pinned her hopes on was treating her like something loathsome.

And it was beginning to exact a toll she no longer wanted to pay.

"How long are we going to keep this up?" she asked, directing her question at the twelve-foot ceiling.

"As long as it takes."

She shifted her head against the vinyl mat, stared at him, then sat up and wrapped her arms around her knees. "Well, I've decided this sourpuss attitude of yours is over. Barking orders and acting as though I'm a contagious disease isn't going to make me a better kung fu fighter or shoot-'em-up girl. My grandma always said—cliché as it may be—that you can catch more flies with honey than with vinegar."

"You can catch them with shit, too, which is what you're up against, darlin'."

To her absolute horror, tears welled in her eyes before she could even try to stop them.

Grant started to turn away, then froze, his gut twisting. He nearly snapped at her to turn off the waterworks, but he saw what the vulnerability cost her. Despite her delicate features and uptown-girl persona, she wasn't the type of woman who used tears to get attention or have her way.

He'd put her through hell these past four days, and other than peppering him with questions and vocalizing her very definite opinions, she hadn't complained.

"Damn it." He stepped toward her.

"Just get away from me." She scrubbed at her face. "I've had enough—of you and this whole pile of crap."

He sat down on the mat, scooped her up and held her on his lap. Her struggles were pitifully easy to subdue. She wasn't a tiny woman, but she felt that way in his arms.

Almost instantly, she relented, buried her face in his shoulder and sobbed.

Man, oh man, he didn't know what to do.

"Shh, baby, don't do that. Come on now." He laid his cheek on her head, disgusted with himself because he knew he was partially responsible for breaking her spirit. She was facing life-and-death stakes, and handling it better than most of the soldiers he'd trained with in the army.

"I can't bear to think about losing Jolene. I don't know what's right anymore. I feel so selfish because I want to stay. But what if I put her in danger? The FBI found me. Anyone else can, too. I suck at shooting a gun, and—"

Grant did the only thing he knew to stop her tears and rambling. He cupped her head in his hands and kissed her.

The moment his lips touched hers, he knew he was in trouble. Four days of pent-up frustration came pouring out, and though he'd intended to soothe, all he could think about was inciting.

He wanted her response, her surrender, wanted her to ache as deeply as he'd been aching.

After a moment of surprise, she returned the kiss, her lips soft and mobile beneath his. Moaning deep in her throat, she wrapped her arms around his neck and speared her fingers through his hair, putting her body and soul into that single meeting of mouths, stunning him. Something he hadn't thought possible.

Instead of surrender, she charged, taking over with an avidness that stripped his mind, leaving nothing but naked sensation. He was drenched in the warm vanilla scent of her skin, the sweet taste of her lips, the soft, smooth feel of her body. Need clawed like a savage beast in his chest, his heart racing like a Thoroughbred's crossing the finish line.

But they were nowhere near the finish line, he reminded himself, easing back.

They weren't even supposed to start this race.

Convincing his body of that was no easy feat—especially with her sweet derriere planted squarely in his lap.

Her green eyes were dazed as she looked up at him. With his thumb, he wiped away the tears that he'd had a hand in causing.

"I'm sorry," he said quietly.

Her eyebrows drew together. "For kissing me?"

"No. For being an ass. And you don't suck at shooting a gun."

"I'm no dead-eye, either. Why have you been so moody with me? Sometimes I feel as though you hate the very sight of me."

"Hell, Abbe. I don't hate you. I want you. I want to take you to bed, or better yet, right here on this mat."

"Oh." She glanced away, shifted in his lap.

He stifled a groan. "Teaching you self-defense has turned out to be a little more hands-on than my libido can handle. You're so damn beautiful. My head is filled with the scent of your perfume—"

"It's lotion."

"Well, it drives me nuts and keeps me awake at night. I've constantly got my hands somewhere on your bare skin, or your body plastered against mine, and instead of accepting the contact as a necessary part of instruction, all I can think about is getting you naked. It ticks me off that I have so little control around you, and so I've been taking my frustration out on you. For that, I apologize."

She groaned. "I really wish you hadn't put that carnal image in my head. You're not the only one reacting to body contact. But things are way too complicated to add sex to the equation. You realize that, don't you?"

"I'm fairly sure that's what I was just saying." He felt amusement tickle the back of his throat.

"Saying and doing are two different things," she said. "And that kiss felt pretty darn complicated to me."

"Too late to take it back."

She shifted off his lap to sit next to him. "True. But we probably shouldn't repeat it."

"You don't sound real convinced."

"Not being able to have what I want is new to me." She laid her cheek on her drawn-up knees. "That sounds awful, doesn't it."

"I have a feeling we're no longer talking about kissing."

She shrugged, her lips curving slightly. "Maybe not a hundred percent."

"We're all a product of our upbringing and lifestyle," he said. "Can't apologize for being fortunate."

"My life wasn't always that way—but I did get used to the comfort of wealth."

Yet he imagined she still knew how to squeeze a dollar when necessary.

He shouldn't encourage this line of conversation because he hadn't completely come to terms with the radical swing of emotions that ate at him when he thought about the years she'd spent with the father he'd never known. Irrationally, one of those emotions was jealousy, which had its roots, he was sure, in the skewed memories of a scared little boy who'd worn the label of "bastard" for the first six years of his life. Even after Fred Callahan had adopted him and his brothers, the ugly epithet remained branded on his soul.

But curiosity festered like an infected wound, and he decided he might as well lance it.

"What was it like growing up with Stewart Shea?"

She lowered her legs, folded them beneath her. "Like being a princess. I was spoiled. Indulged. But I appreciated it, you know? I didn't *expect* things. I didn't believe that I deserved to have the world handed to me on a fancy platter."

"That was pretty clear the first day you got here and helped Iris Brewer serve supper."

She nodded. "My mom met Stewart on a trip to Las Vegas. A friend of hers was getting married, and the reception was held at Villa Shea's—Pop's restaurant. We ended up staying several days longer than planned. Within two weeks, we'd moved out of my grandmother's house in Texas and into Pop's place in Vegas. A month later they were married, and Stewart had started the adoption process to change my name to Shea." She picked at a snag on her sweatpants, remembering how elated she'd been, how she'd felt as though she'd finally *belonged.*

"Until then, Mama and I had lived frugally, and it was exciting to suddenly have closets full of clothes and toys, and to travel. Pop owned his own plane and he flew us to Disneyland, the San Diego Zoo, shopping trips—anywhere we wanted to go."

"Is that where you got the bug to be a pilot?"

She smiled. "Yes. Mama wasn't a good flier. She sat in the back with the windows covered so she wouldn't have to see outside, which left the copilot's seat open for me. By the time I was ten, I was flying the plane—Pop still handled the takeoffs and landings. He was a patient and encouraging teacher."

As Fred Callahan had been, Grant reminded himself, feeling his animosity diminish.

"What about your real father?"

"He died before I was born. My mama said he was on his

way home when the throttle stuck on his motorcycle. He crashed into a house two blocks away."

"That's rough." The wall clock ticked audibly as the second hand advanced in jerky increments around the face of the dial. "Interesting that you took up both of your fathers' hobbies—piloting aircraft and motorcycles."

"I never thought about that. I guess you're right. I was always a bit of a tomboy—in some ways," she added sheepishly. "Clearly, shooting, fighting and ranching weren't introduced in my world—thus my ineptness in those areas."

"You're catching on quick. I'm sure it took you more than four days to master the plane and the motorcycle."

"That's a nice way of looking at it." She paused, sought his gaze. "I really do appreciate you teaching me to be prepared. I was only objecting to your attitude."

"I think I figured that out," he said dryly. "So where is your mom?"

"I don't know. Lord, that sounds terrible."

"Not really. I lost track of mine for a while, too. I was fifteen when we finally got word that she'd died."

"I'm sorry." She reached out and touched his knee, then drew her hand back. "I have no idea if my mom's even alive. She's a hard person to explain. I guess you could say she's the stereotypical southern belle—soft-spoken, perfect etiquette, a fragile beauty who needed a man in her life to make her happy, someone who would put her up on a pedestal and take care of her. She pretty much fell apart when she and Pop divorced, but I had a hard time showing any compassion. I was so angry at her for not making the marriage work, and I resented having to go back to Texas."

"Tough move for a kid about to enter high school," he said.

"Very. I rebelled the whole four years. Las Vegas is a town that never sleeps, and it naturally pulls you into a faster pace of life. After living there in a huge villa, I felt claustrophobic in my grandmother's modest, craftsman-style house, and totally bored in a town that rolled up the sidewalks every day at five."

"You realize you could easily be describing Shotgun Ridge."

She tucked her short hair behind her ear. "What I want from life has changed considerably since I was a teen. Nowadays I'd rather nest than party. Shotgun Ridge would be my idea of paradise."

He noticed that she said "would be." As long as danger followed her, she would have one foot out the door. Another good reason why he should not be thinking about repeating that kiss.

"Anyway," she continued, "I don't think Mama knew what to do with me. She'd always been ill equipped for single parenthood. Before she married Pop, she'd been in one relationship or another, then of course there was Grandma Jane to help out. I hate to admit this, but one of the major draws of living with Pop was that he took care of Mama."

"Isn't that what husbands normally do?"

Abbe straightened her legs and smoothed her sweatpants. The air conditioner blew frigid air from the vent above them, drying the perspiration on her arms and making her shiver.

"Not in the way—or to the extent—that my mother needed." She shrugged, remembering the woman who could, at times, be more child than adult. "After the divorce, she sort of lost interest in pursuing any kind of social life. Things got worse when I was a senior in high school and Grandma died. From then on, Mama rarely came out of her room. I fixed her meals and brought them to her on a tray."

"Was she sick?"

"Not that I knew of. At least, not physically. She always had her hair styled and her makeup flawless and wore silky negligees. It seemed like that's all she did—primp and smoke, lying propped up in bed staring at the walls. Some days she was sugary sweet, and others she was downright ugly. I dreaded finding out which was the mood du jour. Two days after graduation, I celebrated my eighteenth birthday by boarding a bus headed to Las Vegas. That's the last time I ever saw her."

"Did you tell her your plans?"

"Yes. I told her I'd call and check in with her when I got to Pop's place. But she didn't answer my phone calls. I finally got in touch with one of the neighbors and found out that she'd left in a taxi and hadn't told anyone where she was going. Pop arranged for someone to take care of the house in case she returned, but she never did. I feel guilty. Mama wasn't all that stable to begin with. I think my leaving might have pushed her over the edge. It's just…I was constantly searching for a sense of belonging and normalcy that seemed to be missing from my life, and I thought I could find that by going back to live with Pop."

"Did you?"

"I believed so at the time. After Pop's initial shock at seeing me on his doorstep, he took me in, doted on me, put me through college, bought me the Baron when I graduated. I was independent and happy, with the world at my feet." She shrugged. "And it all turned out to be a lie."

Silent, he studied her for a long moment. "You haven't had a lot of people in your life to lean on."

"Oh, I think I've leaned too much—on Pop and Tommy. I was perfectly happy to let them take care of me."

"You're selling yourself short. You went to college, flew around the country. You've been raising a daughter mostly as a single parent. Just because someone else supplemented your income doesn't mean you let life sweep you along. If you weren't strong, you'd have never left after finding out about Stewart's deception."

He had a point. She'd been so caught up in feeling foolish for not realizing what was going on around her, chastising herself for being so easily taken in, that she'd lost sight of all the things she *had* accomplished over the years, and the responsibilities that had been—and still were—on her shoulders.

"Do you trust me?" he asked.

The switch in subject caught her off guard. She almost gave an unequivocal yes, but hesitated. Her emotions were still a little shaky from her crying jag. And the kiss. Before she could form an answer, he got to his feet.

"That's what I thought. I don't blame you, after the way I've acted the past few days."

"Grant, I didn't say—"

He held out his hand. "I need you to know that you *can* trust me."

"I do." She took his hand anyway and stood, then frowned when he stepped behind her. "What—?"

"Don't turn around." He put his hands on her shoulders to hold her in place.

She gave a small, nervous laugh. "Even though Jolie believes I have eyes in the back of my head, I really don't. What are you doing?"

"An experiment. When you work as part of a team, you trust your partner to be your eyes. I want you to fall straight back and let me catch you."

His hands were no longer touching her, and she could tell by his voice that he'd moved away. Wary and a bit confused, she glanced over her shoulder. His raised eyebrows told her he understood her reluctance. The look in his blue eyes, though, begged her to comply. It seemed as though what he asked of her was somehow more important to him than to her.

"This is silly. You're too far away to catch me."

He shook his head. "Trust that I'll be there when it matters."

"Given what I've been through in the past six months, that's a tall order."

"I know. Trust me, Abbe. Without looking, just spread your arms and let yourself go."

She turned back around, stared at the latte-colored wall. Obviously, facing her away from the mirror had been deliberate. Her heart sped up as she contemplated his request. Her mother hadn't been around to catch her. Neither had Pop or Tommy—they'd pretty much *pushed* her.

"I don't think I can do this," she whispered, feeling like a total coward.

"Yes, you can. Come on, Ace."

She hesitated, thought about it, her mind trying to dial in on the imagery of what might happen if she was crazy enough to go through with the exercise. Probably wouldn't be any worse than being flipped onto the mat. But in that, she didn't have a choice. This, however, required a conscious choice. And her conscious mind was insisting she'd be an idiot to deliberately put her backside in jeopardy.

Still, a small part of her wanted to prove something.

She started to raise her arms, then hesitated. From behind her, she heard Grant sigh.

"Hasn't Jolie ever jumped from a high place and expected you to catch her?"

"Yes, but that's different. For one thing, she weighs quite a bit less than I do. Plus, I'm her mother."

"It's the same principle."

She didn't think so. And darn it, his voice sounded even farther away. She started to turn, to give up.

"No," he admonished. "Don't look. Just leap."

"I'd feel a lot better if you'd come closer." Lord, where was her backbone when she needed it?

"That would defeat the point of the exercise. Do this for me, Abbe."

She hadn't always been so cynical. At one time she'd been vibrant, full of joy, looking forward to each new day and experience. Was that same woman who'd viewed the world through rose-colored glasses still inside her?

Yes. Just buried under the weight of disappointment and fear. She wanted to be that trusting woman again.

Hands shaking, her insides jumping, she stiffened her knees and slowly leaned backward. A natural, ingrained sense of self-preservation fought the movement. She tried to shut her mind against the part of her brain that was screaming caution.

Somewhere during her mental battle, she realized she'd reached the point of no return.

For a split second, she felt herself free-falling.

She opened her mouth and nearly strangled on a gulp of breath. It was too late to bend her knees and break her fall.

Every muscle in her body knotted in anticipation of impact, of pain. Because that was what she expected. Always before, when it really counted, no one had ever been there to catch her.

As the thought registered, strong arms slid under her, banded around her. The room tilted as Grant swept her into his arms and held her against his chest.

Her heart was pounding like a piston, yet she suddenly felt elated and giddy.

"I'm glad to know you're fast on your feet." Her voice came out in a breathy whisper. Whether it was from exertion, or his nearness, or the intensely tender look in his eyes, she couldn't seem to draw in enough air.

Much more of this and she'd be hyperventilating and needing to breathe into a bag.

They'd already decided that kissing wasn't a good idea. Yet that was exactly what he looked like he wanted to do.

She licked her lips, and his eyes widened.

With a heavy sigh, he lowered her to the ground. "Now it's your turn."

She frowned. "For what?"

"To catch me."

"You're kidding, right?" Her body was still quaking like an aspen.

"No. Just as you need to trust me to catch you, I need to do the same with you."

"That's not such a great idea. What if I can't hold you? There's a sizable difference in our weight. Plus, if I drop you, your trust in me will do a final crash and burn."

"I have faith in you."

"Obviously more than I do," she murmured.

He turned his back to her, and held his arms out to his sides. Without hesitation, before she was even ready, he was toppling as though pushed by a gale-force wind.

She raced forward, slid her hands under his arms, took his weight against her chest and lowered with him onto the mat.

"See?" he said. "Piece of cake."

Her cheek was against the side of his head, his hair tickling her skin. "Don't be too quick to give me credit. I think momentum had a lot more to do with that successful landing than any finesse or skill on my part."

He turned his head, met her gaze. "It doesn't matter how you get the job done. Only that you have confidence that it *will* be done. That's what teamwork is about."

"Is that what we are? A team?"

His blue eyes were intense and probing. And hungry. "With a little more practice…we could be."

CHAPTER THIRTEEN

"I'M TIRED OF PLAYING Chutes and Ladders," Jolie whined. She was lying on her stomach, propped on her elbows, Lambie-pie under one arm, Harley under the other. Saturday-morning cartoons played on the big-screen television built into the wall, but nobody was watching them.

Ever since they'd arrived in Shotgun Ridge a little over two weeks ago, Abbe had been determined to spend every possible moment with her daughter, the fear of their time together being suddenly cut short riding her like a shadow. But true to the nature of children, Jolie was beginning to feel smothered.

And she wasn't above letting that be known in typical three-year-old fashion.

A knot the size of Texas tightened in Abbe's chest—and the grandfather clock hadn't even announced 8:00 a.m.

Sitting on the tea-green and ivory Aubusson rug that covered the hardwood floor in Grant's family room, she rescued one of the little cardboard game people from Harley's mouth, groaning when the movement stretched her sore muscles. Thank goodness Grant had given her a weekend reprieve from boot-camp torture.

"We've hardly been playing for ten minutes, sweetie babe."

Jolie shrugged. Although it wasn't her turn, she spun the plastic arrow that determined how many spaces each player could move, waited until it almost stopped, then flicked it again. And again.

The constant *dddrrrrr* of plastic against cardboard was about to strain Abbe's last nerve.

She took a calming breath. "Okay. We can play something else. How about The Cat in the Hat puzzle?"

Jolie rolled her eyes. "We do that one all the time. 'Sides, it's for babies."

"Who said?"

"Lambie-pie." She sent the plastic arrow spinning once more.

"Well, *I* like the puzzle." This was new information to Abbe. Granted, there were only twelve puzzle pieces, each about three inches square, but the box clearly stated ages three and up. And until now, Jolie had entertained herself for hours fitting the spongy pieces together. "Does Lambie-pie think *I'm* a baby?"

Although Jolie's eyes flickered with a brief sparkle, she quickly looked away.

Abbe knew what was at the root of her daughter's moping. The moment she'd opened her eyes, she'd wanted to know if Katie could come over, or if she could go play at Katie's house. When Abbe had said no, Jolie acted as if she'd been grounded for a month. Even Harley had been slinking around with his tail down.

As she watched her daughter bounce her leg up and down, the toe of her slipper striking the rug harder on each downward swing, Abbe's emotions vacillated between annoyance and hurt. Darn it, Jolie spent plenty of time with Katie and Ryan. It wasn't fair to pawn her daughter off on Dora all the time.

Besides, she never knew if—or when—a particular moment might be the last she'd have with Jolie. Her life could be altered forever in the blink of an eye.

But Jolie didn't understand that. And Abbe couldn't explain it to her, either.

"Katie gots a TV that goes into a Batman cave."

"A Batman cave, huh? I thought it was a bookcase." When the Callahan men were living together as bachelors, they'd equipped their home with every state-of-the art gadget imaginable—including a wall of bookcases that slid back and turned electronically to reveal a stereo and theater system.

"Nuh-uh." Jolie shook her head. "Dora calls it the Batman cave. But we're not 'llowed to touch the buttons."

"I know. And I'm proud of you for remembering that. How about we play with your Barbie?"

Jolie dramatically sucked in a breath. "I left her at Katie's house! Can Katie come watch cartoons wif me? And bring Barbie?" Harley, reacting to the excitement in Jolie's voice, popped up from under her arm and licked her in the face.

"Not right now, hon."

Jolie hissed out a breath, her bottom lip trembling as the toe of her slipper *bonk, bonk, bonked* against the floor. With her thumb and middle finger, she thumped one of the cardboard tokens, sending it skidding across the board.

Abbe shot a warning look at her daughter and caught the game piece—the red-haired girl with the green T-shirt and blue, star-printed shorts, she noticed. It was the token she was using—or *had* been. Jolie always insisted on being the blond boy in the overalls.

The knot in her chest worked its way to her throat. So much for Chutes and Ladders. She upended the board, folded it and shoved it in the box.

"How come you don't go do your knitting or something?" Jolie asked, resting her cheeks on her fists.

A zing of both anguish and annoyance shot through Abbe's chest. "I just thought we could spend some time together."

She raked the remaining pieces off the rug, dumped them

in the box and slapped the lid in place. "You used to *like* playing with me." Her voice nearly broke. Dear God, she was about to cry over a stupid child's game. What the hell was wrong with her?

Jolie's foot paused on its descent toward the floor. "I like to play wif you."

Abbe raked her fingers through her hair, trying to get a grip, and forced a smile. The last thing she wanted to do was worry her little girl.

"I know you do, sweetie babe. I think maybe we both just got up on the wrong side of the bed. Suppose we go jump under the covers, then hop back up again and see if that'll straighten us out? I bet that'd be just the thing to make us pert as a couple of crickets. Ya think?"

At last Jolie giggled and rolled into a sit.

Harley, obviously seeing an opening, snatched Lambie-pie, shook the toy wildly, then tore off toward the door.

"Hey!" Jolie shrieked. "Lambie-pie!"

"Harley!" Abbe made a grab for the puppy and missed. She jumped to her feet, raced out of the family room, rounded the corner and plowed right into Grant.

"Whoa." His arm hooked her waist, keeping her upright as her feet slid on the polished wooden floor and her legs tangled with his. Jolie, half a second behind, bounced off the back of Abbe's knees, then giggled as she scrambled up off the floor.

Grant chuckled. "That was some greeting. Everybody okay?"

"Um…hmm." Flustered, Abbe stepped back and brushed her bangs out of her eyes. She was still in her pajamas—a tank top and drawstring-waist bottoms. And though he'd seen her in tank tops plenty of times, she usually had on a bra. This morning, that wasn't the case, and the feel of her chest colliding with his had left her breasts tingling.

Naturally he was dressed for the day in his usual cowboy attire, and it was difficult for her not to drool.

"I found a grinning, canine mop on the loose, making off with a sheep," he said. "Anybody missing either one of those?"

"Lambie-pie, Lambie-pie," Jolie sang, jumping up and down impatiently, her arms reaching for her beloved—*bedraggled*—stuffed animal.

Grant passed her the toy, which she hugged to her chest. "Bad puppy," she admonished, tilting her head way back to frown at the dog. "You don't hurt Lambie-pie."

Harley, appearing even tinier against Grant's broad shoulder, looked most unrepentant.

"Yeah," Grant said next to the little dog's ear. "Pork chops are off-limits, buddy. Got it?"

Harley licked him on the chin.

Grant nodded and set the puppy on the floor next to Jolie. "He said he'll try to remember."

Jolie rolled her eyes. "He always says that. Then he forgets. But Mommy says it's cuz he's a baby. And he's a *boy*."

Grant's eyebrows rose. "Do boys forget things?"

"Yep. All the time."

"I see." He glanced at Abbe as if expecting her to explain her daughter's statement.

She folded her arms beneath her breasts, refused to defend herself. Call her sexist, but in her experience, boys were forgetful.

Truthfully, formulating a credible argument right now would have been next to impossible. Seeing him interact so gently with the puppy had quite simply moved her beyond words.

And now, watching as he turned his attention once more to her daughter, well…she didn't dare allow those thoughts to run amok. One of the biggest dangers to a single mother's emotional well-being was a hunky guy who easily interacted with her kid. Stuff like that had a tendency to make a woman read more into feelings than might actually be there.

"What about girls?" he asked Jolie. "Don't they forget things?"

"Nuh-uh. We're very smart." Her brow furrowed. "'Cept, I forgetted Lambie-pie on the pottie chair. She had to go tee-tee. But Mommy 'membered for me."

Grant seemed at a loss for words. "Hmm," he murmured after a moment. "Guess it's a good thing she didn't fall in— the lamb, that is."

Jolie nodded seriously.

His blue eyes were filled with amusement when he glanced back at Abbe. "So how come you ladies are still in your nightclothes?"

Abbe took a breath and found her voice. "Because a certain drill sergeant was nice enough to give his soldier the weekend off."

"What's a dwill sergeant?" Jolie asked, protectively hugging her lamb.

"Someone who hollers and snarls and makes people exercise until their muscles are so sore they can hardly pick up a fork." Thankfully, Jolie wasn't aware of what she and Grant did during the time Dora watched her, so Abbe could get away with the teasing.

"Big Bird does exercises. We hafta touch our toes and stretch way up to the sky. Is he a dwill sergeant?"

Grant smirked and folded his arms, clearly interested to see how she intended to dig herself out of this one. She should have known better than to start this. Jolie was smarter than her years, and one question turned into a perpetual string of questions.

"Of course not, sweetie babe. Big Bird never snarls."

"Oh. Okay…" Jolie paused, cocked her head toward the sound of animated voices spilling from the TV. "Tweetie and

Chopper! C'mon, Harley!" Scooping the dog into her free arm, Jolie raced back into the family room.

Abbe watched her go. Without Jolie as a buffer, she felt practically indecent standing here in her pajamas, alone in the hallway with Grant. Finally she looked at him.

He was staring at her breasts.

His gaze slowly lifted to meet her eyes. "When have I ever hollered?"

He was so close she could feel his breath on her face. She bit her bottom lip. Ever since that kiss—less than forty-eight hours ago—all she'd thought about was repeating it.

"Um…I suppose you haven't. But you *do* snarl, and that makes it seem like you're hollering."

Had he moved closer? It felt as though she was having to tilt her head even more to look up at him. Flustered, she took a small step back, raised a hand to her shoulder and massaged her sore muscle.

For crying out loud, she wasn't the kind of woman who went stupid at the nearness of a sexy man. She really needed to get a grip.

"Did I snarl yesterday?" he asked.

"No, but you were operating under a handicap."

His eyebrows rose. "I was?"

"Of course. You were scared to death I'd start bawling again, so you were on your best behavior."

He shifted behind her and replaced her hand with his, gently kneading her sore muscles. "Might want to rethink your reasoning, Ace. I wasn't all that unhappy with the results of your crying jag."

His fingers worked like magic and she didn't even try to suppress her moan. "Well, don't expect to steal any more kisses via that method. Crying embarrasses me to no end and I try to do it as little as possible."

"Tough girl," he murmured close to her ear. "Are you really sore?"

"On a scale of one to ten? I'm a twenty."

His fingers paused. "Seriously?"

"Maybe that's a little exaggerated. I'm probably only eighteen and a half."

He leaned around to look at her. "You really aren't joking. Baby, how are you even functioning? Why didn't you say something?"

Baby. It was an endearment, pure and simple, and Lord help her, she liked the way he said it, the way it made her insides melt. He'd called her that Thursday when she'd gone all watery on him—right before he'd kissed her. Something had shifted between them since then, something she couldn't quite name, something she had no business even *trying* to name.

"I did tell you. I said I've never stepped foot in a gym." And, she recalled, he'd told her she had a great body for someone who didn't exercise. "Besides that, the only time I've ever run on purpose is to chase after Jolie or the dog." She wiggled her shoulders. "Don't stop."

This time, he was the one who groaned. For about half a second, she felt guilty, as though she was playing with fire, sending him the wrong signals. Then she got over it. The massage simply felt too glorious. His hands kneaded her shoulders, her biceps, all the way down her arms.

Her eyelids had barely slid closed when he whirled her around to face him. Startled, she swayed, her eyes now agog. "What in the—"

"Bad timing on my part," Clay said.

Abbe gave a start and looked over her shoulder, but Grant held her in place, facing him.

"Perfect timing," Grant countered. "Jolie's in need of company while she watches Tweetie Bird battle the cat."

Clay winked and grinned. "Then I'm her man. I never miss an opportunity to see Chopper pound the whey out of Sylvester." He continued past them toward the family room. "You two keep an eye on the time. We're due out at the Bodines' place by ten o'clock."

Clay disappeared into the family room, and Abbe realized her mouth was literally hanging open. She closed it. Glared up at Grant.

"What is the matter with you?" she said in a whisper. "Do you realize the impression you just gave him? Now he thinks—"

He slid his hand down and entwined his fingers with hers. "Come on."

She started to dig in her heels, but realized that would only cause a scene, so she let him pull her toward the stairs. Once there, out of hearing range, she put up some resistance.

"I won't be able to face your brother without turning red in the face." She tugged back on her hand, but might as well have saved her energy. "And if you think I'm going up these stairs with you to just hop between the sheets, you better think again, pal." He continued to haul her up the stairs and down the hall, and she kept right on talking.

"I'm sorry if I led you on, but I wasn't kidding when I said I was sore. I darn near became crippled sitting on the floor to play Chutes and Ladders. My legs were killing me. There's no way I'm going to wrap them around you, and it's your own damn fault—"

Beveled mirrors, gold faucets, a tub the size of a small swimming pool…she only had a fleeting moment for her brain to register that they were in Grant's master bathroom before his lips covered hers.

Then every other thought dissipated like vapor hitting a fan. What began as a surprise onslaught softened almost immediately into what could only be described as an enthralling seduction. Where before his lips took, now they gave. Oh, how they gave.

He kissed her with gentleness and reverence and a single-minded purpose that made her want to weep. The purpose of soothing, of apologizing, of telegraphing a need.

And the need inside her was becoming way too strong. She eased out of the kiss, noted that he didn't try to hold her.

"Grant…"

He stopped her words with two fingers against her lips. "Your top says Kiss Me. I was merely obliging."

She'd forgotten about the words emblazoned on her tank top just beneath the curve of her left breast, glanced down and noticed that the outline of her nipples clearly showed through the fabric. Chances were very good that they'd been just as visible downstairs in the hallway.

She lifted her gaze back to his. "So were you protecting my modesty or your interests by turning me around when Clay walked in the room?"

His eyes were steady on hers. "Maybe a little of both."

"Haven't you ever heard of subtlety? I'm horrified about what your brother is thinking right now."

"I imagine he's laughing his ass off over the cartoons."

"Don't be dense. You know good and well you deliberately gave him the impression that we're up here fooling around."

"I did nothing of the kind. You have sore muscles and I have a spa tub and some miracle salve that'll make you feel like a new woman."

"You could have told him that." She glanced at the oversize tub surrounded by a sea of mocha marble.

He chuckled. "Now *that* would have given him the impression we were up here fooling around."

"Why?" She was having a great deal of trouble thinking straight. "Do you often bring women up here to take a bath?"

"You're the first."

"Then why would he—"

"Baby, he's a guy, okay? And if we stand here much longer talking about this subject, *I'm* going to be crippled."

He turned and twisted the faucets, adjusted the temperature and set the drain. Steam rose as the tub began to fill. From beneath the cabinet, he retrieved an opaque blue bottle, removed the cork and poured a generous stream into the running water. A blend of ginger and wintergreen fragrances filled the moist air.

From the medicine chest, he took down a tin that looked as though it had come from a nineteenth-century pharmacy.

"After you soak in the tub and let the jets work on your muscles, rub this on. You should be able to do the splits down the banister."

She opened the tin and sniffed. "Doubt it. I've never been able to do the splits to begin with. This stuff doesn't have any scent. What is it?"

"Beats me. Little Joe Coyote, the medicine man over on the Cheyenne reservation, turned me on to it years ago after I'd been shot and screwed up the muscles in my shoulder. The wound healed in a week and totally blew the doctors away. They'd predicted several surgeries and only a forty percent chance of fully recovering the use of my arm."

"You were shot?"

"Yeah." He stacked fluffy, ivory towels on the wide marble ledge of the bathtub. "Damn embarrassing."

Her jaw dropped. "Don't joke."

"I'm not. Strip before you flood my bathroom."

For a moment she thought he meant for her to undress for *him.* Worse, he was such an authoritative, larger-than-life man, she nearly jumped to comply. But in the brief space of time that her brain paused in stunned inaction, he turned and left the room, closing the door behind him.

Abbe let out the breath she hadn't realized she'd been holding and moved to turn off the water.

Lord have mercy.

That was one dangerous man. In more ways than one.

She undressed, inched her way into the steaming hot water, then turned on the jets and let them knead her sore muscles. The reminder that he'd been part of an elite special forces team, a type of mercenary polite folks didn't talk about, made her shiver.

He'd been shot, for goodness' sake.

Yet he could be gentle. As he had been when she'd fallen apart on him. As he was moments ago, running her a bath, concerned over her sore muscles—even though he was the cause of them.

She was terribly afraid she was falling for the man.

And that would be stupid. Because nothing would ever change that fact that she was Stewart Shea's daughter—adopted or not.

And as it had been clearly pointed out, world-renowned horse breeders and relatives of the Mafia simply did not—could not—mix.

In the master bedroom, outside the bathroom, Grant leaned against the wall, waiting for his rock-hard erection to ease. No sense going downstairs with a bulge in his pants, giving Clay even more ammunition to quiz him about Abbe Shea.

Hell on fire, he'd never been so obsessed with a woman that he couldn't control his baser instincts. Yet all he could think about was getting his hands on her, getting *inside* her.

By God, the woman could kiss like nobody's business.

And she opened up all the dark, secret places inside him where he yearned, hungered.

He could hear the sound of rushing water still filling the bathtub, fought with himself not to turn back around and join her there. He was pretty damn sure she wouldn't refuse him, and that knowledge wasn't doing a thing for the stiff ache in his jeans. Nor was the sight of his unmade bed mere feet away.

A bed he'd never shared with another woman.

He'd built this house soon after Ethan and Dora had married. Watching their profound love and contentment had made him all too aware of the vast emptiness in his own life.

When he allowed himself to admit it, deep down what he wanted most was a family. A wife, kids, in sickness and in health and all that.

Yet something had always held him back from making that kind of commitment. He'd seen and done a lot in his thirty-three years—more than most men did in a lifetime. He knew a hundred ways to kill a person, and he'd used many of them.

If fate had stepped in, preventing him from accepting that last assignment, perhaps he'd have been able to put all that behind him. But he'd made that trip, and the gruesome results had damaged something inside him, made him wonder if a man with his background was even worthy of love and happiness.

Yet here he was, desperately wanting those very things.

He didn't know how or when the tide had turned, but Abbe and Jolie were no longer just a mother and daughter needing his protection.

Somewhere along the way, he'd begun watching them the way a wolf watches its mate, with a territorial possessiveness, as though they were bonded to him for life.

And that scared the hell out of him.

CHAPTER FOURTEEN

IF ABBE EVER GOT the opportunity to meet Little Joe Coyote, she intended to bow down and kiss his feet. Whatever the Cheyenne medicine man put in his potions and salves worked miracles on her aching muscles—as Grant had promised they would. Executing the splits down the banister was still out of the question, but she was happy to claim lack of skill as her excuse rather than sore muscles.

Leaning against one of the white, floor-to-ceiling Corinthian columns in the foyer, she watched as Jolie stood in front of Grant like a little soldier, looking incredibly tiny in the immense, two-storied entryway.

Evidently, while she'd been soaking in healing waters, Grant had gotten Jolie dressed—and even done a nice job of matching the colors. Blue jeans, a pink T-shirt appliquéd with Barbie princesses, and her pink tennis shoes with the blinking lights on their soles. Hopefully the intermittent flashes wouldn't scare Cheyenne Bodine's horses.

"Got the pork chop?" he asked.

Jolie giggled and her little arm shot out, Lambie-pie clutched in her hand.

"Check," Grant said seriously. "Got the dust mop?"

Jolie rolled her eyes and her other arm shot out to show Harley's leash, the puppy dancing at her side.

"Check. Everybody finished doing the potty thing so we don't have to stop and find a bush?"

Jolie's head bobbed up and down in an exaggerated movement that set her off balance.

He caught her shoulders and righted her. "Check. Got your mom?"

"Nope," Clay said, coming up behind Abbe. "But I do." He slid his arm around her waist, grinned down at her and swept her toward the front door where he deposited her next to Grant. "Found her hiding behind the column."

"I wasn't hiding."

Clay shrugged. "Whatever you say. I smell ginger. Has my brother been working you too hard?"

"Nothing I can't handle."

"You just let me know if he gets out of hand. I'll take care of him for you."

"In your dreams," Grant muttered. "Did you get the trailer hitched?"

"Ready and waiting. Come on, short stuff," Clay said to Jolie. "Let's go make sure Clarabelle's behaving herself. She might have gotten impatient waiting for you girls to quit primping and decided to walk over to Cheyenne's house on her own."

As soon as Clay took Jolie and Harley out the door, Grant turned to Abbe.

"How are your bones?"

"Still holding up my skin."

"Muscle soreness one to ten?"

"A two."

He nodded. "Powerful stuff, isn't it? A two's a damn sight better than eighteen and a half."

"You better believe it." She sniffed her arm. "I don't stink, do I? Clay said he could smell me."

He leaned down, his breath warm against her neck. She could practically feel his lips against her skin.

"Reminds me of gingerbread cookies," he murmured. "Good enough to eat."

She stepped back, cleared her throat. "Um…as long as the horses don't decide to munch."

"How about me?"

"*You* should behave." What had gotten into him lately? She looked out the front door, nerves humming along her skin. She wasn't sure if the reason was Grant's nearness and the carnal images that sprang to her mind when his voice went all low and sexy, or the prospect of leaving the safety of the ranch. "Are you sure we should go?"

Each month, Cheyenne Bodine's uncle, John White Cloud, brought the children from the reservation to his nephew's ranch to spend a few hours riding horses, eating burgers, roasting marshmallows and going for hay rides in the wagons. Grant had thought the outing would be a good one for Abbe and Jolie, as well.

"Baby, you can't keep yourself and Jolie cooped up in the house. If you let these people have power over your life, what then? Besides, you saw how it was when the feds showed up. Strangers don't come into Shotgun Ridge without being seen. And they sure as hell wouldn't have the balls to show up at the sheriff's house."

"You're right. I'm being paranoid."

He touched her arm. "Trust me, okay?"

She did. Strangely enough, she must have trusted him on some subconscious level since she'd first opened the compiled dossier on his life.

Otherwise, she wouldn't be standing here now.

Grant set the alarm and they left the house, joining Clay and Jolie who were waiting for them in the truck. A white horse trailer, waxed to a brilliant shine, sported the same green Callahan and Sons logo as the pickup.

"Do you always take your own horses for these outings?" she asked.

"Just Clarabelle and Miss Lily. They're sweet old girls, and the kids love them."

"Will it just be the children from the reservation riding?"

"Doubt it." He opened the passenger door so she could climb in back with Jolie and Harley. Clay was already at the wheel, which left Grant to ride shotgun. "Ever since Cheyenne married Emily, she's turned the monthly riding event into a big to-do. She used to be an executive for an advertising agency out of Washington. She still does consulting for them, but now Shotgun Ridge is her playground, and she considers every occasion a personal challenge."

Abbe smiled. "Has she used her advertising skills and taken the matchmaking geezer's efforts global yet?"

"Shh," Clay said from the driver's seat. "Don't be carrying any of those ideas to Emily."

Grant shut the door then got into the front seat. "Afraid they'll go after you next?" he asked his brother.

"Since I'm about the last unattached guy around, yes. But I have plans of my own, thanks, anyway."

"Are you involved with someone?" Abbe asked from the back seat.

"He's working on Wyatt Malone's neighbor, Cherry Peyton," Grant answered for him, flashing a grin. "An older, widow woman."

"Hell, you're making her sound like my grandmother," Clay complained. "She's not *that* much older. And if people would stop drawing attention to the age difference, maybe I'd get somewhere with her."

"Nobody draws attention to it, bro. You're just touchy."

"*She's* the touchy one," he grumbled. "Drives me nuts."

Abbe sat back and listened to the brothers jab good-naturedly at each other. She hadn't realized Clay was smitten with someone, and felt bad that she'd inadvertently taken up a lot of his free time lately. He'd been sticking close to the ranch, as had Ethan, all three brothers acting as hers and Jolie's personal bodyguards.

She noticed that Clay hadn't included Grant in the available targets for the matchmakers, nor had Grant mentioned himself as a candidate.

Because of her? People *were* treating them as a couple, and God knows there was enough sexual chemistry between them to light a prairie fire.

But they weren't a couple.

Grant deserved someone who could settle down and grow old with him, give him babies and a lifetime of unconditional love.

Through circumstances beyond her control, Abbe wasn't that woman.

She wasn't going to dwell on maudlin thoughts and waste a perfectly beautiful day. When they reached Cheyenne's ranch, things shifted into high gear.

"My gosh, it looks like the county fair," she said as she got out of the truck.

"Told you Emily likes a challenge," Grant said.

Pickup trucks were parked everywhere, even on the front lawn. Men hauled saddles from the barn while horses milled in the corral, some gathered in little knots like ladies at a weekly coffee klatch exchanging juicy gossip. A huge steel barrel, cut lengthwise and fashioned into a barbecue, belched smoke into the midmorning air, while children played tag in the dirt or stood quietly in line, waiting for a turn on horseback.

"I'll go see what I can do to help in the kitchen." She held out her hand for Jolie.

"Leave the squirt and the coyote snack with me," Grant

said. "I promised her a ride on Clarabelle, and I'll make sure
Harley doesn't get eaten or stepped on."

She glanced around at the ranch, recognizing several of the
neighbors. Clay had parked next to Ethan's truck, which
meant that Dora was already here. Jolie would be fine, she told
herself.

"Quit worrying," he said.

"Worrying is a mother's job." But she left Jolie with him
and headed toward the house.

The kitchen was a hive of activity, with food covering
practically every available surface. Eden Stratton was pulling
a cookie sheet from the oven, and the aroma caused Abbe's
mouth to water. Dora sat at the table, flipping through an
album of photographs with Amy Lucas.

"Y'all need help in here?" she asked.

Emily rushed forward and gave her a hug. "We never turn
down an offer of help. Get yourself something cold to drink
first."

Abbe declined the drink and accepted hugs from the rest of
the women, then spent the next hour hauling huge bowls of sal-
ads and platters of condiments and food to the tables set up outside, keeping an eye on Grant and Jolie. She noticed that Harley
was running off leash, frolicking with a Siberian husky who
could probably squash him with one paw. The little Maltese
seemed to be holding his own, though, so she didn't interfere.

As though she was wearing a homing device, each time she
appeared outside, Grant looked in her direction, proving that
he was constantly watching her, too. Invariably, when their
gazes collided, her stomach fluttered.

Having him as her constant bodyguard and living in close
quarters had raised the sexual tension between them to a fever
pitch. She hadn't been off the market so long that she didn't
recognize when a man wanted her. And Grant clearly did.

She wondered, though, if his feelings ran any deeper than mere lust. She couldn't tell.

What she *could* see was how taken he was with her daughter. Watching him carry the little girl around the corral or lead her by the hand, talk to her about the horses, kiss her chubby cheeks, or soothe her when she tripped over a rope and began to cry, touched Abbe's heart.

This lifestyle was the complete opposite of what she'd had in Las Vegas with Tommy. Tommy had never doted on Jolie this way. Where before, she was the one solely responsible for Jolene's basic care, now she saw what it was like to have someone who was around to share the load—who seemed to *want* to be involved in her child's life.

It made her dream when she knew she shouldn't.

The Bagley widows showed up, bickering over who got to hold the babies, and ended up shooing everyone out of the house, admonishing them to see to their men, claiming they intended to turn the living room into an impromptu day care and didn't need all the kitchen noise disturbing their peace.

The absolute love in this town was palpable. Abbe wanted so much to be a part of that, to have a piece of it to call her own. Absolute trust, the knowledge that someone was looking out for them always—not necessarily from danger, but out of consideration, concern and a wish to have only good things touch their partner's lives.

It just made her sigh. As the day wore on, she was forced to admit that she'd done the unthinkable.

She'd fallen in love. Not only with the town and its people, but with Grant Callahan.

Needing a few moments to herself, she wandered off, stood alone by the fence and looked out over the land, trying to get a handle on the bittersweet longing that swelled in her chest until she thought she might split apart at the seams.

Along the clean lines of the horizon, there was no haze. Armies of cumulus, fair-weather clouds, moved across the immense blue sky, their bottoms as even as if they'd scraped against the flat green earth.

The day had been so perfect, yet she kept expecting to discover that it was all an illusion, a painted picture no more real than the props a magician used when working one of the clubs on the Vegas Strip.

This place was a far cry from Las Vegas, she mused. The very drama of the landscape was in the sky, pouring with light and constantly moving. All the money in the world couldn't compare to Montana's great outdoors.

Or more specifically, to Shotgun Ridge.

Looking at the vastness and beauty of the land, the good hearts and friendships of the people, made her realize that the best things in life really were free.

Lost in thought and in the visual feast before her eyes, it was a moment before she realized she wasn't alone. She turned her head and nearly jumped out of her skin.

"Oh! Mr. White Cloud. I didn't hear you come up."

"You may call me John. I did not want to disturb your commune with nature."

"It's beautiful here."

His head dipped in acknowledgment, yet he remained silent, as though he was content to just stand there with her. Slightly nervous, Abbe searched her brain for conversation, although she wasn't sure if he wanted to talk.

She glanced at his weathered face, at the squint lines that fanned out toward his temple. Wise brown eyes gazed off in the distance, giving away none of his thoughts. He was a tall man, proud. Long, steel-gray hair was tied at his nape with a thin strip of leather. He wore a red bandana knotted at his neck, a white T-shirt, jeans and well-worn boots that had con-

formed to the shape of his foot. His age could have been anywhere between sixty and eighty, yet his body was fit and mus-
cular.

Like Grant, this man had presence.

"I notice you have sampled Little Joe Coyote's liniment,"
he said, turning to look directly at her.

"My gosh! I *do* stink, don't I?" Mortified, she sniffed her
upper arm, the back of her hand, then fanned the neck of her
sleeveless top to see if she could detect any odor between her
breasts where perspiration was trickling from the summer heat.

Why the hell couldn't she smell what everyone else obviously did?

"Tell me the truth. I mean it. There's got to be some kind
of tribal law that bars you from lying—even to save a woman's dignity."

A ghost of a smile twitched at his lips. "The scent is barely
detectable, and not at all unpleasant."

"Are you sure? It's not like Ben-Gay or anything?"

"That would be a bad thing?"

"Oh, yes. In college, I was kidnapped on my birthday. It
wasn't embarrassing enough that I was wearing bunny pajamas—those one-piece jobs like babies wear with the feet in
them," she explained when he looked at her in confusion,
"but I'd been helping a friend paint her room and my muscles were so sore I could hardly move, so I'd slathered on
practically a whole tube of the stuff. I reeked."

His gray eyebrows were drawn together in concern. "Were
you harmed?"

"By the Ben-Gay?"

"By the kidnapping."

"Oh. Oh, no." She laughed, startling a meadowlark off the
fence post. "It wasn't that kind of kidnapping. It was a bunch of
college girlfriends with a crazy way to celebrate my birthday."

"Ah. Party-going with extreme alcohol consumption."

She shook her head. "It was much tamer than that. More like a slumber party playing truth-or-dare, then a very public breakfast, which I had to attend in my pajamas, nearly making me late for my first class. And I did smell pretty strong."

"I see. You may rest assured that you do not have an unpleasant odor. Only those who have used Little Joe Coyote's liniment would recognize the healing aroma. I do not know the ingredients, but it is strong medicine, with the power to reach a person's soul."

"It worked wonders on my sore muscles."

"Perhaps it will do the same for your bruised spirit." He was silent for several long moments. "The land has a way of mesmerizing. One can learn a lot by stillness, listening to it speak."

Abbe sighed. "There's so much going on in my head, I doubt I could hear a freight train trying to communicate with me, much less the trees and bushes."

He turned to face her, his eyes serious, looking at her as though he could see inside her, ferret out all her secrets.

"You must learn to quiet those voices. There are not many women with your heart and bravery, Abbe Shea. Mothers who would offer such deep sacrifice."

She frowned. How did he know what she was willing to sacrifice?

"You must stay and fight. Victory will not be gained by the teachings of battle, but by trust. You will remember that I told you this."

Before she could ask him what he meant, he turned and walked away, leaving her confused and dazed.

Good Lord. Had she just had her fortune told?

She saw Grant coming toward her. For an instant, her heart

somersaulted. Jolie wasn't with him. A quick scan of the ranch had her relaxing. Her daughter was happily riding on Clay's shoulders.

Grant paused a moment to speak to John, shook hands with the man, then continued forward.

"I thought you were inside with Emily," he said, stopping in front of her.

"I felt like taking a walk."

"Then you should have come and got me." His tone held a hint of censure. "I don't like looking around and not being able to find you."

"Sorry. Y'all were busy with the horses." She glanced past him, saw John White Cloud gathering up the children.

"You about ready to call it a day?" Grant asked.

She nodded. "Thank you for talking me into coming. I've had a wonderful time. And so has Jolie. It would have been a crying shame to miss this."

He put his arm around her shoulders and guided her toward the truck. "What can I say? When I'm right, I'm right."

"Don't trip over your ego."

He grinned down at her. "How can I when I have you around to tromp on it?"

"As if." She saw the last of the children climb aboard the reservation's van. "Did you tell John White Cloud my reasons for coming here? To Shotgun Ridge?" *To find a safe haven for my daughter?*

"No. Why?"

"Just something he said."

"Regaled you with one of his cryptic riddles, did he?"

She shrugged, then nodded. "I guess."

"He has visions. But he's stingy with the details. Whenever he gives advice, though, it's usually pretty solid."

The words flipped through her mind. Stay and fight. Victory would be gained by trusting.

But trusting whom? Or what?

ALTHOUGH IT WAS still light outside, Jolie was in bed by seven-thirty, both she and the puppy utterly worn out by their adventurous day at the Bodines' ranch. After dropping them off at Grant's house, Clay had gone back to the stables with Ethan, making sure Clarabelle and Miss Lily were properly bedded down for the night.

"Hungry?" Grant asked, pouring iced tea into two glasses, then returning the pitcher to the fridge.

"Are you kidding? I ate enough to last me a week." She noticed that Grant had suddenly gone still, was staring out the kitchen window toward the guest house.

An inkling of dread lodged behind Abbe's breastbone.

"What's wrong?" Moving up beside him, she searched for something out of place.

The door to the guest house was open.

She sucked in a breath, the vague concern now a full-out roar rushing through her veins. "Oh, God. Someone's been in there."

"Maybe. Maybe not. Clay could have gone inside for something. I'll go check it out. Stay here." He reached for his gun.

"Wait!" She grabbed his arm. "Why don't you call Clay first?"

For an instant the look he gave her was so tender, she nearly wept. Obviously he realized that she was worried about him walking into a potentially dangerous situation.

He checked the clip in his gun, then unhooked his cell phone from his belt.

Something inside Abbe gave way. She couldn't explain it, even to herself. That he'd heeded her suggestion, cared enough to honor her feelings, made her feel valued.

He could have just told her she was being silly.

As Tommy had whenever she'd expressed concern over his late-night outings.

"Clay's on his way back here with Ethan," he said when he disconnected the call. "If someone was inside the guest house, they'll likely be long gone by now, but I want to make sure. I don't like to take chances."

On impulse, she slid her hand down his arm and twined her fingers with his. "I'm so sorry I dragged you into this mess."

He looked down at her for a long moment, lifted their joined hands to his mouth and kissed her knuckles. "No one drags me anywhere I don't want to go."

She melted. On the other side of the locked doors, seventy-five feet away, potential danger lurked. Yet all she could focus on was that this onetime Special Forces soldier had just kissed her hand.

She slid her arms around his waist and held him, not wholly sure why she was initiating more intimacy.

Perhaps she was taking comfort, or perhaps she was merely keeping him there, making sure he didn't go off on a solo mission before his backup arrived.

She didn't know, and for a few minutes, she didn't want to think. She simply wanted to feel the beat of his heart next to hers, rest against his solid chest and shut out the world.

The sound of the front door opening sent a jolt of adrenaline through her. She jumped back like a guilty teenager caught necking with her boyfriend, and saw Clay and Ethan walking toward them. How in the world had they driven up without being heard?

Grant reached into the overhead cabinet, took down a second gun and handed it to her. "I want you to go wait up in Jolie's room until I get back. I'll set the alarm. If it goes off, you're to assume it's a foe, not a friend."

"One of us can stay with her," Ethan said.

"No." Abbe shook her head. "Both of you go with Grant. I'll be fine." She wanted him to have as much help as possible in case he ran into trouble.

She released the magazine on the gun so that it wasn't shoved in all the way but would only take a quick push to ready it, then sprinted up the stairs.

Jolie was dead to the world, her arm curved around Lambie-pie, her lips slightly parted, her arm flung outside the covers. Harley raised his head from his curled position on top of the quilt, one eye squinted, the fur on the side of his face sticking up like the hair on an old man's head who'd just been rousted from sleep. Abbe patted the puppy's silky tummy and whispered for him to go back to sleep, then tucked Jolie's arm under the covers.

She moved to the window, silently, not wanting to wake her daughter and have to explain the gun.

Luckily, the room was on the back side of the house, giving her a perfect view of the guest house. She didn't see any movement, so Grant and his brothers were probably already inside. Although she told herself that was a good thing, her whole body still shook, and she felt a bit nauseated.

The window was shut because the air-conditioning was running. She examined the latch, mentally going through the motions of sliding open the glass, popping out the screen. If it came down to it, she could possibly be of some help from this vantage point. Sort of like a sharpshooter.

She nearly laughed at the melodrama of her imagination. She seriously needed to get a grip.

It seemed like an eternity before Grant and his brothers reappeared on the porch, shutting the guest house door behind them. They spent a few minutes in conversation, then Grant headed across the pathway separating the two houses. Ethan and Clay walked around the driveway, obviously going back to wherever they'd parked their truck.

Glancing to make sure Jolie hadn't stirred, Abbe quietly left the room and hurried down the stairs. Unless a stampede of horses came roaring through the house, the little girl would be out until morning.

"Well?" she asked, meeting Grant in the kitchen as he punched in the code to reset the alarm.

"Somebody trashed the place. Pretty much turned the decor into a pile of matchsticks." His features were rigid, as lethal as the weapon he laid on the counter.

"But why?" Abbe was horrified that anyone could be so malicious. She handed him her gun so he could put it away. "If they were looking for me, they'd clearly be able to tell that I wasn't living there. Why hang around to destroy the furniture and chance getting caught?"

"Hard to tell with these kind of people. Assuming it was Ziggmorelli's thugs. I've seen that kind of mess before. They were looking for something. You don't slash the cushions to see if a body's hiding in the couch."

"Looking for what?" She didn't give him a chance to answer. "How did they get in? How could this happen? You said it wouldn't!" Her voice started to rise, her body quaking. "You said nobody gets into Shotgun Ridge without someone in town seeing them—"

He put his fingers against her mouth to stop the flow of words that threatened to escalate into hysteria. Then he cupped her shoulders and drew her against his chest. With a hand at the back of her head, he cradled her against him, rocked lightly on his feet.

"I can't answer those questions, babe." His lips pressed the top of her head, her forehead.

She had no idea how long they stood that way. Her body

relaxed by slow degrees, bringing with it a different kind of awareness. She could still feel the angry tension coiled in his body. Some fool had made a lucky escape tonight. Even a cocky Mafioso wouldn't want to come face-to-face with this man when he was in a fighting mood.

She tilted her face up to his. His blue eyes were intense, held her more surely than the arms around her waist.

It seemed like the most natural thing in the world to rise up and meet his lips.

He looked like a predator, dangerous and unpredictable, yet his kiss was gentle, soothing, made her feel cherished and safe. Yes, safe, she realized. In his arms, she felt as though no harm could ever touch her.

He eased out of the kiss, brushed her bangs from her forehead. "I'd give anything to be inside you right now."

She stared up at him, frozen mute at the shock of his words. No one had ever expressed their desire for her in quite that way. A rush of hunger, so carnal it stunned her, washed over her. She'd dreamed of knowing him—all of him—but hadn't allowed herself to consider the reality.

Now the reality was staring her in the face.

"Is Jolie still asleep?" he asked.

She nodded, whispered, "For the rest of the night."

"You better say no."

How could she? The longing inside her was too huge to deny. She should. She knew it.

But she couldn't.

Her eyes spoke what she was unable to vocalize.

He took her hand, led her out of the kitchen and up the stairs.

CHAPTER FIFTEEN

GRANT SHUT the bedroom door, pulled her tank top over her head and unhooked her bra, slipping it off her shoulders and letting it fall to the floor between them. He was surprised by the tremor in his hands. It wasn't visible, thank God, but he could feel it.

At last, he rubbed his hands over her breasts, stroking, learning their shape, the way they fit in his palm. "You're so soft."

This time when he kissed her, he didn't think he could be gentle. The need in him was so great he shook with it. Her skin was soft and warm and smelled like a dream. He ate at her lips, plunged his tongue into her mouth, held her hard against the ridge of his erection. He wanted to rush, knew he had to slow down. He tore his mouth away from hers, breathing hard.

"I have condoms," he said, knowing they needed to have this conversation, "but it's been a long time since I've had anything other than solo sex, so I hope to God they aren't expired."

For a brief moment, she seemed taken aback by his declaration, but she didn't shy away from the subject, looked him straight in the eye. "I took out an insurance policy after Tommy died, and they do a mandatory blood test. I'm healthy. And I'm still on the pill. How about you?"

"Can't say as I'm on the pill," he teased, earning himself a light pinch and narrowed eyes. "But I give blood at the Red

Cross every three or four months—in support of my military family. It's been longer than that since I've been with a woman."

Her eyes widened. "Later, I'm going to want to know why. Right now, though, you can forget about expiration dates and condoms, and just kiss me." She grabbed the hem of his T-shirt and yanked it over his head, then wrapped her arms around his neck and initiated the kiss rather than waiting for him.

Her breasts rubbed against his chest, driving him mad.

He reached between them and unsnapped her jeans, wanting to touch all of her, everywhere at once. He managed to get her zipper down, then thrust his hand inside her panties, curled his fingers up inside her while his palm rode the sensitive tip of her clitoris. She bucked against him, gasped in surprise and desire.

Her body was like a cauldron of slick heat, pulsing around his fingers. She moaned into his mouth, panted, whimpered as she pressed harder and faster against his hand. In a matter of seconds, she climaxed.

"My gosh," she whispered. "What did you just do to me? I've never..." Instead of finishing her sentence, she grabbed his face between her hands and kissed him—a kiss of gratitude, and a kiss that demanded more.

Given the length of time since he'd been with a woman, Grant was highly concerned he was about to embarrass himself and come before he could even get his pants off.

He stripped off the rest of her clothes, then his, and bore her down onto the bed, spreading her legs.

"I'm sorry, baby. I can't wait. I promise I'll make it up to you." He rubbed the head of his penis against her wet opening, then pushed inside, feeling as though the top of his head was going to blow. Her body closed around him like a fist, her feminine muscles squeezing him, throbbing.

As he pulled back and thrust again, he gritted his teeth, watched her, astonished when he realized she was teetering on the edge of another climax. He grabbed her hips, tilted them up, and pumped into her, hard and fast, wringing another orgasm from her as his own release shuddered through him.

Slumping on top of her, his skin wet with sweat, he wondered if he'd ever felt anything quite like that, quite that quickly. Wondered if he would ever be able to breathe normally again.

Abbe locked her legs around his waist, still rubbing against him. She wanted more, and didn't understand it. He'd satisfied her twice, yet she was still aching to go another round...or three.

"That was incredible," she whispered against his neck, tasting the salt on his skin.

He braced himself on his elbows, gazed down at her. "If you think I'm through with you, you're sadly mistaken."

"I was hoping you'd say that." She writhed against him, surprised when she felt him begin to grow inside her. "Mmm, I like your powers of recovery."

He chuckled. "I'm a little impressed myself."

She shifted slightly, causing his penis to slide out of her. He reached between them and filled her with his fingers.

"This time it's going to take a good long while," he warned, taking her nipple in his mouth, sucking, pushing his hand against her mound until his fingers reached the back of her womb. "This time, I'm going to make you scream."

GRANT SAT on the grass by the pond in front of his house, content to just watch as the ducks waddled up from the banks and surrounded Abbe and Jolie. The little girl tossed a handful of bread, and the ducks dived and fought over the morsels. For once, Harley wasn't in the middle of things; the puppy had opted to stay inside with his bone.

The sound of Jolie's sweet giggle and Abbe's returning laughter caught at his chest. He was getting in deeper than he'd intended, but he couldn't seem to stop the tide of emotions.

Especially after last night. He considered himself an experienced man sexually, but he'd done and felt things with Abbe that he'd never done or felt before with another woman. It was a wonder either one of them could even walk.

Abbe hummed a little sound of distress as the greedy ducks advanced, closing in. "Grant…" Her voice trembled on a laugh. "Come and save us."

Grinning, he got to his feet. He should have been bored, spending so much idle time, time away from the horses. But he wasn't. He could be content just passing his days in the company of this enchanting woman and her daughter.

He waded into the gaggle of ducks and playfully swept Abbe into his arms. "What do you mean, save 'us'? Looks to me like the squirt's perfectly happy and holding her own."

"I know." She sighed and rested her head on his shoulder. "Pitiful, isn't it? Why is it that the older I get, the more chicken I become?"

"Baby, you can be as chicken as you want. Gives me a good excuse to get my hands on you." He lowered his head and nibbled on her lips.

"Are you kissin' my mommy?" Jolie asked.

He glanced down at the grinning little girl, then set Abbe on her feet, shooing the ducks with his booted foot. "Yeah. Want me to kiss you, too?"

Jolie giggled and turned her cheek up. He bent down and placed a loud, smacking kiss on her round, baby face.

"We could get my floaties and swim," she suggested slyly. She'd been dying to get in the water.

"You want to go swimming in my fishing hole?"

She vigorously nodded her head.

"Think you can catch us some fish for supper?"

Jolie thought about that for a moment, eyeing the water. "Do they gots big snapping teeth?"

"Naw. They're nice fish."

"The sharks gots big teeth. Nemo's daddy and Dory had to tell them not to eat little fishies and kids."

Grant looked at Abbe for translation.

"Finding Nemo," she said. "A movie."

"Ah. No sharks in this water. Come to think of it, though, little girls shouldn't have to go swimming with the fish. Looks like I'll need to build you a regular swimming pool—one where you can touch the bottom without your floaty things."

Jolie's eyes went round. "You can? Right now?"

He'd spoken without giving it much though, forgetting that kids had memories like elephants and a penchant for holding adults to their promises—even if they were mere musings rather than promises. Swimming pools weren't built in a day, and several months to a kid was a lifetime.

And despite their incredible night in bed, he wasn't sure Abbe was willing to stay for a lifetime.

Trying to figure a way to wiggle out of his offer, he heard the sound of a plane overhead. His senses went from relaxed to alert in less than an instant.

He grabbed Jolene and tickled her ribs. "Bet we can beat your mom to the bridge."

Caution turned Abbe's skin pale and she understood immediately. "Last one there's a troll!" she said, and was only a step behind them. The bridge was about fifteen feet away, and it took only seconds to reach the shaded arch and duck beneath it.

"Mommy's the troll," Jolie sang happily, clapping her hands.

The plane circled low over the ranch. Grant reached out and hauled Abbe back when she craned her neck to get a look at it.

"That's Pop's plane," she said.

His gut tucked itself right up under his rib cage. "How do you know?"

"It has his *S.S.* monogram on the tail section."

Grant took another look at the plane. "I'll go check it out. I don't want to leave you and Jolie here alone, so I'll drop you at the barn with Ethan and Clay."

"Don't you think I should go with you to meet him?"

"We don't know if it *is* Stewart flying that plane." He swung Jolie into his arms and headed away from the pond, across the expanse of grass to the front driveway.

"I'm the best one to determine that in the shortest amount of time," Abbe said, jogging to keep up with him. "You wouldn't recognize him. We'll leave Jolie with your brothers."

"I believe we discussed who was in charge of this show."

"Well, I'm second in command—"

"No. My brothers are."

"Then I'm *somewhere* on the team. For crying out loud, we're wasting time."

They piled into Grant's pickup. Since Jolie's car seat was in the other truck, Abbe held her daughter on her lap. A cloud of dust billowed behind them as they sped toward the barn.

"Where are we going?" Jolie finally asked, clutching her lamb under her arm. She looked worried, as if sensing something might be amiss with the grown-ups.

"To see the horses," Grant said. "It's time for Miss Lily and Clarabelle to eat some carrots."

Ethan and Clay were already outside, watching the Citation circle and line up with the runway.

Grant left the truck running and reached for Jolie. "Come on, squirt. You get to be a cowgirl. Don't let that sheep be eating Miss Lily's carrots." He quickly got out and passed the little girl to Clay. "Heard you needed some help doling out snacks," he said to his brother.

"Got you." Clay nodded and immediately moved back inside the barn.

"Want me to ride shotgun?" Ethan asked.

"Abbe's insisting on that spot. Just watch Jolie."

"Done."

Ethan followed Clay. Grant jumped back in the truck and put it in gear. They made it to the airstrip just as the wheels of the plane chirped against the asphalt.

The Citation was a honey of an aircraft, but Grant had little time to admire it. His senses were razor sharp, his mind calmly and methodically plotting his plan of action.

"There's a loaded .38 in the glove box." He reached under the seat for the spare key and handed it to Abbe. "Go ahead and unlock it in case you need to cover me."

She did as he instructed. "I don't think that'll be necessary. I'm sure that's Pop's plane."

"Maybe so. But we don't know if he's alone. He could have been hijacked."

"God, I hate this."

He lowered the window and opened the door, using it as a partial shield as he got out and stood behind it. "Stay put. And keep down."

"You don't know what he looks like, Grant. I do."

He spared her a quick glance as the engines on the Citation shut down. "Being a team player means you take directions without question. I need to be able to count on that."

She sighed and scrunched down in the seat. "You're right. I won't distract you. But for God's sake, don't shoot Pop."

Grant noticed that she didn't say "my" pop. Technically, Stewart Shea was *their* pop.

The man who got out of the plane was tall and fit, his light brown hair beginning to turn gray, his skin tanned from the desert sun. He chocked the tires but didn't bother with tie-downs, then turned.

Grant raised his nine millimeter and pointed, bracing his arm against the frame of the open window.

Stewart stopped and raised his hands.

"Anybody else in that plane?" Grant asked.

"No. I'm alone."

Abbe's head popped up, and she scooted across the seat. "That's him."

Grant's back teeth clamped so hard it was a wonder he didn't break them. "You don't follow orders very well," he muttered as he made room for her to get out of the truck.

"He said he's alone and I recognize his voice."

"What's the verdict?" Stewart asked. "You going to shoot or can I come ahead?"

"Are you carrying a weapon?"

"Of course."

"Planning to use it?"

"Not on you."

Grant lowered his gun. "Then I suppose you should come on ahead."

As Stewart moved closer, Grant searched for a resemblance. He had this man's DNA. They were close in height, both had blue eyes. But that was all he could see.

Stewart held out his hand. Grant kept his by his sides, not yet ready to play nice.

Lowering his hand, Stewart nodded. "Can't say I blame you for your animosity. I debated showing up here—could have made a phone call. But I wanted to meet you in person. Just once. Selfish of me, I know. And I wanted to see for myself that Abbe was okay." He turned his gaze to Abbe, his features softening. "Hello, punkin."

Abbe slipped out from behind Grant and went to her father, putting her arms around him, forgetting about the rift between them.

"Pop." For a moment, she rested her cheek just above the open button of his white shirt, felt the springy chest hair give against her skin, smelled the familiar scent of Brut aftershave. Pop had worn the same cologne since the day she'd met him twenty-two years ago. Despite all that had come between them, she suddenly felt like a little girl again in her daddy's arms.

She knew Grant was behind her, watching the reunion, and a twinge of guilt shivered over her spine, as though she were claiming something—*someone*—who was rightfully his.

She eased out of her father's arms and stepped back. "Why are you here?"

Stewart looked past her. "Is there somewhere more private we can go?" He addressed his question to Grant. "I don't intend to stay, but there are things the two of you need to know."

Grant tugged the brim of his hat lower on his forehead and tipped his head toward the truck. "Get in. We can go to my place."

"Should he put away the Citation?" Abbe asked Grant.

"I won't be here that long," Stewart answered for him, and got into the back seat of the truck.

Grant hesitated with his hand over the ignition key, looked at Abbe. "What about Jolie? Do you want to pick her up, or leave her with Ethan and Clay?"

Again, Stewart answered a question that wasn't posed to him. "I hope you'll let me see my granddaughter before I leave, but it would probably be best if the three of us got our business out of the way first."

Grant nodded and started the engine, then took out his cell phone and punched the automatic dial for Ethan's number. The tires on the pickup spit dirt and gravel as he spun a

U-turn while giving his brother a spare update and asking him to keep Jolie a little longer.

The short drive was silent, the tension in the cab so thick you could practically see it. Stewart watched out the window, noticing every detail of the ranch around them. When they arrived at the house and entered through the front door, the expression on his face showed he was impressed.

Grant felt his chest puff with pride. The grandeur of the entryway, with its two-story white columns braced from the wooden floors to the ceiling, made an immediate impression of wealth and success. He imagined he could pit his bank account against Stewart's any day of the week and come out ahead.

And *his* finances had been gained legally.

"You've done well for yourself, son."

"Don't call me that." The words were reflexive and rapid-fire.

Stewart nodded, looking old and sad. Grant felt a twinge of shame, but wasn't sure if he could—or if he even wanted to—make amends.

He didn't know this man. Had *never* known him. Putting his emotions aside, though, he realized there was really no reason to hold animosity toward a stranger, no reason not to treat him hospitably like any other new acquaintance who could potentially become a friend.

He wasn't looking for a replacement father. No one would ever fill Fred Callahan's shoes.

But he certainly had room in his life for friendships. All he had to do was to stop thinking about the part Stewart Shea had played in his birth.

"Well," Abbe finally said into the silence, "if the two of you have decided not to draw pistols in the foyer, shall we act like civilized folks and sit down over a glass of iced tea?"

Stewart's features relaxed into a smile. He reached out and brushed her short hair with his fingertips. "You reminded me of your mother just then. The consummate hostess and peacemaker."

"Mama was a peacemaker?"

"Yes. She didn't like dissension—despite the opinion you formed of her as a teenager. When did you cut your hair?" he asked.

"Right before I came here." She shrugged, and led the way into the kitchen. "I needed a change and figured it'd make me less visible."

Grant nearly snorted. This woman would be noticed wearing a burlap sack.

Stewart sat on one of the bar stools and accepted the tea Abbe poured into an ice-filled glass. Grant stood by Abbe on the other side of the counter, facing Stewart.

"Why are you here, Pop?" she asked again.

"I need to know if you still have any of Tommy's belongings—or if you found any computer disks when you went through his things."

"No. I donated most of his stuff to the Salvation Army. There were some personal items I packed up and sent to his sister in California, but nothing to do with computers—he didn't even own one, that I know of. You took care of the rest of the things in the house."

Stewart sipped his tea, his shoulders slumping. "That's what I was afraid of."

"What was on the disks?" Grant asked, shifting closer to Abbe. He was getting a bad feeling.

"Incriminating names and dates—information the Ziggmorellis wouldn't want falling into the federal prosecutor's hands."

"Where did it come from?"

"My computer." Stewart met Grant's steady gaze. "These last few years, I've pretty much stuck to running my restaurant—legitimately. Donato wanted more action and bigger stakes. He put the information on my computer, made a copy, then went to Lucca Ziggmorelli with what he had and tried to make a deal. He asked them to make a hit on me." He glanced at Abbe, apology in his eyes.

"Pop…" she whispered.

"He'd decided he wanted to take over my position, but he didn't want to handle the dirty work himself, didn't want it getting back to you," he said to Abbe.

Grant slid his arm around her, a move born out of the ease and familiarity gained through intimacy. Stewart noticed, the look in his eyes turning speculative, then mildly approving.

Grant didn't give a damn whether or not the man approved. He only cared about Abbe, what she was feeling as she learned the true depths of her late fiancé's soul, the extent of his betrayal.

"Tommy was whacked because of his cockiness. Gil Ziggmorelli took a dislike to him, felt he was a loose cannon and a disgrace because he'd proved he couldn't be trusted—even though he was from a rival family. Gil places great store in loyalty. I knew Tommy wasn't happy, but I didn't know he wanted my place. As long as he was with you, I wouldn't have allowed him that kind of power."

His hand tightened around his glass as he held Abbe's gaze. "I know that sounds stupid considering you're my daughter and I was the head of a crime family. I just figured I could shield you better than he could. I made it a point to stay low profile. Tommy would have dragged every one of us into the spotlight."

"How'd you find out about the hit?" Grant asked.

"Gil came to me—out of respect—and told me. To show good faith, because he'd had the father of my granddaughter offed, he agreed to let the matter of the computer information drop, trusting that I wouldn't rat out anyone as long as I was left to fade quietly into the woodwork and out of the game."

"Men in organized crime aren't usually such a trusting bunch," Grant commented. "What makes him so accommodating to you?"

"That's personal between me and Gil. The point is, I agreed to turn over the goods when I got out of the game. We never found the disk Tommy claimed to have, but I had the computer. Last week, Gil came and asked for the machine. With his son facing prison and their lives being scrutinized, he doesn't like loose ends. He's not exactly up on the latest technology—I could've easily made a backup copy of the information before turning over the machine. But I'm a man of my word. The problem is, when I checked to make sure the file was still there, it became corrupted. Tommy programmed it to destroy if it was opened more than once."

"My God, how would he know how to do that?" Abbe asked. "I never saw him even use a computer."

"He was a whiz on the things. There were a lot of things you didn't know about him, sweetheart." Stewart said it gently, but the words fell like giant boulders dropping off a cliff.

"Why didn't you tell me?"

"Because then I'd have to give myself up, too. And I couldn't stand the thought of seeing the love and respect in your eyes turn to hatred."

"Maybe it wouldn't have. If I'd had a chance to understand instead of it being dropped on me by the Las Vegas P.D."

"I've made a lot of mistakes that I can't take back. That I'm ashamed of." Stewart traced the beads of condensation on the side of his glass. "All these years, I've tried to protect you from my world, and here you are, square in the middle. Gil has honor, but he's not stupid, and he has to protect his ass. He wants possession of that information, and he won't stop until he gets it. I knew if he found out I didn't have it, he'd come looking for it from you. It would appear just as logical that you found the disk Tommy stole, that you're keeping it to ensure your own safety, or to use as blackmail."

"The guest house," Abbe said, reaching out to clutch at Grant's arm. "Do you think…?"

Stewart raked a hand through his hair. "I'm not ruling it out, but I don't see that as a job by one of Ziggmorelli's guys. Until this morning, Gil still believed I had the information he wanted."

"Then who?" Abbe asked.

"I don't know. And I'm no longer in a good position to put an ear to the ground."

"The break-in was only yesterday," Grant said. "How'd you hear about it so quickly?"

"I have excellent sources."

"Ozzie Peyton?" Grant had called Ozzie himself, just to make sure the townsfolk were on extra-sharp lookout. He hadn't expected Ozzie to contact Shea.

"Yes," Stewart admitted. "And I still have a few associates of my own who are loyal. I left a message for Gil this morning. Told him the deal was off and that I'd decided to keep the information. I told him I have the missing disk."

Stewart looked at Abbe. "I've caused enough of a mess in your life, punkin. They'll come after me now."

"What about the trial? I still saw Lucca kill Tommy."

"The trial's about drugs and money laundering. You're no threat to them."

"But I am. The FBI has been here. They wanted me to testify. They're afraid Lucca will get off on a technicality and they want to add an airtight murder charge to the case."

"Did you agree to testify?"

"No. I stuck to my story about not seeing the shooter."

"Good girl."

"The feds claim they have someone who saw Abbe witness the hit," Grant said. "There's a possibility they could subpoena her."

"Are they offering to put her in the witness protection program?"

"They mentioned protective custody, but no solid deals. Frankly, I wouldn't trust them to guard a hamster."

"Neither would I," Stewart said. "You've got to get Abbe and Jolene out of here."

Abbe slapped her palm on the countertop. "Would you two quit talking about me as if I'm not here?"

"Sorry," both men said at the same time.

"All this time, I've been thinking that Lucca's people were after me and Jolie. Now you're saying they only want something they think I have?"

Stewart nodded. "I doubt the feds would tip their hand about wanting you to testify. And unless they actually follow through with a subpoena, there's no reason to disclose their plans to the defense."

"What about the dead canary?"

"That was merely a reminder."

"That I'm another loose end."

"You haven't talked in the last six months. I discussed that with Gil myself the day you left Texas. I made sure he understood that I raised you right."

Grant could feel Abbe's discomfort at that statement. For the past few minutes, he'd almost forgotten exactly who Stewart Shea was.

"But I'm still a loose end," she insisted. "Especially with the angle the feds want to take."

"Gil doesn't know that, punkin. The only beef they'll take up with you is if they believe Tommy gave you the disk. I've taken care of that by shifting the heat onto myself."

Abbe sighed and leaned against the counter. "This won't ever be over, will it?"

Stewart's eyes were incredibly sad. "I hope it will. As soon as Lucca's trial ends, one way or the other, this should all blow over. With me retiring, I'm no longer competition for Ziggmorelli. He's pissed off at me right now, so he'll be eager to track me down—which will buy you enough time for Lucca's trial to get resolved. While I'm laying low, I'll re-create as much of the information as I can remember, then I'll mail him the disk and computer, see if that'll pacify him."

Grant could tell by looking at the other man that he didn't believe anything would pacify his enemy.

Abbe seemed to realize the same thing. "Oh, Pop." She rounded the counter and put her arms around her father.

The man had marked himself for death, and they all knew it.

He'd done it to save Abbe's life.

"Do you have a plan of action?" Grant asked. "Someplace you intend to go?"

"Nothing concrete. Perhaps Sicily. I have a lot of contacts throughout the world, but it's difficult to know anymore who to trust."

"Then why don't you use the benefit of my Special Forces training and let me map out a strategy for you? I'm somewhat of an expert on moving in and out of countries without being detected. And I *do* have contacts I trust."

"I should get going," Stewart said. "The less time I spend here, the better it'll be for Abbe and Jolene."

"I'm not only good, I'm fast. The information's in my study." Grant told himself he was offering strictly for his own purposes. It was always better to know where your enemy was.

CHAPTER SIXTEEN

ABBE FOLLOWED THEM into the study and listened as Grant gave instructions to her father, sketching a route on paper. The chart looked more like a game of "connect the dots," with the occasional square or triangle representing one country or another.

Stewart understood the meanings, which was all that mattered. Watching the two of them, their heads bent over the desk, Abbe couldn't help but notice the resemblance. How bizarre that she and the man she loved shared the same father. But not the same blood, thank God.

"Do you have access to a passport under an alias?" Grant asked, straightening.

"Yes. Several."

"Figures," Grant murmured, and made another notation on the chart.

Stewart shoved his hands in his pockets. "I appreciate what you're doing for me, Grant. Especially after..." His words trailed off as though he couldn't figure out how to finish.

"Forget it," Grant said.

"I don't think that's possible. I'd like to explain about the past thirty-three years, if you'll let me."

The pencil in Grant's hand snapped. He calmly picked up another one. "Not necessary."

"It is to me. This might be my only chance."

Grant shrugged, then straightened, crossing his arms over

his chest and leaning a hip against the desk. His body language couldn't have been any less inviting.

"If it'll make you feel better to unburden," he said, "knock yourself out."

"I didn't know your mother was pregnant."

Grant's eyes narrowed. "That's not what I heard."

"What did you hear?"

"That you gave her money for an abortion and she never saw you again."

"I gave her money, yes. Two thousand dollars to pay her rent and buy herself and her little boy—your brother—some clothes and food. I was living in Chicago at the time, about to relocate to Las Vegas and open my restaurant. I left town for several months, and when I returned, she was gone— she'd been kicked out of the apartment. The super didn't have a forwarding address, and he was pissed because she'd stiffed him for the rent."

"Hard to believe my mother wouldn't latch on to you if she knew you had money."

"She didn't know."

"You just said you gave her two grand."

"She thought I'd borrowed it from my family. My own mother was still alive then—a strong-willed Sicilian matriarch—but her health was failing, so I'd recently had to take over the Shea family business. I didn't tell Anne—your mom—about my private life. Part of me was egotistical—enjoyed the money and power. The other part of me, the biggest part, hated the lifestyle. The lack of choice. I wanted to be an astronaut or an airline pilot, not the head of an organized-crime family. I'd always known what was required of me, though."

"I didn't think the Mafia followed the rules of royalty, where only heirs succeed as dons," Grant said.

"Most don't. But in my family, there's always been a blood Shea or Cappino—my mother's people—running the show. Anyway, I had a short affair with Anne even though I didn't approve of her lifestyle—the constant need for drugs and alcohol. I figured that was the reason she didn't stick around— because I wouldn't party with her."

"So when did you find out about me?"

"When Social Services called—after she dropped off you and your brothers in Idaho. She gave them my name and they tracked me down. I knew about your older brother—he was just a baby when I was seeing Anne—but I didn't know she'd had another child—you—or the one after you. The woman at Social Services said I was the only man that Anne knew for sure—could prove paternity through blood tests—that had fathered any of her kids."

"God, she was a piece of work," Grant said. "We were on our way somewhere—to Washington, I think—with her latest boyfriend. Halfway there, he decided he didn't like having three kids tagging along, so she dumped us off at the next county they stopped in. She didn't say goodbye or even look back. Just left us sitting there, holding hands in a dingy building that smelled like stale coffee and copier ink, watching the pity on the faces of the employees who walked by or stopped to stare at us through the glass like puppies tossed in the gutter."

He shook off the vivid memory, looked up at Stewart. "You know she died, don't you?"

"No."

"When I was fifteen. She'd finally married a guy with money, gained a conscience, I suppose. My brothers and I inherited a wad of cash from her."

"You deserved it."

"That's what my dad said. That it was our due." He didn't feel awkward speaking about another father to Stewart. Anyone could make a baby. It took a true man to actually be a father. And Fred Callahan had been that man. Grant realized that he wanted to brag. Not to make Stewart feel small, but to honor the man who was his dad, a giant of a man, both in stature and in heart. A man who'd been a bachelor all his life, yet hadn't hesitated to take in three orphaned little boys, fought to make them his own, then patiently taught them about horses, family and love.

"I didn't want the money, and neither did Ethan or Clay. Dad talked us into taking it, though, said we could give away a big chunk of it to help other boys in situations like ours. He coached us with shrewd investing advice so our nest eggs would grow, telling us the amassing fortune meant we could give even more to those in need."

"That was good solid advice. You were lucky to have him."

"Very." Grant stared at the man in front of him, realizing how different his life might have been if his mother had hung around and waited for Stewart, used his money to pay the rent instead of doing whatever she'd done with it. A single alternative decision, a single day walking down another sidewalk at another time, would have altered the entire map of his life.

"I hated you, you know," Grant said. "I'd formed an image of you in my mind, and every day my brothers and I were forced to dig through trash bins for recyclables, or beg for money on the streets, or when one of my mother's boyfriends wanted to buy me for his own personal use, I bounced between hating you and fantasizing that you'd show up in a fancy limo to rescue us."

Dimly, he heard Abbe gasp. He hadn't known he was going to say all this, hadn't known the pressure of old, buried feelings were so close to the surface, ready to spew.

He could still remember—vividly—the squalor of the different places they'd lived in, the stench of garbage on his clothes, being so hungry he'd thought his ribs would collapse into his spine. The terror of smelling alcohol on Ralph Zuckerman's breath, of fighting off the hands bent on removing his pants. God, even now, the rage filled him.

It had been Ethan who'd saved him that day—and Ethan was only older than Grant by eighteen months. Ethan had been punished for wasting a full bottle of cheap Scotch by smashing it over the boyfriend's head. The guy had decided Anne wasn't worth his trouble—despite the enticement of her having *three* little boys—and all Grant's mother had said when the boys defended their actions was, "Just shut up, you little liars. You always ruin everything for me."

Grant shook away the ugly images. He hadn't realized how many emotions and dark memories a boy could store up at such a young age—six years old.

The same age as Dylan Quinn had been. The innocent little boy who'd lost his life because Grant had screwed up.

"God, I'm sorry," Stewart said. "If I'd known…"

Grant looked up sharply. For an instant, he wasn't sure which atrocity Stewart was apologizing for. Then his mind cleared. "You'd have what? Enacted my fantasy and showed up to make it all better? Believe me, I'm glad you didn't."

"So am I," Stewart admitted quietly.

Abbe put her hands over her face, peering at both men over the tips of her fingers. Watching the two men she loved verbally cutting each other to shreds was twisting her up inside. But she didn't know how—or if she even had the right—to jump into the fray and try to restore peace. Before she could make up her mind, Stewart spoke again.

"By the time Social Services tracked me down in Vegas, you and your brothers were already wards of the state. I was shocked and dismayed to find out I might have a son. I had to weigh the two evils—a crime family versus foster care. I didn't think you'd want to be separated from your brothers which meant if I stepped in, I'd be dragging *three* boys into a family that expected male children to enter the business. Also, that was before I married Cynthia—Abbe's mother— and the thought of caring for three boys on my own seemed too daunting to even contemplate."

He picked up a glass paperweight, set it back down. "I might have chosen differently if Fred Callahan hadn't come along. I was there in Idaho the day he showed up on the Treechmans' farm. I'd been there once before, but couldn't make myself act. You cut yourself on a roll of chicken wire and a scrawny little kid gave you a napkin to wipe the blood."

"Scott," Grant said. "The Treechmans' only son. He was sick a lot, so they didn't make him do physical work, but old man T had a mean tongue in his head and he used it on Scott at every opportunity. The kid would have been punished if he'd been caught giving me that napkin. I'd have been punished if I'd gotten blood all over my clothes."

"So that's why you hid the evidence," Stewart said. "Later that night, I retrieved the napkin from where you'd buried it in the dirt and sent the sample to a lab. Back then, they didn't have DNA technology, but they could match blood types. You have the same as mine."

So that was where the blood-test results in the folder had come from, Grant thought.

"It ate at me," Stewart continued, "the way you boys were made to work at such young ages. I told myself it was good for you, that a little hard work wouldn't hurt you. The rationalization didn't make me feel any better, so I went back, still not sure if I was going to break Treechman's legs, snatch just you or all three of you. Callahan gave me another excuse to stall. I hired a private investigator to keep tabs on you. Then I came here to Shotgun Ridge to see for myself how things were going. That's when I met Ozzie Peyton. When he assured me that you and your brothers were settling in with a good man who wanted to adopt you, I was glad I'd hesitated. You were much better off with him and this lifestyle than you would have been with me."

Now that his storm of emotions had been spent, Grant was able to listen to Stewart's words and really hear them. He found that he couldn't hate the man, after all. In his own screwed-up way, Stewart had been trying to do the right thing.

And he'd done it. Grant couldn't imagine a life without ever having known Fred Callahan.

If Stewart truly hadn't known he'd gotten Anne pregnant, then the anger Grant had harbored all these years was misplaced. One more sin to place at his mother's feet.

After a moment, he unfolded his arms, relaxed his stance. "Thank you," he said, and meant it. "For making the right decision."

Stewart nodded, his eyes moist. The unguarded emotion removed another brick in the wall between them. Who would have thought a Mafioso would allow himself to be caught on the verge of tears?

"I've touched bases with Ozzie over the years and kept the investigator on retainer, as well. I've been discreet, but I've watched you grow up through the reports he compiled."

"I know. Abbe showed me the file."

Stewart's gaze rested on Abbe. "I wondered if you'd made a copy. Ever since your phone call, when you gave me the veiled hints on where you were going, I've been racking my brain to figure out how and why you'd chosen Grant."

"I printed a copy from your computer. If you think about it," she said, glancing at Grant, "it's kind of cool to have an autobiography written by an impartial observer. No messy emotions. Just an unvarnished truth that shows the true depth of a man."

"I think you did some creative reading between the lines."
Grant felt his insides soften just looking at her. Making love
to her last night had been an experience unlike any other, stunning him. He'd thought his feelings were only the product of
lust. Now he realized they went much deeper.

"What made you leave a career in the army?" Stewart
asked, interrupting his thoughts.

Grant dragged his gaze away from Abbe. "Dad got sick. I
came home to lend my support to Ethan and Clay, to talk him
into going to the doctor. He was stubborn about that kind of
thing. Being back reminded me how much I loved working
with the horses, and when Dad was diagnosed with cancer, I
requested a discharge, wanting to spend whatever time he had
left here on the ranch with him."

"You still did freelance assignments. Seemed like you had
the best of both worlds. What made you stop? If you don't
mind my asking."

"It's not something I usually talk about."

"I understand. Forget I asked."

Grant realized that Stewart probably *would* understand.
Being trapped in a lifestyle he hadn't initially chosen, he'd
likely experienced his own share of ugliness. Jobs that had
gone sour and cost lives.

The Special Forces unit Grant had been part of had basically been an elite killing squad. Formed by the army, yet not
wholly recognized by the U.S. government lest it shed them
in a bad light. And in some ways, not all that different from
the Mafia's way of "evening the score."

"I went to Myanmar in Southeast Asia," he said quietly,
moving to the window to stare out into the bright sunshine,
needing the light and warmth on his face to counteract the
darkness of memories. "The six-year-old son of an American
executive had been snatched for ransom, and we were sent to

bring him home. Our recovery mission was almost complete when a kid of about nine pulled a gun on me. I hesitated— even though I knew Myanmar had more child soldiers than any other nation. The kid soldier pumped three rounds into our 'snatch'—the child we were sent to rescue—before my backup drew a bead on him. I was still holding the little boy's hand."

"My God, Grant." Abbe was at his side in an instant, sliding her arms around him.

He stood stiffly, not making any move to accept her comfort.

"Surely you don't blame yourself," she said, her palm stroking his back. "You could see the soldier was just a child."

"A child trained to kill." He stepped away from her compassionate touch. "Remember what I told you about never aiming a gun at something or someone you aren't fully prepared to destroy? I broke that rule, lost my edge, and cost an innocent little boy his life. I would have lost mine, too, if my partner hadn't stepped in and saved my ass. Ended up, all I got was a bullet in the shoulder."

"And now I've put you in an intolerable position," she said softly. "By asking you to take on the responsibility for another child's life."

His whole body jerked. He glanced down sharply. "Are you afraid I'll choke when it comes to protecting Jolene?"

"No! That's not what I meant. I *don't* think that."

The muscles in his jaw tightened, ached. He made himself relax. He was projecting his own fears on to her, and he knew it. Reliving nightmares that woke him in the middle of the night with his heart pounding and sweat pouring down his face.

He'd never gotten back on that proverbial horse, never again tested himself in the high-stakes arena of life and death decisions.

By God, he would *not* be bucked off again.

He rolled up the chart he'd prepared for her father, scribbled a phone number on the outside and handed it to Stewart.

"You're losing time. Follow these instructions and it'll seem as if you've fallen off the face of the earth. I've written down a code that will scramble your phone line, make your location undetectable. Place a call to Ziggmorelli every other day, play cat and mouse, give him false hints. I'll leave the details of that part to your imagination. Hopefully the Ziggmorellis will stay busy for a while, tracking you, and forget about Abbe."

Stewart hesitated, then held out his hand. "Thank you."

After a beat, Grant accepted the gesture. Nodded. "I'll take you back to the airstrip. If Abbe's okay with it, we'll pick up Jolie and let her watch you take off."

"Yes," Abbe said, her heart breaking when moisture appeared in Pop's eyes.

Stewart hugged her, then set her away from him. "At the risk of ruining our relationship all over again, there's one more thing I need to tell you, and I might as well do it now while I'm unburdening—even though I'll be breaking my word."

Abbe frowned. "What is it?"

"I deliberately screwed up my marriage to your mother. I sent the two of you away to protect you."

"You didn't want the divorce?"

"Not in a million years. It broke my heart. But your mom needed more than I could give her. She wasn't like you, who took my odd hours and absences in stride. I was dealing with a messy situation at the time, and she was getting too close to finding out the truth about me."

"Would that have been so bad, Pop?" Abbe didn't understand.

"For me, yes. I was ashamed of what I did. Just as you didn't want the ugliness touching Jolene, I felt the same about your mother and you. When I met Cynthia, I was bowled over by her. I was so in love I convinced myself that I could lead a double life, that there would be no danger to either of you. One night your mom followed me and nearly got herself killed. She was…fragile, had been growing even more so over the years, and she didn't understand what she'd walked into the middle of. I knew then that the marriage had to end, so I lied to her, told her I needed more freedom and sent her away." He reached out and tenderly brushed the bangs off Abbe's forehead.

"Then, lo and behold, you came boomeranging back four years later. I was dismayed, but I loved you, too. And you were so strong. Stronger than me, because I couldn't make myself send you away again."

"Why didn't you just get out?" she asked. "Quit the Mob life?"

"Walking away from organized crime isn't an easy thing to do. Once you're in, that's it. You know too much to be trusted on the outside. For years, I've eased back, little by little, trying to find the right time and circumstances to fade into the woodwork. In order to successfully make a break, there's such a delicate line to walk if a man in my position wants to live to see more than a week of retirement. And I wanted to live, punkin. I wanted my family back. *Want*," he amended. "You and Jolene…and Cynthia."

Abbe frowned, her palms beginning to sweat, her heart thudding heavily in her chest. "What are you saying?"

"I know where your mother is, Abbe. I talk to her several times a month, see her when I can."

"What!" Unconsciously, she took a step back, hit the wall of Grant's chest. From behind, his arms wrapped around her upper chest, across her heart, as though he was offering her any of his strength that she might need.

"You've known all these years and never said anything? Why? Where is she?"

"In a medical facility in Florida. Assisted living for people who are…" He hesitated. "People who don't function well in society unless someone is there constantly to see that they take their medication."

"How could you keep something like this from me? I had a right to know if my own mother was alive or dead."

"She made me promise not to tell you. I wanted to. I've argued with her over the years, but she's adamant. I still love her, Abbe. I couldn't break my word to her." Stewart shook his head sadly. "We make a fine pair, your mother and I. Both of us ashamed of who we are."

Tears backed up in Abbe's throat, spilled over the rims of her eyes, splashing onto Grant's arms. Arms that tightened subtly as though he was determined to hold her together.

Dear Lord, her mother was alive. Abbe's emotions ran the gamut from elation to despair. Her immediate impulse was to fuel up the Baron and head to Florida.

But she couldn't do that. Not with the threat of danger still hanging over her life, and the FBI scrutinizing her.

"Does Mama know about Jolie?" she whispered.

Stewart nodded. "I bring pictures of our girls every time I go." His blue eyes watering, he glanced at Grant, almost in apology, then back to Abbe. "You might be mad at me," he said softly, his voice catching on emotion, "but you *are* my girl. You always will be."

Grant's arms loosened and his hands came up to cup her shoulders, urging her forward. Toward Stewart.

"Trust your heart, baby," he whispered.

That was all the urging she needed to step from his arms and into her father's. She wasn't sure how long they stood there, holding each other, not speaking. Finally Stewart eased back.

"I have to go."

She nodded. "I know." She rose on tiptoe, kissed his cheek. "Please be careful. I mean it. Don't you dare get yourself killed."

He rested his forehead against hers. "Likewise." Then he whispered, "God, Abbe, I'm so sorry. I'm so, so sorry."

He stepped back and squared his shoulders, his features settling into the self-assured, no-nonsense man she was used to seeing.

He nodded to Grant, indicating that they should go. "You take care of them…and yourself, too."

"I'll do my best."

Stewart nodded again. "That's all anyone can ask."

They were speaking their hearts now, their goodbyes, saying what they would not be able to say once Jolie was with them. As they walked out to the truck, Abbe felt as though a scream was lodged in her chest, clawing to get out.

Forgiving her father, letting him know he was welcome in her life, had put her between a rock and a hard place.

If Pop's plan worked, if he could re-create the computer disk and the Ziggmorellis would be satisfied with that, if the trial ended and they no longer viewed her as a threat to Lucca, if this whole mess somehow blew over and had a happy ending, what then?

Would she be forced to choose between her father and the man she loved? And how would she make that choice, not even knowing Grant's feelings toward her?

Grant and his brothers' business might survive being associated with a woman estranged from her adoptive father who happened to be part of the Mafia.

She doubted it would stand a snowball's chance in hell if the crime boss himself was in the picture—retired or not.

CHAPTER SEVENTEEN

THE NEXT MORNING, the security alarm went off before daylight.

Abbe bolted straight up out of bed, her heart pounding. Her first and only thought was to get to Jolie.

Her bare feet hit the floor before her eyes were fully open or her brain cleared of sleep. Fighting vertigo, she was in Jolie's room in a flash.

The little girl, her lamb clutched to her chest, was sitting in the middle of the bed, her eyes wide.

Abbe scooped her up just as Grant and Clay appeared in the doorway, both in their boxer shorts, bare-chested and barefoot, weapons in their hands.

"Stay put," Grant said, and quietly shut Jolie's bedroom door, closing them in.

Her arms trembled around her daughter. The only illumination in the room came from the night-light plugged into the outlet in the wall. It would have been funny—seeing both virile men half-dressed and armed to the teeth—if there had not been the ominous shrill of the alarm.

"Why is that loud noise going?" Jolie asked, her voice sounding small in the dimly lit room.

"That's the security alarm on the house. It does that when it thinks something moved, or if someone forgets to turn it off before they open the door. Don't worry, sweetie babe. Probably some little old field mouse was playing around and wandered someplace he wasn't supposed to."

"Like in *Cinderella*, when they come out and play in the nighttime?"

"Just like that." She pressed her lips to Jolie's silky hair, inhaling the lingering scent of shampoo.

"Is Gwant going to shoot the mouse?"

"What?" She realized Jolie had seen the guns. "No. He probably just wants to scare it a little, let it know he means business. Then he'll tell it to go outside."

"It could come play in my room."

"That might not be a good idea. Harley would end up chasing it all night, and nobody would get any sleep." With her brain starting to clear, she looked around the room, just now realizing the puppy wasn't climbing all over them. Her heart jumped into her throat.

"Where's Harley?" she asked, patting the bunched up quilt.

Jolie shrugged. "Maybe he wanted to play with the mouse."

Before she could work herself into a tizzy, the alarm silenced. A moment later, the bedroom door opened, and Grant appeared, backlit by the hall light, Harley curled against his wide chest.

The traumatized puppy was shaking as though he'd been afflicted with palsy.

"I thought he was afraid to navigate the stairs," Grant said, his voice a rusty growl.

"So did I." Which was why she didn't bother closing Jolie's bedroom door at night. She'd figured Harley would stay on the second floor with no problem.

Biting her lip, trying to stifle a smile, she held out her hands as Grant transferred the trembling dog into her arms. "Did he set off the alarm?"

"Yes. Tripped the motion sensor."

"Oh, baby dog. Did you get scared?" She hugged the puppy

against her breasts. "You were a brave puppy and went down the stairs all by yourself, didn't you? What a big boy. Then that mean old alarm scared you half to death." She kissed his head. "Are you scarred for life?" Two kisses on his ears. "Should we call the doggie doctor and put you into therapy?"

Jolie giggled. "Silly Mommy. He doesn't hafta go to the doctor. See? Him's not shaking. Poor puppy," she crooned, showing him Lambie-pie, evidently as some kind of reward because everyone knew he was forbidden to so much as lick the stuffed animal. Scooping him into her arms, Jolie buried her face in his fur, then looked up at Grant. "Did you shoot the mouse?"

His eyebrows drew together. "No."

Abbe noticed that his hand was behind his back. Obviously hiding the gun. Although her adrenaline hadn't quite settled down, she wasn't so shaken that she couldn't appreciate the sight of him wearing only his pale blue boxer shorts.

"Did Uncle Clay shoot the mouse?" Jolie asked persistently.

"Nobody shot any mice, squirt. What's got you so bloodthirsty before breakfast? And why the obsession with mice in the house?"

"It's a Cinderella thing," Abbe explained. "The mice come out to play at night."

He looked utterly at sea, then leveled a thoroughly annoyed look at the puppy who was sitting in Jolie's lap as though nothing at all was amiss.

"Only close call we had," he said darkly, "was that I nearly turned the coyote bait into buzzard food."

"What's coyote bait?" Jolie asked, teasing the puppy with her lamb.

"Never mind!" Abbe and Grant said together.

Abbe laughed. "I think we'll shut the bedroom door from now on."

"Good idea."

She scooted off the bed and tucked Jolie under the covers. "It'll be a while yet before morning. Think you can go back to sleep?"

Jolie nodded her head against the pillow. Harley made several circles atop the quilt until he found a place to settle.

"Will you be okay if I close your door? Or do you want me to take Harley into my room?"

"You could close my door. Lambie-pie doesn't like to look in the hall no more. She said it's too noisy."

"Well, we can't have anything disturbing Lambie-pie's beauty sleep." She kissed Jolie's cheek. "Night, sweetie babe."

"Night—kisses, Gwant!" she demanded when he started to back out of the room.

"Beg your pardon, squirt." He leaned down, his gun hand still behind his back, and smacked a kiss to her cheek. "See you when the sun's up."

"'Kay."

As soon as they stepped into the hall, Grant hooked an arm around Abbe's waist, hauled her against his nearly naked body.

"Kisses," he said, mimicking Jolie, and bent his head to fulfill his own demand.

Abbe smiled against his lips. "I thought I gave you every kind of good-night kiss imaginable only a few hours ago." Yesterday, after Stewart had said a tearful goodbye to his granddaughter, Jolie's spirits had flagged. She'd gone to bed shortly after supper, leaving Abbe and Grant to do the same— although not for the purpose of sleep.

"Mmm," he murmured. "I'm a greedy man. Makes me hard just thinking about that clever mouth of yours."

"You're pretty darn skilled in that department, too."

"Pretty darn?" He backed her against the wall, moved his

hips from side to side, his erection rubbing her pubic bone "Is that all?"

She was having some trouble breathing. "Sugar, that's real high praise. Besides, you know well and good you don't need a performance rating."

"Every man needs a performance rating. It's wired into our DNA."

"You're off the charts. And that's as specific as I intend to get, even though you *are* holding a gun in your hand." They were both still whispering. Although they were on the opposite side of the wide hallway, Jolie's room was across from them.

"Come with me to my bedroom so I can put it away."

"Nuh-uh." She kissed his neck, his jaw, desperately wanting to climb right up his body—into it if that were possible. "Jolie might have a delayed reaction to the alarm fiasco and come looking for me. And before you suggest it, you're not coming to my room, because I don't want to have to explain to a three-year-old why you're in bed with me." Both times they'd made love, Abbe had gone back to her own room for that very reason.

"You're a heartless woman," he complained.

One minute she was so turned on she could barely think, and the next she wanted to cry. She leaned her head back against the wall, swallowed the sudden lump in her throat.

"I wish I had a little *less* heart."

He stroked her cheek with the back of his fingers, tucked her hair behind her ears. "Baby, what's wrong?"

She sighed. She couldn't tell him that her heart was so filled with love she feared it would burst.

"I don't know. I'm worried about Pop, I guess. And feeling guilty because the few short hours of sleep between the time I left your room and when the alarm went off were the most restful I've had in a long time. It's like...I can let down my guard for a while, because all the bad guys are gunning for Pop, instead of me. And *that* makes me feel like a shit."

He kissed her forehead, her eyelids, the corner of her mouth. "He can take care of himself, sweetheart. It's okay for you to relax for once. You've been dodging virtual bullets for longer than anyone should be expected to."

She'd never had a man use so many endearments with her, so genuinely. Sweetheart, baby, babe. She could almost believe that he loved her. Then again, her track record in that area wasn't so great. She'd believed that Tommy loved her, too.

But Grant wasn't Tommy.

He was dangerous, yes. For crying out loud, the quiet ease with which he held a gun at his side while wearing nothing more than cotton boxer shorts drove that point home in a heartbeat. Yet he had an incredibly gentle side, too.

He was a guy whose kiss was soul-stealing. A guy with deep emotions that he kept hidden. A guy who'd harnessed his sensuality into something explosive that only time and experience could accomplish, tempering it with a tender touch and a protective streak. A guy who would go to the mat for what he believed in, and for those he loved.

He was the man Abbe had been searching for all her life and hadn't truly known it until just now.

They would be so perfect together. As a family. If only…

Anxiety blindsided her, bringing with it an urgency that seemed out of place, an urgency to say everything that needed to be said. Perhaps it was the exchange they'd had with Pop yesterday that caused words to rise up, spill out in a rush.

"Grant, if anything ever happens to me, promise me you'll take care of Jolie. Promise me—"

He snatched her to him, cutting off her words. "Hush,

baby. Don't talk like that. Nothing's going to happen to you. I won't let it." He kissed her with a desperation that bordered on anger, then tore his mouth from hers. "Damn it, I *won't* let anything happen!"

"Don't." She held him as tightly as he held her, which left little room for either of them to breathe. "Life doesn't come with guarantes. I don't want you ever again blaming yourself for things you can't control." Like the little boy in Myanmar he'd been unable to save. "Do you hear me?"

"I hear you. And I hear what you're not saying, too. You're safe here, Abbe. So don't start in again about leaving. You can't go."

"Actually, I can." She said the words half in seriousness, half out of pure orneriness.

"Fine. In the literal sense, you *can*." He paused, shrugged. "Unless I tie you up first," he said in a perfectly conversational tone.

She smiled against his chest, halfway surprised that she could do so. "I'm not sure I'm into that kind of thing."

"We could give it a trial run, see how you like it."

She gave his back a playful pinch, then simply allowed herself to rest quietly against him. With her cheek pressed to his warm chest, she listened to the sound of his heartbeat, her own heart yearning for peace, wanting the guarantees that life couldn't offer. "I just wish…"

"What, baby? What do you wish?"

"That things were different." She closed her eyes. "I just want to put down roots. Be normal. Feel like I belong. Stop having to look over my shoulder. I want to plant myself, and I want to plant a garden. I just want to be free." *Free to love.*

He held her to him, pressed his lips to her hair. "Soon, baby. Soon."

OTHER THAN CARRYING on a love-hate relationship with a headstrong wheelbarrow, Abbe was getting pretty darn good at mucking out stalls.

Of course, she'd been to Arletta's beauty shop twice this week to have her acrylic nails fixed from all the wear and tear she was putting them though. Arletta was making darn good money off of her. Abbe figured she at least deserved a frequent-visit discount.

In the four days since Pop had left, there hadn't been so much as a ripple of drama in Abbe's life—other than being half-buried beneath a stinking pile of horse manure when the wheelbarrow insisted on going left when she was trying to make it go right. There weren't many sane people who would actually admit out loud that they were having an all-out battle of wills with an inanimate piece of equipment, but by dog, Abbe would willingly put her name at the top of the list without an ounce of shame.

Well, maybe she would admit to a pinch of embarrassment.

She was sure that the deceptively innocent-looking shit hauler was deliberately trying to make a mockery of her driving abilities.

She was doubly demoralized at having stooped to the un-civilized level of conducting a one-sided cussing match with the thing, earning herself a nice-size audience of ranch hands who appeared highly entertained by her struggle.

And wouldn't you just know it, Grant was among the watchers, standing there with a grin on his face and her daughter perched on his shoulders.

"Good morning, gentlemen. Little lady." She'd intended to redeem herself with a little dignity.

Instead, she probably gave them the best show of their lives, because the front tire chose that very moment to deposit itself smack-dab in the middle of a mud hole. The wheelbarrow came to a bone-jarring halt, pitching the handle end straight up.

Not right—as she'd wanted it to go.

Not left—as *it* had been determined to go.

A dead-center, straight-as-an-arrow headstand, propelling her up and over the tipped-up end of the wheelbarrow, her fisted grip still wrapped around the handles.

The tricky part of this aerial gymnastic was in trying *not* to land headfirst in the pile of shit.

How was she supposed to know that the fool thing would flip over completely if she didn't let go of the handles?

When the dung finally settled, Abbe was absolutely sure of only one thing—steer clear of maniac wheelbarrows that clearly fancied themselves demons starring in a Stephen King novel.

She heard male laughter and a little girl giggle before the wheelbarrow was lifted off of her.

"The object is to shovel the stuff, babe. Not wear it."

She leveled a warning look at Grant that had him backing up a step.

"Uh-oh," Jolie whispered, patting Grant's cheeks from her perch atop his shoulders. She knew when her mother was operating on a short fuse.

Abbe managed to keep her glare in place as she looked at Clay. He swallowed his mirth midlaugh.

Ethan was the only male who had sense enough to control himself in the presence of a clearly upset, manure-covered female. Obviously his wife had taught him well.

Looking at these three, sexy-as-sin cowboys was enough to ruin a perfectly good snit. They were simply too cute to stay mad at.

Especially Grant, with his hands wrapped around her

daughter's pudgy legs, the little girl, in turn, resting her small hands on his hat.

Each day, the bond between Grant and Jolie grew stronger, and Abbe loved watching it. Nothing was sweeter to a mother's pride than seeing someone genuinely love and enjoy her child the way she did.

Manny came out of the barn carrying several shovels, reminding Abbe that she still had work to do.

"I'll only need one," she told him.

"We'll help," Clay offered.

"No, thank you. Me and this wheelbarrow have a bit of a power struggle going on, and I'm determined to win."

"You're competing with the ranch equipment?" Grant's expression was both mystified and amused.

"Apparently so. More accurately, *it* seems bent on competing with *me*."

His hat shifted nearly an inch as his eyebrows shot up. "Well, I'll be damned. If I'd known my everyday tools were such fluent communicators, I'd have paid more attention."

She raised her chin. "This is not your everyday, run-of-the-mill wheelbarrow. It's a sadistic mule posing as a kiddie-cart. Give it a spin, sometime, and *then* come talk to me. But not today. It's my turn."

He shook his head and grinned. "You are a crazy woman. I like that about you. A little too much, maybe."

For a long moment, he held her gaze, his blue eyes filled with such sexy, masculine intent, her knees nearly gave out.

For crying out loud, they still had a small audience.

"Y'all may have given yourselves the day off, but I still have work to do. So would you please run along and let me get to it?"

"We can at least help you shovel the poop back into the misbehaving monster," Grant said, mindful of his language with Jolie sitting on his shoulders.

Abbe shook her head, flicked her hand at them. "Shoo. Go back in the barn and make yourselves useful doing something else. And don't be spying on me, either. After I best this stupid wheelbarrow, I'm going home to change clothes."

"Give me and the squirt a shout when you're ready to go," Grant said. "And if that beast of a wheelbarrow gets out of hand, just holler and I'll rush right out here and tame it for you."

"If you know what's good for you, Grant Callahan, you'll hightail it into that barn before *you* end up smelling like the underside of a horse's tail."

"Go!" Jolie advised, pounding his hat with Lambie-pie. "Hurry! I don't wanna get timed out."

"Aw," Grant said. "She wouldn't give us a time-out."

"Uh-huh," Jolie said, bouncing her feet against his chest. "That's her mean look."

"Her mean look?" Grant made a show of studying Abbe's face. "Yeah, I suppose she does look pretty ferocious. Maybe I better ease off on her boot-camp training. She's liable to whip both of us."

Abbe pretended to lunge.

Grant whirled and ran for the barn as though being pursued by snarling dogs, which thoroughly delighted Jolene. Childish squeals and giggles mingled with deeper, masculine laughter.

Abbe felt a smile bathe her from the inside out. Lord, it felt good to simply let go and just be in the moment.

Especially the moments with Grant.

Once again, the giddy, life-is-wonderful feelings washed through her.

Even though she was covered head to toe with manure.

Clearly, she was rediscovering her inherent optimism.

Either that, or she needed some serious therapy.

ABBE SHOWERED, put on clean jeans and a pale coral tank top, plucked her bottle of scented lotion from the counter and walked barefoot out of the bedroom. Jolie had fallen asleep on top of her bedcovers, which gave Abbe the perfect excuse to stay home in case Grant had planned on going back to the barn.

Funny how she kept calling this house "home." Without thought, the word swept through her mind with an ease that was scary.

Each day that passed without a reminder of lurking peril, it seemed that another piece of the old Abbe came creeping out—the happy-go-lucky, joyful part of her.

Oh, she'd never again be as blind to the people and world around her as she'd once been, but the new maturity she'd found within herself, the independence, would simply complement the best parts of who she used to be. The girl full of fun and laughter who could invariably see the glass as half-full rather than half-empty.

She squirted scented lotion into her palm, then tucked the bottle under her arm, massaging the silky scent into her skin as she carefully navigated the stairs without holding on to the banister.

Being suspicious of everyone and everything, unable to trust, was incredibly draining. It sucked the joy out of life, robbed a person of friendships...of love.

Joy is what Grant made her feel. And she'd decided to embrace that feeling.

Sure, there were still insurmountable hurdles between them, but darn it, if the sky fell in tomorrow, she'd deal with it then. No sense wasting precious days in anticipation of what could or might happen.

She squirted another dab of lotion in her palm as her bare feet touched smooth wooden floors.

No one knew when their time on earth was up. If today was

her day to die—or tomorrow, or ten days from now, or in sixt
years—she didn't want to be standing at the Pearly Gate
wearing her couch-potato clothes and no mascara, account
ing for a life lived in fear and pessimism. No way.

She wanted to talk a mile a minute, expounding on every
thing wonderful she'd seen and done and felt and embraced
The good Lord would have to open the gates and let her i
just to shut her up.

She smiled, thinking Pastor Dan would get a kick out o
that image.

Grant immediately looked up from his desk when sh
walked into the study.

"Mmm. Nothing like the scent of a woman right out of
bath. You smell good enough to eat. Come here."

She skirted his desk and slid into his lap.

He sniffed her neck. "Sugar cookies?"

"How in the world do you get sugar cookies out of vanill
and *musk?*"

"Beats me. Maybe I've been smelling horses for so man
years, my scent glands are ruined."

She picked up his hand and squirted a generous glob of lo
tion into his palm.

"Hey!" He jerked back as though she'd handed him a live
snake. "What the hell?"

"Oh, stop it." She tugged his hand back, placed her ow
over his palm and began spreading the thick lotion over his
callused skin, massaging each individual finger and their pres
sure points.

"You've got me smelling like a girl," he complained. "My
own horses won't recognize me."

"Mmm. They'll probably think you're me."

"Now, that might get interesting. Especially when it comes
to the up-close-and-personal part where we have to lend

hand in order to get those twenty-inch penises lined up with their target."

She tsked, used her thumbs to work at the muscles in his hands. "You're just looking for an excuse to talk dirty. I know that you scrub clear up to your armpits with disinfectant before you handle any of those barkers."

"Now who's talking dirty?" He nearly dumped her off his knee when she smeared another huge glob of lotion in his palm. "Would you cut that out?"

"Don't be such a baby. Your skin's drinking this moisturizer like a bone-dry cactus. You ought to take better care of your skin."

"Is this a polite way of telling me you've got complaints about my hands?"

"Absolutely not. I love your hands. As for who's talking dirty, I can repeat my statement at a ladies'-auxiliary tea. Can you claim the same?"

Before he could answer, the phone rang. He looked at his slippery hands, sighed, then poked the button that activated the speakerphone.

"Grant here." He frowned when Abbe slid off his lap. He made a grab for her back pocket, but his lotion-slick fingers thwarted him. Giving him a saucy grin, she moved to the other side of the desk.

"All hell's broken loose, boss," the caller said.

"Hang on a sec. Who am I speaking with?"

"Uh, sorry," the kid said. "It's Junior Rawlings…the groom…uh, I mean one of the grooms."

Grant grinned as the young man stammered. "Okay, what kind of hell is messing with my horses, and what's wrong with my brothers that they're allowing it to happen?"

"We've got a mare in trouble—she's got a gash on her leg that'll probably need stitches. Ethan's got the Sully Farms mare at the teasing rail, and she's about good to go. Plus, the Thoroughbred Racing Bureau is out here asking questions about our breeding procedures…and about Abbe Shea. Any way you can come back to the barn? At least to stitch up the mare?"

Grant looked at Abbe, and she nodded.

"I'll be out there as soon as I can." Grant punched the button to disconnect the speakerphone.

Abbe's idyllic bubble, the one she'd been riding high on most of the day, lost a little bit of air. She'd been here barely three weeks, and her presence in Shotgun Ridge was already casting suspicion on the Callahans' breeding farm.

Grant came around the desk, tipped her chin up with his vanilla-scented finger and kissed her. "Stop worrying about the racing bureau." He kissed her again, lightly bit her bottom lip. "Clay can handle them."

"Who said I was worried?"

"Those green eyes. Dead giveaway every time. You ready to head back over to the barn?"

"Are you nuts?" She toyed with the buttons on his shirt, smoothed the material over his chest. "Don't you think that'd be a little like waving a red cape at a bull?"

He had the nerve to laugh. "Baby, they wouldn't know you from Dora or Emily or any other woman in this town. Besides, all they need to do is talk to you for five minutes, tops, and they'll be begging our pardons, and hunting down whoever it was that put a bug in their ear, itching to punch the guy in the mouth."

"That was a whole bunch of b.s., Callahan." She grinned. "But thanks for saying it, anyway. I'm not afraid of running into one of those 'suits.' I'm barefoot, my hair's still wet, and Jolie's down for a nap. She'll be a real crab if I wake her up in the middle of it. You get going. See to that poor mare needing stitches. Jolie and I will be right here waiting when you get home."

He cupped her cheek, slid his fingers over her ear, in her hair. "I like the sound of that." His voice was low and raspy, his lips warm and seductive.

Abbe had to force herself not to get greedy, not to pour herself into the kiss and start something neither one of them had the time to finish.

"Hold that thought," he said, kissing her once more, then grabbing his hat and shoving it on his head. And don't let Jolie sleep too long where she won't want to go to bed tonight. I've got this craving, you see, to toy with every inch of your sweet body, taste every pore of your skin, head to toe. It's going to take a while to satisfy that craving, so we'd be smart to start early."

She could have cheerfully strangled him for leaving her on the verge of melting into a quivering puddle of desire right there on his sculpted area rug.

She was sorry she hadn't followed through and given him a dose of *her* erotic medicine.

She went upstairs, making as much noise as possible as she fixed her hair and makeup, then rummaged through her closet for shoes. She took out a pair of sandals and slid her feet into them, admiring the way the color matched her coral toenail polish.

Harley barked, the sound barely carrying past Jolie's closed door. He wasn't a yappy dog. He had more of a deep, one-note bark, and rarely cut loose loud enough to make anyone jump. He barked at the birds, and at the reflection of himself in the windows—mostly because it took him by surprise and scared him.

Abbe opened the door and waved at Jolie who was awake—barely—then looked at the puppy. "What are you barking at, silly dog?"

He darted past her and down the hall to the top of the stairs. "What is it? Do you hear Grant?" she called to the puppy. He answered her with a one-note *woof*. She let him be. Sometimes he just felt the need to act a bit ferocious. If such a thing was even possible with tiny dogs who were so cute you just wanted to squeeze them.

"Hey, sleepyhead," she said to Jolie. "Did you have a good nap?"

Jolie nodded, still rubbing her eyes.

"How about we go down to the kitchen and fix up a dessert to go with supper?"

"Okay! What can we make?" She hopped off the bed, snatching Lambie-pie on the way. "Cookies?"

"Hmm. I suppose we could." She took Jolie's hand and headed down the hall. "We can do some big fat chocolate-chip ones and squish ice cream between them, make cookie sandwiches. Sound good?"

"Yum. Can I whack the eggs."

"Sure. You can whack 'em." At the top of the stairs, she snapped her fingers for Harley. "You coming downstairs with us, baby dog?" Now that she knew he could do it, she didn't carry him as often.

He didn't seem inclined to brave the steps, instead lay at the very top rung, his nose barely hanging over the edge, as though he intended to guard his upstairs domain.

"Okay," Abbe warned. "You'll be sorry once you start smelling food." She and Jolie went down the stairs and into the kitchen. While Abbe rummaged through the pantry for the cookie ingredients, Jolie dragged a chair over to the center island where she knew the main mixing and stirring took place.

She butted the chair against the cabinet, but instead of climbing onto it, she trotted toward the back door.

"Where are you going, sweetie babe?"

"I gotta let Katie's daddy come in."

Abbe dropped the package of chocolate chips and spun around, her sandaled feet already carrying her across the kitchen. "Jolie! No! Don't open the door!"

Jolie froze five feet from the door.

Abbe scooped her daughter into her arms just as the kitchen door swung wide open and slammed against the wall.

CHAPTER EIGHTEEN

GRANT WAS SELF-TAUGHT in the art of suturing wounds, a sort of baptism by fire he'd gotten while serving in the Special Forces. The type of guys he'd hung out with during those six years had a tendency to show up at a rendezvous with gaping holes in their bodies and seriously low blood counts. The board of plastic surgeons wouldn't note his before-and-after results in their medical journals anytime soon, but he could get the job done.

He gave Sunday's Best a cube of sugar and a piece of carrot for being a good patient, then sterilized his instruments and stowed the supplies. Putting stitches in an animal wasn't all that different from sewing up human skin—except he didn't have to get the animal drunk in order to proceed.

Mission accomplished, he walked over to the breeding shed to check in with Ethan and Clay. Evidently, Clay had satisfied the racing bureau, because the men hadn't stayed long. They'd poked around some in the breeding records, checked out the stalls and supplies, talked to the grooms and handlers.

Grant had steered clear. He was too touchy when it came to Abbe, too protective. One wrong question, posed in the wrong tone, even, and the likelihood of him inflicting bodily harm on someone would have pretty much been a given.

So, it was a good thing he'd had Sunday Best's puncture wound to keep him busy.

When he entered the breeding shed, Ethan was readying the blood-bay mare—another horse they were boarding and breeding from Sully Farms.

"She's a beauty," Grant said. "Any weaknesses?"

"A slight restriction in the shoulder, but hardly anything to talk about."

"Duke'll compensate. He's got excellent, free-flowing movement. What's her name?"

"Lady Anne."

"Great. Let's hope her temperament's nicer than our mother's was. Just to be on the safe side, lock up the booze."

Ethan chuckled. "Here comes our boy."

Duke of Earl was already prancing, having caught Lady Anne's scent.

"Might've known you'd show up," Clay teased, grinning at Grant. Controlling the stallion with a firm grip on the lead shank, Clay kept his voice even and low. They all did, since it was important to keep the breeding process as relaxed as possible.

Had to have the right ambience.

He smiled to himself, making a mental note to tell that to Abbe. He could already imagine her laughter. She'd probably suggest candles, champagne, chocolate and flowers be delivered to the equine couple.

"You a voyeur, today, or a participant?" Clay asked.

"I hadn't planned on being either. How'd it go with the racing-bureau guys?"

"Piece of cake. Just like I told you it'd be."

"So they asked about Abbe?"

"Yeah…" Clay paused as Duke curled his upper lip, straining his powerful neck forward. "Ethan, are you going to take all day wrapping that mare's tail, or what?"

Ethan flipped his brother the bird.

"No need to get vulgar." Clay gave a soft chuckle. "I told the bureau boys if they were bobbing for spoiled apples, they wouldn't find any on this ranch. Said if my word wasn't good enough, they were more than welcome to come on over and pitch a tent, or set up a cot, watch over our shoulders and see for themselves. We shook hands and they left happy."

Grant nodded. "Thanks for taking care of it."

"How come you're thanking me? If anybody's talking smack on us, they're stepping on *my* boots, too. Besides, I could handle those two yahoos with one hand tied behind my back."

Ethan snorted. He was finished with Lady Anne's tail, and Manny stood close, ready to help him get the mare in place.

"If you're so good, hotshot, why'd I have to come back and pick up the slack? And in case anyone's interested, I took care of Sunday Best's rear hock. Put three sutures in—hardly worth the effort. It probably would have healed fine on its own."

"Then why'd you stitch it?" Clay asked.

"Junior called and said you *wanted* me to come stitch her up."

"I didn't tell Junior to call you," Clay said, frowning.

Grant's spine went ramrod stiff. "Ethan?"

Ethan shook his head.

Panic hit him with the swift and immediate force of a lead pipe smashing against his head, his feet already moving.

"Damn it! Somebody find that kid and make him talk. I don't care if you have to beat the shit out of him, or ship him out of here in a pine box." Grant sprinted toward the door.

"Grant! Goddammit, wait," Clay yelled, spooking the stallion.

But Grant wasn't waiting for anyone. "Stay with the horses," he called back. "And find that son-of-a-bitch kid."

God, he was an idiot. How could he have left Abbe and Jolie alone? He hadn't even set the fucking alarm.

He jumped into the truck, slammed it in gear almost before the engine caught, stomped the accelerator to the floor, and didn't let up. Adrenaline pumped through his veins like molten fire, making him wonder for a fleeting instant if his foot would push right through the steel firewall.

He didn't glance down to see if the speedometer needle was pegged. Even if it was, he felt as though he could *run* faster than the beefy, big-block Chevy engine in the pickup could carry him.

These past few weeks with Abbe and Jolie had given him a taste of what it could be like for them as a family.

He wasn't sure when or how it had happened, but he knew without a doubt that he was no longer willing to settle for a taste. He wanted the whole meal.

By God, he couldn't lose them before he'd even had a chance to make them his—in every way.

All he could do now was pray that his screwup hadn't already cost them their lives.

He almost missed the black sedan parked beneath the copse of sycamores next to the guest house. He slammed his foot on the brake, leaving a black trail of rubber on the pristine concrete, reversed, then peeled down the driveway leading toward the back.

Snatching up his Colt .45 from the seat beside him, he got out of the truck, and stealthily circled the Lincoln Towncar, noting the license numbers on the Montana plates. The side windows were tinted black. Through the windshield, he could see that the vehicle was empty.

But his own back door wasn't. He ducked behind a sycamore.

Two men, wearing black business suits that fairly screamed FBI, were leading Abbe from the house, one of them gripping her biceps. She held Jolie in her arms, the little girl's limbs locked around her mother like a spider monkey's.

"This isn't right," he heard her say. "All I need is five minutes to make arrangements for my daughter. Please," she implored. "She's only three. Let me call someone to come take care of her. We don't even have to wait. I'll leave her in the house and go with you."

"Just keep walkin', lady."

She jerked against the grip on her arm. "She's only a baby, for crying out loud! There's no reason for her to be involved."

Grant stepped into their line of sight, slowly raising his gun. "Mind telling me what's going on here?"

Two guns appeared, one trained directly at his heart, the other pointed at Abbe's side. For that transgression alone, he could have plugged the guy between the eyes without an ounce of remorse.

"Grant!" Abbe cried. "Thank God. You have to take Jolie."

"Stay right where you are." The tallest of the two men stepped in front of Abbe, both his words and his .357 Magnum aimed at Grant. "We don't want any trouble from you, Callahan, so why don't you do us all a favor and put down your weapon."

"Not until you identify yourselves." At a glance, he could calculate the amount of firepower he was up against. He dismissed the .357—he'd had a cannon aimed at him once, and that tended to put every other caliber into perspective with regard to his own level of anxiety and mortality odds.

He doubted Abbe had ever had a gun pointed at her ribs, though, so most of his interest zeroed in on the .38 Special, and the short, plump man who held it there. This dude was a cool customer. He hadn't so much as batted an eyelash.

Tall guy—the spokesperson so far—reached inside his suit jacket. "We're with the FBI." He withdrew a leather badge holder, flashed the shield, then tucked it back in his pocket. "I'll take that gun, now, if you don't mind. Set it on the ground, nice and slow, and move away."

If you don't mind. Grant minded a great deal. He kept the gun in place. "You still haven't said what you're doing here."

"We have a warrant for Ms. Shea's arrest."

"On what charge?"

The man reached in his jacket once more and produced a trifold piece of paper. "I'll be glad to *show* you, just as soon as you lower your weapon. And if that doesn't happen within the next five seconds, I'm going to shoot you for obstruction of justice."

Grant was screwed, and he knew it. Showing them that his finger was well away from the trigger guard, he set the .45 on the ground. He still had a small, .25-caliber Beretta strapped to his leg, but didn't intend to volunteer that information. They could damn well work for that discovery.

The agent gestured with his gun for Grant to move away from the weapon on the ground and continued waving him on until they'd executed a semicircular shift and exchanged places, the agents and Abbe closer to the car, Grant with his back to the main house.

"Let me see that warrant."

The agent took a step forward and stretched out his arm, handing over the document. That was a good sign. In the movies, they usually waved the paper in the air, and nobody took the time to read it.

He wasn't certain he'd even recognize the real deal. He'd never had a warrant sworn out for his own arrest, and legalities didn't apply to "black ops," which were generally conducted outside the country *and* the law.

Opening the folded sheet, Grant scanned it. Las Vegas federal court. The charges were accessory to money laundering, counterfeiting and murder.

Murder? Good God. Shock filled him, but didn't alter his expression. He knew how to hide his emotions.

This whole thing was a crock of shit. Several weeks ago, he might have hesitated, entertained doubts. But not now. Abbe was as genuine as they come. Her artless awe of the world around her, especially her recently recaptured sense of optimism, had forced him to take a fresh look at life, to see and appreciate the beauty and love around him that had been so easy to dismiss most of his life, blurred by layers of cynicism that had become all too easy to hide behind.

The kind of unspoiled innocence, generosity and kind spirit she portrayed were traits that couldn't be feigned.

She would *never* have assisted in any of the crimes she was charged with.

A sixth sense he never ignored cautioned him to stop and think. To look again. Something was missing here—he just wasn't seeing it.

Both men still had their guns pointed...

His mind did a fast rewind. The guns, he realized. They hadn't been holstered.

And Abbe wasn't handcuffed. Even if they'd decided to leave the cuffs off—perhaps being decent guys with families and wanting to allow her time with her child until Social Services came for the girl—they wouldn't be marching her to the car at gunpoint.

They also hadn't frisked *him* for additional weapons—which feds were trained to do. Even without a weapon, he could easily take down these men—but not without injury to Abbe and Jolene.

"Do you guys mind lowering your weapons?" he said. "There's no threat here that I can see. Everything seems to be in order. I just need to call your field office and confirm your identities. You understand. Can't be too careful these days."

He plucked the cell phone from his belt.

"Drop the phone!"

The gun at Abbe's ribs was now jammed against her temple. "Mommy!" Jolie screamed. "Mommy! Mommy!" Her terrified screams grew in volume, turning to hysteria.

The tall guy was crouched in a shooting stance, both hands gripping the stock. "Back away."

Grant held up his hands, his chest feeling as though there was a beast inside it, clawing to get out. "Okay. Easy. Take it easy. Let's everyone just calm down, now."

He could see Abbe's terror, her struggle to subdue the screaming child without making any drastic movements that might cause the gun to discharge. He felt utterly impotent that he couldn't reach them, that he couldn't stop the madness. That he couldn't protect them.

He stepped back and to the side until his boots sank into the grass next to the driveway—the same side as where the black sedan was parked. If he'd backed away on a straight course, he would have ended up on the other patch of lawn between the guest house and the main one, with the width of a driveway between them, and the gunman would have the advantage of not only a cleaner line of fire, but of forcing even more distance between them. He couldn't let that happen.

Although it tore him up to hear Jolie's screams, her near hysteria served as a distraction, gave him an edge.

Abbe, meantime, didn't know whether to breathe or hold her breath. She had to completely isolate herself from the gun at her head, the feel of the barrel bumping her cheek as she struggled to calm her daughter.

My God, she'd never been so scared in her life. But she couldn't afford to think about anything except keeping Jolene and Grant safe.

The gun was at her right temple. Jolie was screaming in her left ear, practically climbing up the front half of her body.

"It's okay, sweetie babe. It's okay. Mommy's fine. Hush now. Let go of Mommy's neck."

She tried to pry Jolie's arms from around her neck, cooing and shushing, desperate to get her daughter's head beneath the line of fire. If a bullet was going to pass through her head, by God, it wasn't going to hit her daughter's.

She could see Grant inching to the side—not really away from them, she noticed, merely following directions and moving. Sweat slicked her body. Her face was burning hot, both from adrenaline and from wrestling with an overwrought toddler. Her hands kept slipping off Jolie's skin.

Finally she managed to get a hold of Lambie-pie, nearly ripping off the stuffed animal's head as she used it to break Jolie's grip and yank her arms down.

Now what? If she set Jolie on the ground, she knew her daughter would latch on to her legs and cling.

These men were not FBI. She knew that now. But what did it matter, really? She'd been living in fear of both organizations.

The bad guys wanted to kill her before she could testify or leak information she didn't even know.

The good guys wanted her to testify about the information she didn't know, before the bad guys killed her.

Either way guaranteed an urn of ashes.

She couldn't subject Jolie to witnessing whatever horrors might happen. Abbe was the only one they wanted, and the fear of them needing Jolie to get to her was no longer an issue. They wouldn't want the baby now that they had her.

The men flanked her now, backing her toward the car parked beneath the trees beside the guest house. Grant had backed away as he'd been told, but only a few feet, and he was still moving, slightly to the side, instead of directly in front of them.

She caught his gaze, held it and made a split-second decision, a decision born out of fear, love and absolute trust.

Trust that the person you need most will be there when it counts.

Her gaze never leaving Grant's, she dug her heels into the grass, her feet slipping off the sides of her sandals.

"Jolene! Stop that crying this instant!" She'd never before raised her voice at her daughter in this manner.

Jolie was so stunned she stiffened and hushed immediately.

Ziggmorelli's man lost his hold on her arm.

And Abbe did the unthinkable.

She hooked her hands beneath Jolie's armpits and hurled her daughter into the air.

Almost simultaneously, Ziggmorelli's men grabbed her upper arms and yanked her backward. She had no concept of time or feeling, wasn't sure if she'd managed to completely let go of Jolie before she was literally jerked out of her shoes.

Had she'd screamed Grant's name a split second before she'd flung her daughter like a life-size rag doll, or after?

She saw him lunge, his arms outstretched. He caught her by the strap of her jumper and her T-shirt. Abbe gasped, whimpered. For a moment, Jolie dangled from his closed fist, then he reeled her in.

Profound relief and utter despair washed over Abbe. Jolene was safe. But they'd probably never be together again. Her heart pounded. She was shaking uncontrollably. As pinpoints of light danced in front of her eyes and bile rose in her throat, one of the men shoved her into the car.

She sprawled across the leather seat, scrambled to sit up. The tall man who'd done all the talking jumped into the driver's seat. The other still stood by the car's open back door.

Abbe saw her little girl clinging to Grant.

And then she saw the thug take aim.

"No!" She screamed the word, launched herself at the man's back, fought like a caged animal, clawing and scratching.

The gun blast rang in her ears.

Blinding pain exploded in her head. And then her world turned black.

GRANT OPENED HIS EYES, found himself staring up at the vast blue sky. He wondered why he was horizontal when he definitely wasn't in his bed. His arm was on fire, felt as though someone was holding a blowtorch to it.

He fought through the fog in his mind, turned his head. Jolie sat beside him on the ground, her face streaked with tears and dirt.

"Gwant?" The tiny voice was barely audible above the snuffling that racked the child's body. "Are you…" *Snuffle* "…'wake?" *Snuffle*.

"Yeah, squirt, I'm awake." He wanted to sit up but wasn't positive he could stay upright just yet, and he didn't want to frighten the little girl all over again.

Something soft was tucked against his neck. He reached for it with his right hand since the blowtorch was still pinning down the left.

His fist wrapped around Lambie-pie.

His eyes stung, his throat closing with emotion. For the first time since he'd been a small boy, he thought he was going to cry.

He distinctly remembered the lamb lying in the dirt halfway between him and Abbe. Unlike Jolie, the stuffed animal hadn't made the entire flight.

Lambie-pie was her constant companion, her comfort. Yet she'd given it to him for comfort, sat by his side and watched over him.

"Did you snuggle this pork chop on me?"

She nodded, devoid of her usual giggle when he called her lamb names. He heard the sound of an engine. Tires skidding. Doors slamming.

He pushed himself to a sitting position, felt his head swim. Reaching out, he lifted Jolie into his lap and kissed the top of her silky hair. "Thank you, sweetheart."

"Where did Mommy go?"

He closed his eyes, beating back nausea, didn't know how to answer.

Abbe. A giant fist squeezed his chest, adding more misery to the fire in his upper arm. My God, she was brave. The strength it had taken—both mentally and physically—to make the decision she had, and to carry it out—had to have been tremendous. She believed Jolie would be safer with him.

He'd seen the trust in her eyes, her intent. No second thoughts. She'd trusted him to be there when she needed him. The look in her eyes had tipped him off that she was about to act. And he'd reacted a millisecond before she'd flung her daughter at him. That single inch head start had made the difference, had allowed a successful pass completion.

The rage he'd felt when he'd seen that thug shove her roughly into the car was coming back to him, building. He had to find her. He wasn't sure how much of a head start they had; he had no idea how long he'd been unconscious. Obviously long enough for this precious little girl to go looking for her lost toy—beyond that, he didn't know.

Before he could go after Abbe, though, he had a more important assignment. He had to take care of her daughter. Abbe was counting on him.

When he opened his eyes again, two pairs of boots were in his field of vision.

"Hell on fire," Ethan said. He squatted next to them. "Are you all right?" He had his cell phone in his hand.

Clay hunkered down next, also holding a phone. "What happened? I—God, Grant. You're bleeding." Clay looked at Ethan, repeated. "He's bleeding."

"I noticed," Ethan said, already lifting his T-shirt, tearing off a strip of the material. "You want to make the call?"

Grant shook away the haze in his mind, closed himself off to the pain and nausea. He needed to get a grip.

"The first one who presses 911 on their phone will be calling an ambulance for himself, not me."

"You're not exactly in the greatest position to hand out orders or threats," Clay said, his tone tinged with anger and concern. "You're looking at two against one, and in case you hadn't noticed, someone blew a friggin' hole in your arm."

Grant didn't speak. He didn't need to. He made his point clear with a single look.

Clay tossed the taunting look right back at him, then stuffed the cell phone in his shirt pocket. "My mistake. I forgot. Only a mortal wound would keep you down."

Ethan clipped his own phone to his belt. "No sense wasting gas in the fire engine and paramedic truck," he said to Clay, then wrapped the strip of cotton around Grant's upper arm. "You know how he is. Thinks he's tougher than God."

"That's taking it a little far," Grant said, scowling at Ethan. "Did you find that groom?"

Ethan shook his head. "Still looking. It's not that unusual for one of the grooms to act on his own volition in calling the vet or anyone else if he needs help. Junior's a good kid."

"The timing is too coincidental." Grant's jaw was clenched so tight, he could hardly get the words past his teeth. His arm hurt like a son of a bitch, and he was so pissed off at himself, he could barely see straight. He shouldn't have left Abbe and Jolie alone under any circumstances. "Besides, you shouldn't have to *look* for one of the employees."

"We'll find him," Clay said. "Manny's working on it. Where's...you know?" Clay had perfected a sort of shorthand language when Katie had come to live with them. They'd all found out that kids understood more than adults thought they did.

"Black Lincoln Towncar," Grant said. He, too, could converse in shorthand fragments. "Two. Bogus FBI. Armed." He glanced over at the driveway. *Damn.* "Including my Colt .45," he continued. "Duped us both. Not sure which direction. I slept through that part."

"Lambie-pie gots to go to the doctor," Jolie interrupted, poking at the toy. "Hers got a hurt tummy." She snuggled into his chest, bumping his injured arm. He winced, toughed out the pain.

Grant knew he was wasting precious moments, that he should be organizing a search for Abbe, but Jolie had been traumatized by all she'd seen today, and she needed solace. She needed to know she was safe. That's what Abbe wanted him to do. Keep her daughter safe.

"Let me have a look." He poked the stuffing back in the grungy animal. "A couple of stitches and she'll be good as new."

"But she ate some'fing bad." Jolie pressed on the lamb's belly.

Since Grant hadn't ever played with the toy, he didn't know if it had a squeaker. He felt the hard spot she pointed to, dug his finger inside the stuffing and pulled out an object that looked like a small cigarette lighter.

"That's a data-storage disk," Ethan said.

No shit. The rage that had been simmering came to a boil. He allowed himself a moment to turn the murderous emotion toward Tommy Donato for using his little girl's favorite toy to hide an object people were willing to kill over. Scumbag. If Donato hadn't already been dead, Grant would have killed the coward himself—and enjoyed doing it.

He took a breath, cleared his mind, steadied himself, allowing his training to kick in. He shut down every emotion. There was no room to feel. No room for error.

"What's the plan?" Ethan asked. "And don't give me any crap. You either clue us in, or we'll dog your ass and figure it out for ourselves. Either way, we're on your team."

Grant nodded. He wanted Abbe safe. And to accomplish that, he needed help.

With icy, robotic focus, he stood and handed Ethan the small zip drive. "Take this to the house and have Dora try to find out what's on it, then head out to the airstrip—I'll check in with Dora later, so don't wait. Clay, put out a call to the neighbors. I want every available plane in the air, including Abbe's Baron. I'll be flying the Ranger, which will leave us with an extra plane. Find a pilot, even if you have to recruit the geezers. I know Ozzie keeps up his license, even though he sold his Piper. Whichever one of you is airborne first should be the point man. Have everyone fan out, take different sectors so you can cover as much ground as possible before dark." He directed his words to both of his brothers. It didn't matter who did what. Just that it got done.

"Have someone get in touch with Dottie over at the post office so she can alert the mail carriers and UPS guys—and any other people who'll be out on the road—to keep an eye out for the Lincoln. All I want is a location. Make it very clear that whoever spots the sedan should radio me immediately with the coordinates. Nothing else. I'll handle it from that point on."

"Alone?" Clay asked.

Grant shook his head. "I won't be alone. You don't want to know any more than that."

Ethan and Clay both understood about his Special Ops days, and respected his boundaries. After Dad's funeral and three bottles of Scotch—a bottle for each man—they'd exchanged stories, shared some of their darkest secrets. Grant had only told them a fraction of what he'd seen and done, but it had been enough to paint a vivid picture. The things said that night had never been discussed again.

"Do you want me to drop Jolie at the house with Dora?" Ethan asked.

"No. I'm taking her to John White Cloud. I know she'll be safe on the reservation—" He paused and made eye contact with both of his brothers. "That information stays strictly between the three of us."

Clay and Ethan nodded in agreement.

"Let's go, then. Clay, you might as well hitch a ride with me to the airstrip since Ethan's dropping off the zip disk."

"That's fine. But I'm driving. Drippy limbs make me a little squirrelly." He shot a pointed look to Grant's arm where blood was beginning to soak through the T-shirt bandage. "Wouldn't hurt you to have Little Joe Coyote take a look at that, either."

"You two carry on with your bickering," Ethan said. "I'm outta here." With a quick grin, he headed for his truck.

Grant lifted Jolie, his forearm creating a perch for her rear end. Her panties were wet, but that was okay. He'd seen grown men piss their pants in less frightening situations.

"I need a couple of things from the house," Grant said. Additional weapons, ammo, and clothes for Jolie.

As they crossed the driveway toward the back door, he palmed his cell phone and made two brief phone calls.

The first, he simply repeated a code into the receiver, then disconnected.

The second call was to the sheriff—a courtesy call only, to keep him in the loop. He gave him the license-plate numbers of the vehicle, and the same instructions he'd given his brothers.

"I've got air and ground support responding, and my own team deployed. I don't want any interference from your end."

"My men are trained in hostage negotiation, Grant."

"Not the way mine are. We don't negotiate. This is my operation, Cheyenne, and I intend to handle it my way...outside of the law. I'll walk right over anyone who gets in my way."

CHAPTER NINETEEN

WHEN ABBE AWOKE, she was alone in an unfamiliar room, tied to a wooden, straight-back chair.

There was no delay in either her memory or her devastation. Pain bolted through her head, throbbing with the beat of her heart. The external wound told her she was alive.

Inside, though, she felt dead.

She wanted to turn back the clock, wanted someone to tell her this was all just a bad dream.

Grant.

Oh, dear God, what have I done?

She'd seen him go down, watched as a bullet had slammed into him, knocked him off his feet. Watched him fall as her daughter clung to him like a burr on a sock.

She didn't know if she could bear the memories. She didn't know if she could bear a world without Grant in it.

She'd stayed too long, selfishly allowed the time bomb to keep ticking. She'd intended to leave before the explosion, before the danger found her and caught her daughter or anyone else in the destruction.

This wasn't Grant's fight, yet she'd allowed him to talk her into getting in shape, learning to defend herself. In the end, the lessons hadn't done a thing for her.

Or maybe they had. She still couldn't believe she'd actually *thrown* her daughter. She hadn't known she had that kind of nerve, that much courage. She'd simply acted with all the strength, fear, faith and trust that only a mother can embody when faced with protecting her child.

She'd trusted, as Grant had taught her to.

And he hadn't let her down. He'd caught Jolie. Protected her. And lost his life in the bargain.

It wasn't supposed to turn out this way.

She tried to shut them out, but the images were so vivid in her mind. Grant had been holding Jolene in his right arm. She wasn't sure if the shooter was aiming at Jolie or Grant. But at such close range, she'd known the bullet was bound to find a target. And it had. Left of center. Grant's heart.

In that single instant after he'd hit the ground, right before she'd been bashed in the head with the butt of a gun, she'd seen Jolie's flailing arms.

Her daughter was alive. That was what she needed to concentrate on now. She couldn't give in to the horrible, empty ache inside her, a pain that simply went too deep for tears. She had to fight, had to get out of here.

She had to get to her baby.

She pulled herself up from the abyss of sorrow, allowed anger to push aside the devastation.

How dare those assholes shoot at her child! She tugged at her hands, struggled against the ropes that bound them, felt like an animal with its paw caught in a steel trap.

She found that she wasn't tied to the chair, after all. Her arms were looped over the cane back, but only her wrists were tied.

Pulling with all her might, she sawed her hands back and forth. *Please, God.* If she could only create some slack. She needed to hurry. Since her feet weren't tied, she doubted her captors would leave her alone for long.

Unless they were stupid.

Given enough time, she could simply work her arms over the back of the chair, walk out and hope to God she ran into a friendly face who could untie her.

She didn't intend to try that until she knew for sure who, if anyone, was in this building with her.

The image of Grant's face crystallized in her mind. My God, she was barely thirty years old, yet *two* men had been murdered right before her eyes. Within the same year.

Tommy's death had traumatized her—primarily because of its gruesomeness. She'd mourned, yes, but mostly in anger. Not out of a deep sense of loss. The kind you feel when you love the person.

This time, she knew the pain of such a loss. The pain of loving deeply, completely, and having it ripped from her so horribly. It was a living, breathing monster that threatened to consume her, a hideous, piercing wail inside her that only she could hear. A raw, bloody wound that would never heal.

She'd lost the love of her life—and it was all her fault. If she'd never come to Shotgun Ridge, Grant would be alive.

But if she hadn't come, would Jolie be alive? Maybe not.

Her shoulders were beginning to ache from the strain of pulling at the ropes, and her wrists were starting to sting, but she didn't stop.

She heard footsteps and froze. A moment later the door opened.

It was the shorter of her two kidnappers. The one who'd shot Grant.

Anger and hatred consumed her. She saw the claw marks bisecting his face, from his forehead to his chin. The skin was swollen, dried blood streaking the center of each welt. Four of them. Compliments of her acrylic nails.

She only wished she'd aimed a little better, managed to dig out his eyeball, instead of just skipping over the socket.

"So what's the deal?" she asked, venom fairly spewing in her tone, very likely from her eyes, too.

"The deal is, we wait for the boss to get here. The pity of that is that he won't let me shoot you before he arrives."

"Oh, yeah. That's just the kind of thing you get off on, isn't it? Does it make you feel like a big man to shoot at an innocent child? At a woman who has her hands tied and can't fight back? You're a fucking coward."

The back of his hand struck her cheek. Her head snapped to the side. She saw stars, tasted blood. Slowly, she turned her head back, stared directly into his eyes with all the hate and determination roiling inside her. She would not be cowed or bested. Not by a piece of scum like this.

She won her point when he looked away first.

Two more men burst into the room—the tall one who'd driven the car, and another man she hadn't seen before.

"What the hell's wrong with you, Carlo? You got a death wish or something? The boss said not to touch her until he got here!"

Abbe twisted her hands, watched as the three men nearly came to blows. Good. Maybe they'd kill each other.

"WYATT TO POINT MAN."

Grant monitored the radio from the command post he'd set up in the hangar. They were using an encrypted frequency used only in Shotgun Ridge, so theirs was the only communication transmitting.

"Point man, go ahead," Clay returned.

"I'm over the Castle Mountains. There's a cabin at the base of the mountains, backed to forest land. Pretty isolated. Gravel road leading up to the structure. Looked like a black Lincoln parked out front, but I'm not sure. I don't want to circle and buzz the place. Over."

"This here's Ozzie. Don't mean to butt in, but me and Lloyd are northeast of Wyatt's position. We'll just make a little left turn and cross him like a T, you bet. Gotta tell you boys, this 185 is a right nice little airplane, you bet."

The radio was silent for a minute—obviously everyone was waiting to see if Ozzie was finished speaking. Grant hadn't known Ozzie was flying one of the Callahan planes, but he wasn't too worried. The mayor was a good pilot—he could use some brushing up on radio etiquette, though.

"Point man to Ozzie. Advise us when you see something. Over."

"You bet."

Grant keyed the mike. "Ozzie, this is Grant. I need as much information as you can give. Roads, number of vehicles, obstacles, other structures or civilians nearby that might require evacuation. Give me a solid visual map. Over."

"Will do, Grant. I got Lloyd ridin' along for just that very thing, you bet. You hear that, Lloyd?" Ozzie neglected to release the mike button. "You keep your eyes peeled and shout out them details." Lloyd's voice interrupted, "I've got ears, you old fool."

Grant listened to some more bickering, then Ozzie finally lifted his finger from the mike. He waited through the radio silence, staring at the pen resting on the pad of yellow paper, ready to write down the details, make a sketch.

It would be getting dark soon, which was perfect for a rescue mission, but not so great for reconnaissance. He hoped to God Ozzie could confirm that they'd stumbled on the right location.

He'd already delivered Jolie to John White Cloud, and had stood impatiently as Little Joe Coyote doctored and rebandaged his arm. It was a good thing the bullet had passed straight through, because he wouldn't have taken the time to have it removed.

Then he'd checked in with Dora. Sure enough, the disk was loaded with pages of documentation that could put away a lot of the players in organized crime. He wondered if Stewart had been intending to inform, despite his words to the contrary.

Manny had found Junior Rawlings tied up in the grain shed. Evidently Ziggmorelli's men had come in with the racing-bureau guys. Junior had just discovered Sunday Best's leg bleeding, and when the men commented about a lack of help, he'd wanted to assure them that everything was under control. He'd told them that Grant was due back any minute, but he would call the house and check for sure. He'd unknowingly played right into the thugs' hands, their hope to catch Abbe alone. As soon as he'd complete the call, they'd forced him into the shed, obviously so he couldn't compare notes with Grant, tip him off and send him running back to the house.

Grant scrubbed his hands over his face, then glanced at his watch for the thousandth time today. He couldn't afford to think about the hours that had passed, the delays it took to put a team together, or what Abbe might be suffering at the hands of her captors.

The planning would still put him on the scene in a fraction of the time it would take law-enforcement officers to arrive with warrants—and it would ensure a safer outcome.

Abbe's life was at stake. And for that, he didn't trust anyone but himself and his team to handle the recovery.

"Ozzie comin' back at you. Yes, sir, I believe we've found our black Lincoln, you bet."

Grant grabbed his pen and wrote down the exact coordinates Ozzie gave. At times Ozzie and Lloyd talked over each other as they called out a surprisingly thorough and vivid account of the scene below them, but Grant managed to capture all of it on paper.

He keyed the mike. "Grant here. All of you did a great job. Thank you. Head on back to base, and I'll take it from here, over."

"Ethan to Grant. Unless anyone's low on fuel, I'd suggest we stick around for a while longer in case the black sedan takes off again. We'll form a holding pattern, keeping our distance so we don't draw attention, operate in a hand-off relay, instead of circling. Over."

"Sounds good, Ethan. Increase your altitude. I'll radio when I'm on scene. Grant, over and out."

He studied the maps laid out before him, then made contact with his team, giving the coordinates for rendezvous. It was impossible to muffle the sound of a helicopter, or the lights he'd have to use for a night landing, so the safest course of action was to set down in the mountains and hike in on foot.

He stood and went outside the hangar where the Bell Ranger was parked. He'd already loaded the supplies he would need for the mission. With steady resolve, he buckled himself into the helicopter, programmed the GPS equipment and put the bird in the air.

By the time he reached the Castle Mountains, it had been seven hours since Abbe had been shoved into the back of that car, and every minute of that elapsed time had built into a highly sensitized hum in his veins, becoming more lethal with each second.

He couldn't afford to become distracted right now. Piloting a helicopter required the use of both hands and both feet, steady nerves and continuous attention to the machine. Especially when forced to set down in a confined area where the rotor would barely maintain clearance with the trees. One small miscalculation would result in a crash.

He circled in a high recon, feeling the bird grow sluggish as the thinner air degraded the helicopter's performance. As the geographical map had indicated, there was a small clearing in the trees. Not ideal landing conditions, but Grant didn't doubt his skill in setting down the bird. He had the unique ability of becoming one with the craft, a heightened sense that allowed him to feel each minute shift and pitch, to compensate for any element, as though he and the Ranger were wired from the same components.

From the illumination of the craft's lights, he noted the direction of the leaves blowing on the trees, then headed into the wind, making a steep approach, his feet controlling the tail rudder to keep the Ranger from spinning like a top, left hand on the collective, carefully adjusting the pitch of the blade as he came down with a level cabin, his slight movements on the cyclic between his legs smooth, steady and precise.

Normally this kind of challenge was exhilarating. Tonight, there was no room for emotions of any kind.

Emotions got people killed.

The moment the skids touched solid ground, he shut down the power, gathered his gear and exited the craft.

As he strapped on his ammo belt, three men materialized out of the trees. Buck, Randy and Marcus. He'd never doubted his old army buddies would be waiting for him. The things they'd been through together had created a bond no civilian could understand. If any of them had a need, Grant would reciprocate without hesitation.

They weren't wearing their usual fatigues. They were dressed in black to blend in with the night—and the plan. Via flashlight, each man studied the map Grant had drawn, then discarded it. A full moon glowed over the mountainside. Although that helped with visual, it was a detriment to their operation.

The bandage on his upper arm was noted by the men and dismissed as they masked their faces, hiked down the mountain to the cabin, reconnoitered, then split up. Randy, Buck and

Marcus disabled the vehicle, plus the ingress and egress routes to secure the perimeter, while Grant took out the sentry.

He didn't kill him. That would screw up the plan. He just made sure the guy would take a nice long nap.

His boots didn't make a sound on the gravel as he crossed to the cabin, flattened himself against the outside wall and looked through the window. Two men were slouched in chairs, one watching a black-and-white movie on the television, the other dozing, his .38 lying on the table beside him.

Abbe sat in a chair in the middle of the room as though she'd been placed center stage awaiting interrogation. Her arms were drawn behind the straight-back chair. A circle of blood-soaked rope dangled from her bent fingertips, the knot still tied.

Emotions threatened to blow his concentration. Good God, she was going to do something stupid and heroic and end up getting killed. The woman was determined and stubborn. She'd proved that countless times—including today when she'd insisted on besting a wheelbarrow full of horse manure.

Now she'd shredded the delicate skin of her hands, literally ripping them from a knotted rope.

His chest was so tight he could hardly breathe. The urge to act on his own was powerful, but he reminded himself that only fools rushed in without backup. From the corner of his eye, he saw Buck coming in low from the north, Marcus and Randy materializing from the east and west.

Let's kick ass.

ABBE'S WRISTS and hands were numb, yet she was aware of the sticky feel of blood trickling down her fingers. She could only hope that any drips would blend in with the dirty brown carpet.

The guy by the window, the one who liked to shoot at children and slap women, was so cocky he'd laid his gun on the table beside him. If she could just get her hands on it, she'd be out of here. She'd already visualized her movements a thousand times in her head.

Her heart was pounding so hard she could hardly breathe. About the time her brain would shout *go!* the thug would shift. The terror wasn't going to lessen, so she'd just have to do it, take the risk and lunge.

Her only chance was in getting her hands on that gun.

If she was forced to shoot someone to gain her freedom, she was prepared to do it.

Her muscles tightened, ready for action. Suddenly the room erupted in chaos. Four men wearing black stocking masks burst in carrying high-powered weapons, scaring her worse than Ziggmorelli's Mafioso soldiers.

For an instant, she was frozen to the chair, unable to decide if they were the cavalry or more of Ziggmorelli's thugs. Chairs scraped against the floor, feet pounded, someone shouted, but she couldn't see what was going on because her vision was suddenly blocked by one of the masked men, crouching in front of her.

Those eyes, staring at her through the holes in the mask, struck terror in her.

They were emotionless, dead.

The eyes of a killer.

Dear God, she was *so* close to escape! She couldn't die now! She had to find her daughter.

Then he blinked.

A sob backed up in her throat. Pinpoints of light flashed in front of her eyes like elusive fireflies. She felt her body slipping from the chair.

Grant's eyes. Eyes she'd despaired of ever seeing again.

He scooped an arm around her back and lifted her to her

feet, placing a finger against her lips to keep her from speaking. Then he led her outside.

The thugs in their bogus FBI suits, and the other man who'd been here when she'd arrived were all tied to the posts in front of the cabin.

Abbe's gaze darted to Grant. She was still angry enough to do some serious damage to these creeps, but she wasn't sure she could condone an execution. The other three men with Grant also wore ski masks. She didn't need to see their eyes to know they were men from his past, and as lethal as he could be.

"Tell your boss he better think twice before screwing with the Sheas," Grant said. He reached to his belt and the men flinched. Instead of pulling another gun, he retrieved his cell phone. "Abbe belongs to us, and we'll be taking her with us. The quiet don's been cordial and respectful toward your family until now. You crossed the line when you went after his daughter."

He pressed a stored number on the phone and lifted it to his ear. "Sheriff Bodine? I figured you might be interested in the whereabouts of three members of the Las Vegas Ziggmorelli crime family. They're wanted for the kidnapping of Abbe Shea. There's a computer disk on its way to your office, loaded with information these boys don't want falling into the hands of the law."

He gave Cheyenne the directions without identifying himself. He knew these scumbags would be out on bond in a matter of hours. He also knew they'd go straight to their boss, trigger fingers itching because four of Stewart Shea's guys ratted them out to the cops.

Damn, he loved it when a plan came together. The feds might not need that disk, after all. Because if he wasn't mistaken, he'd just guaranteed a bloody massacre between the

Las Vegas Shea and Ziggmorelli families. The feds could have who was left.

He disconnected the phone, laughed, then lifted Abbe into his arms and strode away from the cabin. Once they were out of earshot, Abbe looked up at him.

"Jolie…?"

"She's safe. I took her to John White Cloud."

She sagged against him. "I heard those goons say their boss was coming here."

"Cheyenne will pick him up, too."

His face was still covered with the mask. She wanted to see his features. She'd been so sure she'd lost him.

"You made those guys believe you were part of Pop's organization."

"Not that far off the mark, is it?" His voice was strained, as though on the verge of anger.

She looked around, saw the three men following, ammunition strapped to their waists, guns in their hands. "You don't have to carry me. I'm perfectly capable of walking, you know."

"In case you didn't notice, your shoes never made it into the car with you."

"Your friends are going to think I'm a big sissy. How far is it to the car, anyway?"

"The other side of the mountain. I brought the helicopter. You've got bloody wrists and knuckle marks on your face. Nobody thinks you're a sissy."

"Grant, you're not carrying me clear up a mountain!"

"Looks like I am. Would you mind being quiet for a few minutes? I'm having some trouble slotting my emotions. Tends to happen when the woman I love gets kidnapped and I don't have the pleasure of killing the bastards myself."

One of the men behind them gave a muffled laugh.

The woman I love.

Those words were enough to steal her voice.

When they reached the helicopter, he set her in the copilot's seat as though she was fragile china, and buckled her in. Without introducing her, he shook hands with his friends, pulled of his ski mask, then climbed into the pilot's seat. The other three men disappeared into the trees.

Abbe was so emotionally spent, she could hardly enjoy the experience of riding in the helicopter. It was equipped with dual controls and she didn't even ask if she could get her hands on them.

She closed her eyes, not sure for how long, until the pitch of the engine changed and woke her.

"Where are we?" she asked, looking out the window. The helicopter's lights illuminated an isolated grotto surrounded by vegetation and cascading waterfalls.

"Callahan mineral-springs spa."

"But what about Jolie? Shouldn't we—"

"Hang on a sec, babe. Let me get us on the ground."

She watched as he brought the helicopter in from a steep angle, and within moments, had them setting down gently on land. The process was a heck of a lot more involved than landing a plane. But an airplane couldn't have made in into this narrow canyon.

He lifted her out of the helicopter and took her to the water's edge where a light mist of steam hovered above the pool's surface. Her feet had barely touched the moist ground when, without tenderness or caution, he snatched her to him, holding her against his heart, his hands racing over her back and her arms as though checking for more injuries.

"God, baby, I was so scared." He punctuated his words with soft kisses and featherlight touches, carefully avoiding her split lip.

"I wasn't exactly jumping for joy myself."

He smiled at her, reached for the snap on her jeans. "Come into the water with me. It's warm. It'll soothe your wrists."

"We should go get Jolie."

"She's safe, sweetheart, and sound asleep by now. Besides, you'll scare her if you show up with bloody wrists and a bruised face."

She nodded, realizing he was right, and let him undress her, waited while he shed his own clothes, then waded waist-high into the pool of water that felt like silk against her skin.

"How did you know about this place?"

"We own it."

"You Callahans *are* an impressive bunch." She dipped her hand in the water, trickled it over his uninjured shoulder, pressed her lips to the bandage on his arm. "Thank you for rescuing me."

"I'd go to the ends of the earth for you, Abbe. You should know that by now. I think there's a rule somewhere that says when you rescue the right person, they're yours for life. That's what I want. You and Jolie in my life."

She submerged her hands in the water, feeling the sting in her wrists, and looked away.

Grant sighed. "I can see you're going to give me trouble over the Mafia connection. Well, come on ahead, baby. I can fight longer and harder than you can—especially when I want something this badly."

"I wouldn't be bragging if I were you. You're the one with the bullet hole in your arm."

"Yeah, and I'm the one who's got the Shea-Cappino blood running through his veins, which trumps your four-letter surname all to hell."

"Nobody *knows* whose blood you have, so that cancels

your trump. Who I've been for the past twenty-two years is public knowledge."

"Then I'll take out an ad in every newspaper, and at every racetrack, too."

"Oh, for crying out loud. This is getting ridiculous."

"Do you think I care about ridiculous? Don't you get it, baby? I don't give a rat's ass what anybody else thinks or if they approve. Hell, I don't care if the whole friggin' Mafia moves in with us. I only care about you and Jolie. I love you, baby. So much it hurts."

Abbe was stunned at his vehement, impassioned declaration. The words were different from the casual way he's stated them on the walk up the mountain. If she'd ever had any doubts, he'd laid them to rest in grand fashion.

"Fine. You're a stubborn man, Grant Callahan. I'm trying my level best to protect you, and you won't give an inch. Well, you had your chance and I'm not offering it again. I was doted on like a spoiled princess growing up, and Mama used to say that if she offered me an inch, I'd take a mile. That's what I intend to do right now, except I'm older and wiser and can resort to some pretty potent wiles to get what I want. And what I want is you. For a lifetime. In sickness and in health."

His lips came down on hers and he feasted like a starving man. "To love, honor, and cherish until the day we die," he murmured against her mouth. "Will you?"

"Oh, absolutely. I do love you, and honor you, and cherish you beyond reason. So will you marry me?"

"Isn't that what I just asked?"

"Actually, you were shy a couple of words."

His laughter echoed in the grotto. "Do you have a ring to offer me? This is a binding contract, you know."

"Surely you know I'm good for it."

"Sorry. I can't give you an answer until it's done properly."

"Well, that sucks. Look at the corner you've just backed your own self into. I sure don't recall stopping at any jewelry stores on the way here, and you don't appear to have any pockets on you—" Right in the middle of her sentence, he ducked beneath the water and disappeared.

Irritating man.

Several minutes later, he reappeared in front of her, water sluicing off his incredible body, spiking his eyelashes.

He picked up her hand, palm up, and dropped something cool in the center. "Don't lose that."

She looked down, her eyes going wide. "Lord have mercy, Grant. This diamond's got to be at least four carats."

"Five and a quarter, actually. Too gaudy?"

She stared at him to see if he was serious. He was. Poor guy. "Um, I don't believe I've ever met a diamond that was too gaudy. Where in the world did you get this?"

"Payment for a job." He recalled how she felt about ill-gotten possessions, and wanted to make sure she understood he would never do that to her. "A *legitimate* job, baby. For a legitimate diamond supplier."

"I didn't ask. I trust you, Grant."

"I know. But that was *my* first thought when Banksen— the man I did the job for—handed me a loose diamond. Especially one this size. I have papers at the house that trace this little bauble back to the exact spot in the earth it was chipped from."

He kissed her swollen cheek, the corner of her mouth, lifted her hands and placed soft kisses on her injured wrists.

"I've seen and done things I'll never talk about, Abbe. Things I hope someday I'll be able to forget. I'm not anybody's idea of a saint—"

"You're mine."

"Actually, I'd just as soon not be—that's a pretty exalted

title to live up to, and the man upstairs has got a big enough list of my transgressions. I'd be in a lot bigger mess if I screwed up the sainthood thing."

"Can't have that. I take it back. You're no saint of mine, buddy."

"That's more like it." He ran his fingertips over her face as though memorizing it in braille, being careful of the tender bruises. "What I'm trying to say is that my background can be a little daunting, scary for some folks, and I can sometimes be a bit rough around the edges, but I'd die before I'd hurt you, and I'll never lie to you. I'll protect you and our family with every fiber of my being, and love you even more. So how about it? Will you marry me?"

"I thought you'd never ask. Yes, I'll marry you. And have babies with you—you do want more babies, don't you?"

"As many as you want."

"Probably four." She rested her hands against his chest, over his heart. "I think I fell in love with you before I ever met you—through that file. You were doomed and didn't even know it."

"Not doomed, sweetheart. Doom is dark and dreary. You're pure sunshine and joy. *Destined* is a better word."

"Oh, you're right. I like the sound of that." She trickled water over his shoulder. "We need to get this wound taken care of."

"It'll keep. Little Joe Coyote doctored it some."

"I'm sorry I got you shot," she whispered.

"You actually saved my life. When you screamed, I twisted, realizing he was going to shoot. The bullet made a clean exit through my arm. I'm pissed off that I didn't dodge entirely. I think that's a sign that I'm getting too old for these shoot-'em-ups."

"It's just as well you retire that particular hat. Family men shouldn't be dodging bullets." She kissed his chin, his lips. " can't wait to have babies with you. You're so good with Jolie So perfect as a father."

"Speaking of fathers," he said. "I never in a million year thought I'd feel anything toward the man who gave me life Now I owe him a lifetime of gratitude. Because without him I'd have never found you."

"So, you've forgiven him?"

"Yeah. I suppose I have."

"We have to let Pop know what's going on."

"Already done. I have an acquaintance who should be scooping him up in Canada right about now. They'll get him to the right people who can put him in the witness protection program—provided he's willing to corroborate the informa tion on that disk."

"What disk?"

"I forgot. You don't know. There was a small disk hidden inside Lambie-pie."

She would have laughed at him addressing the stuffed an imal by name, but she was too incensed at the thought o Tommy putting his own child in danger that way.

Grant cupped her cheek. "Don't waste emotions on Don ato. It's over and done. Now we have the future to look for ward to."

She nodded, so excited that she could at last look forward to a future. And that it included Grant.

"About that teaching job…I never actually applied. Ozzie sort of tossed it out there like a football and ran with it…"

"Baby, whatever you want to do is up to you, and will be fine by me. Anything that makes you happy. As long a you're mine."

"That I'll always be." She kissed his strong chin, reveled

in the feel of her breasts pressed against his chest. "I love being a mom, and I don't want our kids raised by baby-sitters. I tried teaching once, and maybe it dates back to my rebellious youth, but I'm worse than the kids and can't stand being cooped up inside a classroom."

"Then why'd you pick that field?"

"I didn't. Pop did. I get it now. That was the most normal profession he could think of, and he was determined that I would always be aboveboard—maybe to make up for how far *below* the board he sometimes got. What I truly love, though, is flying. That's my passion."

"I though *I* was your passion."

She gave him a sassy grin. "Oh, you are. But a girl's gotta have her toys."

His eyebrows rose and she laughed. "I've got this idea. Dora wants to become a pilot and—"

"Oh, baby, don't tell me. Ethan'll pitch a fit. He already worries half to death over her. Besides, he's a pilot. *He* can teach her."

"But she doesn't want him to. She doesn't want to look stupid in front of him if she makes a mistake. She'd feel more comfortable with a woman instructor."

"Great. She doesn't want to make a mistake in front of Ethan, so she wants to crash a plane with my wife in it, instead."

"Now, that's not nice."

"I don't feel very nice when it comes to the possibility of losing you. As it is, it'll take me a long time just to get over what happened today." He lifted her hands, kissed the raw skin encircling her wrists. "You were like a wounded animal," he murmured almost to himself, "willing to chew your hands off in order to escape, to find your child."

"Yes," she whispered. "And I found my man."

He looked into her eyes. "I like the sound of that."

"So do I. Since both of us are too stubborn to go to the doctor, why don't we do something constructive."

"Mmm. What did you have in mind?"

"Let's start on making that baby."

EPILOGUE

One year later
Hollywood, Florida

ABBE TWISTED the wedding ring on her finger, nerves jumping in her stomach. She snagged Jolie before she could race down the carpeted hallway, and straightened the pink bow in her daughter's hair, sighed over the grungy lamb Jolie still insisted on taking everywhere.

Grant moved up beside her, holding two-month-old Faith in his arms, her cherub face peeking out of the soft pink blanket Abbe had knitted herself.

"You're both beautiful," he said. "All three of my girls are knockouts."

Sometimes, she still couldn't believe this man was hers. She'd almost lost him once, and it had been the darkest day of her life. She should have known he wasn't a man who would stay down—even if a bullet had knocked him there. The only real reminder of that day was the faint scar on his upper arm, which matched the one on his shoulder.

Thanks to Little Joe Coyote's miracle herbs and salves, there was no lasting damage from either gunshot wound.

"Ready to go show off our kids?" he asked.

"And my handsome husband," she added. When they entered the tastefully decorated room, the first thing Abbe noticed was that it smelled like Charlie perfume—her mother's signature scent. Odd how it only took one whiff of something familiar to open the floodgates and pour out all the precious memories.

Her heart lodged in her throat as the petite, blond woman turned from the window.

"Mama?"

Cynthia Shea's lips trembled, and she opened her arms. Abbe raced across the room and embraced her. "Oh, Mama, I'm so sorry. For being rebellious all those years ago. For being an awful teenager. For not staying. For wanting *things* instead of family. For—"

"Shh, my sweet darling. Don't go on so. You'll ruin your makeup." Cynthia smiled, her expression as loving and innocent as a child's.

"You have two granddaughters," Abbe said, holding her arm wide, inviting Grant and the girls into their circle.

"I know. Your father told me."

"And this is my husband, Grant Callahan."

Cynthia winked at Grant, then bent down to Jolie. "You're my sweet Jolene, aren't you? Come give Grandma some sugar."

Jolie immediately complied, kissing Cynthia's powdered cheek. "This is Lambie-pie," she said. "Mommy had to do surgery on her 'cuz somebody stuffed parts in her tummy that didn't b'long. And her eye got tore out, so Mommy made her a patch. Daddy said she looks like a sissy pirate now, 'cuz the patch is pink, but Mommy and me think she's fashion'bull." Her tongue twisted a bit around the last word.

Cynthia laughed softly. "Quite fashionable, indeed. A trendsetter among lambs." She stood and peeked at Faith, pulling aside the blanket to get a better look. "Another sweet lamb," she said wistfully. "They look like you, Abbe."

Abbe rested her hand on her mother's back, automatically

rubbing as she'd done many times, ages ago. It seemed so odd that her mother would be here, in this medical facility disguised to look like a high-class hotel. Cynthia looked perfectly normal. Slower to speak perhaps, more introspective. But she appeared the same as she had when Abbe was a girl.

"Grandma? Is that your birdie over there?" Jolie pointed to the birdcage sitting on a round end table by the window at the far side of the room. A bright blue parakeet bobbed and danced on his perch.

"Yes," Cynthia said. "His name is Boy Blue. If you speak softly and gently, he might talk to you."

"I can speak *very* soft."

"Then you may be my guest and go have a conversation with him."

"Thank you, Grandma," Jolie whispered, and tiptoed slowly and quietly toward the birdcage.

Cynthia watched for a moment, then turned back to Abbe and Grant. "She is lovely, Abbe. As is Faith. I'm so happy for you. And for you, too, Grant."

As though alerted by a sound no one else could hear, Cynthia looked past Grant's shoulder, her eyes lighting up.

Abbe followed her gaze to the man who stood in the doorway, then watched as her mother moved gracefully across the room, ever the proper hostess, intent on greeting her caller.

Leave it to Mama to draw in the good-looking men, she thought with an inner smile. He appeared close to her mother's age, and though he wasn't someone she recognized, Abbe felt as though she knew him from somewhere.

Grant nudged her with his elbow, leaned in close. "Uh, babe?" His deep voice was barely a notch above a whisper. "I don't know how that guy in the doorway feels, but if you keep staring at him the way you're doing, I might have to start flexing my muscles and marking my territory."

She smiled and leaned her temple against his, turning her head enough to see the amused indulgence in his eyes.

"Mmm. That tactic always works on me. Nothing more menacing than a man holding a baby girl in a pink blanket. Especially when there's muscle flexing involved."

His lips twitched, and as much as he tried to fight it, his smile stretched to match his laughing eyes.

"When's the last time I told you how crazy in love I am with you?" he asked.

"Outside in the parking lot. But feel free to tell me again." She glanced back to the man in the doorway, noticed that he'd taken two steps into the room.

"Okay, now I'm really getting jealous. Here I am, about to profess my undying love to my wife, and she's gazing at another man."

"Well, who does he look like to you? Do we know him, or just *think* we know him because he resembles someone famous?"

"*I* don't know the guy, famous or otherwise. Why don't you put us both out of our misery and go introduce yourself. Or ask your mom to do the honors."

"Whatever happened to our team partnership? You're supposed to be my backup. The least you could do is create a distraction so I can look at him for more that two seconds without him *catching* me staring."

Too late. The man lifted his gaze, locked it with hers.

Abbe sucked in a breath, grabbed for Grant's arm. Those eyes… She knew those eyes.

"Hello, punkin."

"Pop?" My God. That was Pop's voice, his eyes. But that was where the resemblance stopped. "What have you done to your face?"

"Amazing, isn't it? I got an extreme makeover—compliments of the attorney general and witness protection program. Just had to name a few names...and I mean *few*." He glanced at Grant. "It seems my son-in-law instigated a bloody showdown in Las Vegas between two crime families. Damn near wiped out both sides."

Stewart moved forward, engulfed Abbe in a bear hug, then shook hands with Grant.

"You're looking good, Stewart."

"Name's Paul, now. Paul Johnson. Pretty nice face-lift, don't you think? Almost makes me look young enough, and worthy enough, for Cynthia. Let me get a peek at this little bundle of joy." He pulled the blanket away from his newest granddaughter's face and cooed over her. "She's got the look of her grandmother, just like her sister does."

"We think she has your eyes," Grant said, causing Stewart—Paul—to go stock-still. "Same as I do," he added.

The older man swallowed hard, looked at Grant for a long moment, then back down at the baby. "Maybe she does, at that," he said, his voice gruff with emotion.

He stood next to Cynthia and put his arm around her. "I'm moving your mother out of this place, taking her to live with me."

"Can she leave?" Abbe asked, her glance apologizing to her mother. Cynthia didn't take offense, just smiled sweetly.

"As long as someone is around to make sure she keeps up with her meds. I've always been one to take care of people. Can't go into retirement quitting cold turkey."

"Will you go back to Las Vegas?"

"No. I've got a new name and a new face, a chance to start over. Your mom and I were thinking that a pretty cabin in the Rocky Mountains might be nice."

"What about the restaurant?"

"Government helped themselves to the deed."

"Oh, Pop. I'm sorry. I know you loved Villa Shea's. Do you need money? I have an account...the one you set up for me—"

"No. That money is yours. Villa Shea's did legitimate business, honey. I know you didn't like thinking that I gave you dirty money. I tried my best to keep you and your mother completely out of that other world I was trapped in. I didn't do such a great job these last couple of years—"

Abbe held up her hand. "The past is history, Pop. And something very good came out of it. If is wasn't for you, I'd have never gone to Shotgun Ridge and found the love of my life."

"She's got a point," Grant said. "And even if she didn't, there'd be no sense arguing with her. She's so damn chipper, nobody stands a chance against her. A man can't even get in a decent sulk anymore—"

"Oh, hush. You love my optimism, and you know it."

He hooked his arm around her neck and kissed her temple. "I love everything about you, Abbe Callahan."

Jolie interrupted the tender moment, streaking across the room. "Grandpa! Grandpa!"

Stewart bent down and caught the little girl while her feet were still moving. "How'd you know it was me?" he asked.

Jolie rolled her eyes. "I *always* know my grandpa, silly. You just gotta talk. What did you do to your face?"

"I had a little surgery so I'd look as young as your beautiful grandma."

Jolie clicked her tongue, then squinted in a conspiring look and lowered her voice primly. "Ah. You got a lift on your face."

"Who told you about that kind of stuff?" Grant asked, frowning.

"Mildred did. Her and Opal are sisters," she explained to her grandpa. "Mildred said she was gonna have the doctor pull a string on top of her head so her boobies and her face could go way up to the North Pole. She said everything in the Deep

South was just fine. Then Opal called Mildred a vain old woman who didn't have any sense and she'd prob'ly look like a cherry tart and have cat eyes and big water balloons under her neck. I kinda don't think she would look good like that. Prob'ly, you should give her to your doctor, Grandpa. 'Cuz you have pretty eyes, and if ya ask me," she said with grown-up seriousness, "I think water balloons would always be breaking, and it would be awful cold and wet all the time."

Teetering between shock and hilarity over the gossip Jolie repeated, they all began to laugh.

"That's my girl," Grant said proudly. "She's a born natural for small-town life."

Abbe cuddled Faith as Grant passed the baby into her arms. It was almost time to nurse. Grant knew her schedule better than she did sometimes. After a year of marriage, the hunger in his eyes hadn't even begun to wane, in fact, it seemed to grow hotter by the day.

"Just remember," she said to Grant, "we might be getting the latest gossip updates coming in, but you can be sure there are just as many being carried right back out *our* door."

"That's it, then. We're locking her up till she's thirty."

Abbe laughed. "You're such a tough guy." Her laughter became suspended in her throat when he took her free hand and lifted it to his lips. She thought she'd experienced every facet of Grant's tenderness, but in that single, heartfelt brush of his lips against her knuckles, she knew that her husband would always be full of wonderful surprises.

And she was the lucky woman who got to be his wife.

Signature Select™

THE

Signature Select™

SERIES

will bring you more
of the characters
and authors you love.

**Plus, value-added Bonus Features
are coming to a book near you.**

- Your favorite authors
- The characters you love
- Plus, bonus reads!

SIGNATURE SELECT
Everything you love about romance and more.

~ On sale January 2005 ~

Escape with a courageous woman's story of motherhood, determination…and true love!

Logan's Legacy

Because birthright has its privileges and family ties run deep.

Coming in December…

CHILD OF HER HEART
by
CHERYL ST.JOHN

After enduring years of tragedy, new single mother Meredith Malone escaped with her new baby daughter to the country—and into the arms of Justin Weber. The sexy attorney seemed perfect…but was he hiding something?

Where love comes alive™

The men and women of California's
Courage Bay Emergency Services team
must face any emergency...even the
ones that are no accident!

CODE RED

Coming in December...

BLOWN AWAY

by

MURIEL JENSEN

Being rescued by gorgeous K-9 Officer
Cole Winslow is a fantasy come true for
single mom Kara Abbott. But, despite
their mutual attraction, Kara senses
Cole is holding back. Now it's Kara's
turn to rescue Cole—from the grip
of his past.

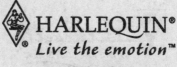

HARLEQUIN®
Live the emotion™

www.eHarlequin.com

CRBA

Celebrate the holidays
in Fortune-ate style!

New York Times
bestselling author

LISA JACKSON

BARBARA BOSWELL

LINDA TURNER

A FORTUNE'S
CHILDREN
Christmas

The joy and love of the holiday season rings true for the
Fortune family in this heartwarming collection of three novellas.

Just in time for the festive season…December 2004.

"All three authors do a magnificent job at
continuing this entertaining series."
—*Romantic Times* on *A Fortune's Children Christmas*

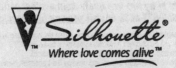

Silhouette®
Where love comes alive™